The Deadly Dispute

ALSO BY THE AUTHOR

The Olive Sisters
Two for the Road
The French Perfumer
The Yellow Villa
Sixty Summers
Lovebirds
The Tea Ladies
The Cryptic Clue: A Tea Ladies Mystery

The Deadly Dispute

A TEA LADIES Mystery

Amanda Hampson

PENGUIN BOOKS

UK | USA | Canada | Ireland | Australia
India | New Zealand | South Africa | China

Penguin Books is part of the Penguin Random House group of companies whose addresses can be found at global.penguinrandomhouse.com

First published by Penguin Books, 2025

Copyright © Amanda Hampson, 2025

The moral right of the author has been asserted.

All rights reserved. No part of this publication may be reproduced, published, performed in public or communicated to the public in any form or by any means without prior written permission from Penguin Random House Australia Pty Ltd or its authorised licensees.

Cover illustrations by Evgeniya Khudyakova/Shutterstock, goldyg/Shutterstock, Andrii Spy_k/Shutterstock, luma_art/Shutterstock, Pretty Vectors/Shutterstock, WinWin Art Lab/Shutterstock, ekler/Shutterstock
Inside cover images: teacups by Aleksandra Novakovic/Shutterstock, frame by Bibadash/Shutterstock
Cover design by Debra Billson © Penguin Random House Australia Pty Ltd
Typeset in Adobe Garamond Pro by Midland Typesetters, Australia

Printed and bound in Australia by Griffin Press, an accredited ISO AS/NZS 14001 Environmental Management Systems printer

 A catalogue record for this book is available from the National Library of Australia

ISBN 978 1 76134 634 7

penguin.com.au

We at Penguin Random House Australia acknowledge that Aboriginal and Torres Strait Islander peoples are the Traditional Custodians and the first storytellers of the lands on which we live and work. We honour Aboriginal and Torres Strait Islander peoples' continuous connection to Country, waters, skies and communities. We celebrate Aboriginal and Torres Strait Islander stories, traditions and living cultures; and we pay our respects to Elders past and present.

For Helen Thurloe with love

SYDNEY, 1967

1
NO PLACE FOR A LADY

Hazel Bates arrives on the docks to the sight of a dead body being hauled out of the water. The scene is chaotic, with police attempting to hold back an unruly crowd of dock workers while two ambulance men lift a stretcher with a blanket-covered body into the back of an ambulance. Slamming the doors closed, the two men pause to watch the police efforts with amusement. They light cigarettes, cradling the match's flame for each other. One cracks a joke, and their laughter reaches Hazel on the bitter wind sweeping off the harbour. She feels a chill that's not entirely weather related.

Her gaze sweeps the dock area and harbour beyond. She should have asked Rex exactly where to find him among the confusing number of large sheds and buildings, all tacked together haphazardly. It's a place on a different scale to the rest of the city. Directly ahead, two enormous cargo ships cast giant shadows over the finger wharves that jut out into the harbour, and long goods sheds lining them. With ships in port, the place would normally be bustling with activity, but the forklifts and stacked handcarts sit idle. Half-loaded trucks are abandoned, tailgates hanging open.

A man stands alone further down the wharf, away from the crowd. He stares out to sea, apparently uninterested in the drama playing out nearby. On a barrow beside him is a stack of wicker baskets, the sort that pigeon fanciers use. The sides of the baskets are open, so he must be waiting for the return of his birds.

Hazel walks over to the man, a wiry, weather-beaten fellow wearing a black donkey jacket and a knitted hat. At her greeting, he turns with a suspicious look. She asks if he knows where she would find Mr Shepperton at the Dockside Workers Union office.

'Mr Jolly? Happy chappie. You Mrs Jolly, are yers?'

Hazel laughs. 'Hardly, he's quite a bit younger than me.'

'Yers look all right. Could probably get a younger fella if yer fancied, like.'

'I'll keep that in mind,' says Hazel. She follows his gaze, shading her eyes against the glare of the winter sun, low in the sky. 'Are you waiting for your pigeons?'

'Nah, waiting for a nice sunset. I catch 'em and sell 'em down the markets.'

'Silly question, sorry,' Hazel says, with a chuckle. 'Do you happen to know which building he works in?'

He points towards a sprawling set of buildings. 'He's in there talking to that bunch of whiners. Never happy, that lot. Any excuse to down tools and bugger off to the pub.'

At the sound of shouting, they turn to watch the ambulance drive off and the police getting back in their cars, accompanied by heckling from the crowd of wharfies.

'Was there an accident here just now?' asks Hazel.

The man gives a bark of laughter. 'Bloke accidentally went swimming with bricks on his feet.' He turns to her with a sly grin, revealing one remaining tooth. 'Accidentally asked too many questions.' He glances at his watch and looks up into the sky, murmuring, 'Come on, me lovelies . . . ah, here they are!' As the birds swoop across the harbour towards them, he nods in the direction of the union office. 'Don't let me keep yer. Me birds don't like strangers.'

Hazel takes the hint and bids him good afternoon. Walking away, she looks back to see the birds land gracefully on his cart. The man takes each bird gently in his hands, places them into the baskets and closes the lid.

She finds the union office and steps inside, relieved to be out of the wind. The reception has a long counter barring entry to the offices. Through the doorway, she can see into a larger room where twenty or thirty men, dressed in rough work clothes, are listening intently. She can't see the speaker and can only hear fragments of what he's saying but realises it's Rex Shepperton holding their attention. After a few minutes, the meeting closes with a sprinkling of applause and a low rumble of grumbling as the men file out a side door. A moment later, Rex walks in, looking his usual dishevelled self in a well-worn tweed jacket. He's a solid fellow with a thick head of hair streaked with silver and badly in need of a trim and his cheeks are ruddy, either from the cold or too many evenings spent at the pub.

'Ah, Hazel. What a pleasure to see your lovely face after looking at those ugly mugs in there!' Rex is followed by another man he introduces as the union organiser. 'I wouldn't be here today if it wasn't for this lady,' Rex tells the man with obvious pride. 'She looked after me as a kiddie, rescued me more times than I can even remember.'

The man raises an eyebrow. 'Mixed blessing, I suppose.'

Rex laughs and turns to Hazel. 'Thanks for coming in. I wanted the chance to show you round and have a chat before you officially start next week.'

He opens the counter to allow her through, points out his own office and leads the way down a dark hallway with pale green walls like a hospital.

'Rex . . . or would you rather I called you Mr Shepperton at work?' asks Hazel.

'I get called a lot worse than Rex.' He chuckles. 'Of course, Rex is fine.' He stops at a door and flicks through a bunch of keys on a ring. 'As I said on the phone, Trades Hall in the city is our headquarters, but we also have this office down here. We come back and forth and are down here for worker meetings all day on Wednesday. So I thought you could spend the Wednesday down here, and Monday and Friday at Trades Hall – if that suits you?'

Hazel nods, relieved she only needs to brave the docks once a week. 'Did you have a tea lady previously?'

'A tea man actually – nickname Cold Tea Jack. Probably tells you all you need to know,' says Rex, trying various keys in the lock. 'He was before my time. The thing is, we're in competition for membership with a couple of other unions, one being the notorious Painters and Dockers mob. Being able to offer workers a hot cup of tea when they come in will do wonders for our public relations. These blokes don't get much for free.'

'Of course,' says Hazel. 'We'll work on it together.'

Rex grins. 'Just like the old days.' Unlocking the door, he pushes it open for Hazel to enter. 'How's your Norma getting on?'

'She's very well. Country life agrees with her,' says Hazel, glancing around.

'You've got a couple of grand-kiddies, I seem to remember?'

'Twins – Harry and Barrie, eleven this year. Lovely little boys.'

Hazel notices a shadow of sadness cross Rex's face and understands why, but there's nothing to be said about the great tragedy in his life. And now is not the time anyway.

'Well, here you are,' he says, looking around the small kitchen. 'Your own little empire. Set it up however you want.' Handing her a couple of keys, he adds, 'That's the front door and the kitchen door. Now, anything else you need?'

'Is there a budget for biscuits?' she asks. 'I have a wholesaler—'

'Of course. Whatever you want.' Rex gives her a warm smile. 'Good to have you on board. You're just what we need to oil the wheels around here.'

'I'll do my best,' she says, returning his smile.

'Good on you, Hazel love. Now I think of it, we're all away at a conference next week, so start the week after.' He pauses at the door. 'You probably know from the news that a variety of activities go on down here. The less you know about them the better.'

'There was a body being removed when I arrived,' says Hazel. 'I spoke to a fellow on the wharves who implied it was . . . murder.'

Rex sighs. 'It's possible. That's the second body fished out of the harbour in a month. Don't take too much notice of what the papers say. It's not the wharfies . . . well, not our members, at least.'

Hazel feels a gentle tingling in her ears. It seems Rex is doing a little public relations work himself, perhaps bending the truth a little.

'It's rival criminal gangs that operate down here and, to be honest, one less of that lot is no great loss. On top of everything else, you might have heard about this gold robbery on board the *Cape Argus* in the papers yesterday?'

'A million in gold coins,' says Hazel. 'Bound to capture the public imagination.'

Rex shakes his head despairingly. 'It's put a lot of people on edge down here. So what I'm saying is, being friendly and cheerful is good, being too inquisitive is not good.' He fills his cheeks with air and blows it out. 'And possibly dangerous.'

Surprised by his serious tone, Hazel says she'll keep that in mind.

Rex lingers in the doorway. After a moment he pulls his wallet out of his back pocket and opens it to reveal a thick wad of cash, peels off a couple of twenties and hands them to Hazel. 'There's no heating in this building. Get yourself a warmer coat.'

Hazel flushes. 'Rex, I couldn't possibly—'

'Let me do this for you, Hazel,' he says. Noting her struggle to accept, he adds, 'Bring me the receipt and I'll claim it as protective clothing.'

'All right,' says Hazel reluctantly. 'Since you put it like that. Thank you.'

He gives her a jaunty salute and heads off down the hall, whistling tunelessly.

Hazel stands for a moment, looking around the cold, cheerless kitchen, which doesn't seem to have been cleaned since Cold Tea Jack went on his way. There's a small bench and sink and a Zip hot water heater. In the floor-to-ceiling cupboards on one side of the room, she finds a filthy tea trolley, along with a couple of dozen heavy white cups and saucers and a battle-scarred, double-handed teapot. She'll have to give the place a thorough going over when she starts work.

Out on the docks, seagulls are tossed about by blustery winds. Hazel passes a team of workers lowering a huge cargo net containing a dozen wooden crates off a ship, using curved hooks with handles to guide the cargo towards the dock. As she reaches the gates, she hears a shout and turns to see the net has ripped open. The load tips heavily to one side. Workers run for their lives as a crate tumbles to the ground, smashing open on the dock, the rest left hanging precariously.

Men come running from every direction. The scattered contents of the crate – car exhausts and mufflers – are snatched up. The broken crate is shoved off the dock into the harbour. Within minutes, the looting is over, men return to their work and the remaining crates are lowered onto the docks as if nothing happened.

As she leaves, Hazel wonders if she has just witnessed a typical day on the docks. She was only there an hour. Clearly not every day heralds a new murder, if that's what it was, but this area is notorious as a hotbed of crime, making headlines with wildcat strikes, pillaging on a grand scale, widespread corruption and violent standover men.

Hazel feels a sudden pang of missing her fellow tea ladies, Betty, Irene and Merl, and their lunch get-togethers in Zig Zag Lane. And the staff of Empire Fashionwear, where she worked for ten years and knew everyone. She gives herself a shake. There's no point in dwelling in the past. Once you start, where do you stop? Rex was kind enough to offer her a job, a great relief given she'd been out of work for so long. Perhaps not her ideal workplace but interesting all the same, and she'll enjoy working with her old friend.

Hazel opens her front door to the fragrant aroma of roasting meat and vegetables. She calls out a half-frozen 'Cooeee!' to let Betty know she's home and gets a warm one in return. Hanging her coat on the hallstand, she goes down to the kitchen. Betty has the coal range heating the room, and she's even filled the scuttle from the sack in the backyard. A friend of many years, Betty Dewsnap really is the perfect boarder.

'I was frozen the entire day,' says Betty, bending over to peek in the oven. 'I washed up all the cups twice just to have my hands in hot water.'

Hazel agrees. 'I do hope this cold snap will be over soon. It was bleak down on the docks with that wind straight off the harbour.'

'And how did it go?' asks Betty, closing the oven door.

'It was fine,' says Hazel, not wanting to expand on the experience, the details of which would only worry her friend.

Betty, now topping and tailing green beans, pauses to look at Hazel. 'I could manage to pay a bit more in board, so you don't have to take the job— oh gosh! I just saw Irene come in the gate. She can probably smell a rolled roast all the way from Lisbon Street.'

A moment later, Irene Turnbuckle gusts through the back door in her tatty black winter coat. She has a limp cigarette stuck to her lip, and a newspaper under her arm. She's also wearing a stripy woollen hat that looks vaguely familiar to Hazel.

'It's bloody freezin' out there!'

'Irene, close the door, for heaven's sake! I hate this dreadful wind,' cries Betty.

'Can't stand the competition, eh?' Irene chuckles, kicking the door shut behind her.

'Very funny, Irene,' says Betty crossly.

Standing with her back to the range, Irene rubs her hands together.

'And now you're hogging all the heat,' Betty grumbles. 'Also, is that Hazel's tea cosy you're wearing?'

Irene takes off the knitted hat and stares at it. 'Wondered why it had two holes in it. Thought they was for yer ears, to hear better.'

Hazel laughs. 'You can keep it, Irene. It suits you.'

'I suppose you're staying for tea, are you, Irene?' asks Betty resignedly as she takes the roast out of the oven.

'Don't mind if I do,' Irene says, pulling out a chair.

The headline emblazoned across the front page of the evening newspaper catches Hazel's eye and she picks it up to read.

MURDER & MAYHEM!

To Sydney's great shame, its port and wharves have become utterly lawless in the grip of criminal unions and communists. On top of the recent million-dollar gold robbery, today an unknown victim was found murdered. Two murders in a month, the first still unsolved. Our fair city now holds the dubious title of Australia's centre of crime and the police seem powerless to control it. Prime Minister Holt has dubbed it Australia's wild west and State Premier Askin has publicly suggested he pull his head in and stick to his own job.

Hazel quickly folds the paper and puts it on the dresser, out of Betty's sight. She finds a bottle of plum wine in the cupboard and pours them each a glass.

'This is the life, eh?' says Irene. She has a good sniff of the meal put in front of her. 'Smells good enough to eat,' she adds with a grin.

'We don't eat like this every night,' Betty says. 'It was on special at the butcher's, so I thought we'd have a little celebration. Hazel went to see about her new job today.'

'I'm not quite sure how I feel about it, to be quite honest,' Hazel admits.

Irene takes a swig and grimaces. 'Yer not taking that job down the docks?'

'I don't really have much choice. I've got to get those broken roof tiles replaced before it gets worse. Both upstairs bedrooms have sinister stains on the ceiling, and I've already got half-a-dozen buckets in the roof space.'

'Yer bloody mad setting foot down there. Commies and crims, the lot of 'em.'

'I don't like the idea of you venturing down there either, Hazel,' agrees Betty. 'It's no place for a lady, everyone says that. It's too dangerous.'

Hazel looks up from her dinner, this conversation spoiling the pleasure of it. 'Think of it as a temporary measure. I know what you're saying, but we're tea ladies. We're no strangers to danger, are we? I'll look out for myself, I promise.'

But neither Betty nor Irene seems reassured.

2
IRENE CATCHES FIRE

Irene stands dead centre in front of the television in the window of Gibson's Electrical. The usual bunch of spotty brats and local louts are gathered around her, waiting for the show to start. As soon as *The Beverly Hillbillies* comes onto the screen, Irene belts out the theme song, as she always does.

One of the louts puts his hands over his ears. 'Who kicked the cat? Shut up!'

'Piss off home, Granny,' says his spotty mate.

'Piss off yerself, Pimples,' says Irene, not taking her eyes off the screen.

Another regular, a skinny girl with frizzy hair, pipes up. 'Give up, yer won't get rid of her. She never misses this or *The Flintstones*.'

'Go home, yer ol' witch,' says the spotty one, not giving up.

'I'll put a bloody spell on yers, if yer don't watch out.'

One thing Irene hates is people talking over her show. She's heard it all before anyway. They're not the only ones to complain about her singing. Most folk around here have no musical taste. A while ago, Mr Gibson put a bigger speaker out the front to try and drown her out. It hasn't put Irene off in the slightest, because singing is a human right. They should be paying to hear her.

By the time her two favourite shows are over, she's built up a thirst and pops around the corner to the Thatched Pig for a quick drink. The usual barmaid is drying the glasses behind the bar. When Irene beckons her over, she slings the tea towel over her shoulder and comes over to dead-eye Irene.

'Which gentlemen are you accompanying this evening, Mrs Turnbuckle?'

'Not this again. Every bloody time,' says Irene. Casting her gaze around the bar in search of a familiar face, Irene clocks Big G and his offsider, Onions, at their usual table and nods in their direction.

'I don't know why you can't go into the snug with the other ladies,' grumbles the barmaid, turning away to pour her a whiskey.

'Told yers before. Yer boss banned me,' says Irene, sliding the coins across the bar.

Drink in hand, she wanders over to Big G and greets him with a raise of the eyebrows.

By the look of the table, these two have been here smoking and drinking for hours. No one would mistake them for anything other than thugs. Big G has a grizzled-looking head like an old bear and a gold front tooth, while Onions looks like someone used his face as a punching bag.

'Mrs Turnbuckle,' says Big G. 'What can I do for you?'

'Yer don't know where I can get one of them little portable tellies, do yer?' she asks.

'Why don't you buy one from Mr Gibson?' he suggests. 'You spend enough time squawking like a strangled parrot out front. He'd probably give you one to get rid of you.'

Squawking? Irene wonders if his hearing is on the blink.

'Too pricey,' she says. 'He's a rip-off artist, Gibson.'

Big G and Onions exchange blank looks. 'What size were you after?'

Irene makes a rough shape with her hands. 'One of them ones with the rabbit ears so I don't need an aerial.'

'I hear yer living at 555 these days,' says Big G. 'On the game, are yah?'

'Thought about it.' Irene grins. 'Nah, I'm on the maintenance side,' she says, thinking that sounds better than cleaning.

'Watchdog,' suggests Onions.

Irene decides to jolly them along. 'Woof-woof.'

'Yer better watch yerself there,' says Big G. 'There's going to be a lot of tart shops opening round here soon. Yanks are about to come in from Vietnam in their thousands.'

Onions grunts. 'Sick of 'em already. Big-noting theirselves around the place.'

This is the most Irene has ever heard Onions utter in one go. He's not the only one upset about hordes of Americans turning up. Local blokes don't like the competition. But there's plenty of others, mostly crooks, who can't wait to hear the *ka-ching* of registers cashing in American dollars.

'Miss Palmer knows what she's doing,' says Irene, with a shrug. 'There's room for all. If anyone's going to make money out of the Yanks, it'll be her.'

'Yer reckon? She'll be greedy for a bundle of hay while the sun shines,' says Big G.

Another thing Irene hates is people talking in riddles. 'Meaning?'

Big G sighs. 'Pretty soon the Yanks are gonna lose that war and go home. The tap will turn off overnight.' He looks to see if she's getting the message. 'We're talking a turf war here. Everyone's after the same hay is what I'm tryna tell yers. Watch yerself at 555.'

'All right, how about that telly?' says Irene, fed up with this conversation.

'I'll see what I can do.' He stares across the room to show he's lost interest.

Irene takes the hint and moves off to a table in the corner where she has a view of the whole bar area. She sips her drink and thinks about his advice. It wouldn't be the first turf war round here. Not long ago, two brothels were firebombed. One was saved but the other burnt to the ground. Every so often wars break out between gambling dens, SP bookmakers and sly grog operations. They always sort themselves out one way or another. But Miss Palmer's a smart lady with friends in very high places. She knows what she's doing.

Irene's the first to arrive at the low wall in Zig Zag Lane where the tea ladies meet most days. In summer they sit about and chat. In winter it's a quick sandwich and a cup of tea from a thermos, and then they're off again. Their get-togethers haven't been the same since Hazel got the boot from Empire Fashionwear. Now it's just Betty, who works at Farley Frocks and blubbers about every little thing, and know-it-all Merl, the tea lady at Klein's Lingerie. That one gets on Irene's wick, but her baking makes up for a lot. Problem is that Hazel was the peacemaker, and since she's gone, they're a bit out of whack.

There's a nasty cold breeze today and Irene's still trying to get her pipe to catch when Betty turns up in a coat with a pink knitted scarf and matching hat.

'Must you, Irene? The embers are flying everywhere,' she says before she even sits down.

Irene tries a couple more puffs and gives up on the pipe. She gets two Scotch Fingers out of her coat pocket and tucks the pipe away.

'I'm not sure Merl will come today, it's probably too cold for her. Which I can understand,' says Betty, unwrapping her sandwich. 'They said on the news that this wind is coming straight off the Antarctic.'

'Bloody sook,' says Irene. 'It's a bit fresh is all.'

'I don't blame her,' says Betty. She fiddles around in her shopping bag and gets out a thermos. 'I've got an extra cup if you want one?'

Irene nods. Taking the cup from Betty, she warms her hands on it. 'I'm thinking of getting a little telly for me room upstairs.'

'You're going to buy one, are you?' asks Betty, sounding suspicious.

'How else am I gunna get one?'

Betty purses her lips. 'I think that's fairly obvious, Irene. Anyway, Mr Gibson will no doubt be pleased about that.'

'Getting one off Big G,' says Irene.

'Hmm . . . talk about a rat with a gold tooth,' says Betty.

'What's that s'posed to mean? He's a mate of mine, I'll have yers know.'

Betty finishes her sandwich and folds up her lunch paper. 'I think you know perfectly well. Didn't you get those dodgy transistors you were flogging around off him?'

'Nothin' dodgy about 'em,' says Irene, not really expecting to be believed.

'Anyway, I'm going back to work. It's too cold for me.' Betty sniffs the air. 'Is that terrible smell the foundry, or an incinerator? It's awful.'

Irene's sense of smell is not the best but even she gets a whiff.

'It's you!' Betty screams and leaps to her feet.

It takes a second for Irene to realise that smoke is leaking out of her coat pocket. But before she has time to work out why, Betty rips the coat off her (nearly ripping her arms out with it), throws the thing on the ground and stamps her feet all over it.

'Gerroff me good bloody coat, will yer!'

Betty drops to her knees. Huffing and puffing, she slaps at the coat with her pink hat. Then, to make things worse, she grabs the thermos and pours tea over it.

'Hardly picnic weather,' says Merl, appearing out of nowhere. Then, noticing that neither of them thinks that's funny, she helps Betty to her feet.

Irene picks up her coat and dusts the dirt off. 'It's soaking wet.'

'Her awful pipe must have set her pocket on fire,' Betty tells Merl.

'Considering the coat and its occupant are likely drenched in alcohol, I'd say that was a lucky escape,' says Merl.

Irene pulls her coat back on. 'There's a hole in the pocket,' she complains. 'That's the one I keep me lunch in.'

'You're lucky to have a coat at all,' says Betty. 'Just keep your silly Scotch Fingers in the other pocket, for goodness sake.'

Irene notices that there's not just a hole in the pocket but a nasty smell as well. But at least she has a coat. She'll get used to the stink.

'I'm going back to work,' says Betty. 'It's too cold out here.'

'I'm not staying,' says Merl. 'I just wanted to pass on information that the cleaner is leaving our firm. They're looking for a new one. I thought Hazel might be interested if she's still looking for work. She'd have to be quick.'

Betty turns bright red. 'Really, Merl,' she splutters. 'Hazel is a professional tea lady.'

Merl gives a huff. 'Don't get all high and mighty, madam. It was just a thought.'

'I'd like to see yer get a cleaning job,' says Irene, also insulted.

Merl's head does a wobble. 'Don't you work as a cleaner, Irene?'

'That's different. We're talking about Hazel here,' says Irene.

'Well, wonders will never cease. I've never known you to agree with anyone before, Irene,' says Merl with a sniff. 'I'm simply trying to be helpful.'

'In any case,' Betty continues, 'Hazel has a new position. She starts next week.'

By Irene's reckoning, Merl's not too happy to hear that news. She's always up to something, that one.

'Well then,' says Merl, still all huffy. 'I'll take myself back to work.'

Betty calms down a bit and says, 'All right. We'll see you at the pub, if not before.'

When Merl's gone, Betty says, 'The cheek of it. Thank you for backing me up, Irene.'

Irene hates this sort of soppy talk. 'Won't be makin' a habit of it.'

Irene lives in the attic of 555, a high-class brothel, getting free board in return for cleaning the place. When Miss Palmer, the madam, is around, Irene has to use the back gate, but when she has the place to herself, she prefers to make a grand exit out the front door, which is rarely used. She likes the way her feet sink into the thick carpet in the entry hall as she walks beneath the sparkling chandelier, and enjoys stepping outside to lock the door as if she owns the place. There's nothing nice about the back gate. It leads into the laneway that stinks of pee and a lot worse, and she has to take a cut-through to Lisbon Street to avoid the side lane. Miss Palmer's clientele enter the building through a discreet entrance in this lane, which is guarded by a big thug Irene remembers from when he was a bouncer at the Venus Room.

This evening, headed down to the corner shop for a packet of smokes, Irene notices a car parked on Lisbon Street with two men sitting in it. From this angle, it looks to her as if they're watching 555. She has a good squiz as she passes but can't see much in the dark. She pauses to speak to one of the streetwalkers, shivering in a skirt the size of a hankie and fish-net stockings.

'Cops?' Irene asks, nodding towards the car.

The girl squints through a cloud of cigarette smoke and shakes her head. 'Seen 'em a few times. Not cops. Just a couple of old guys, foreigners by the looks of them. Probably just having a perve. Plenty of them around here.'

Satisfied with that explanation, Irene continues on her way, cracking jokes with the girls gathered along the street as she passes. The street girls never hang around Miss Palmer's place, Vice Squad make sure of that. They turn up on Friday mornings to collect a fat envelope from Miss Palmer and they look after her interests. Her girls have the reputation of being the best in the business, and she knows how to look after the big boys better than anyone. But, thinking back to Big G's comments, Irene feels a little uneasy. She'll be keeping a beady eye out for anything suspicious.

3

HAZEL HAS A SURPRISE VISITOR

Feeding the last wet sheet into the mangle, Hazel senses someone behind her in the backyard. As she turns to look, her hand is pulled between the rollers. Wincing with pain, she leans over and hits the release to free her arm.

'Sorry, Mrs Bates, I didn't mean to startle you,' says Detective Dibble, standing in the doorway of the washhouse.

'Not the first time I've done that,' says Hazel, rubbing her arm. 'Laundry can be a dangerous business.'

Dibble smiles. 'And not just money laundering, it seems. I tried the front door, and then realised it was Monday and you'd be out back.'

When Hazel last saw the detective, he looked very much the law-enforcement professional, wearing a smart grey suit and matching trilby. Today he looks as if he slept in the suit and sat on his hat, and his coat is long overdue for a dry-cleaning.

'I gather this is not a social visit – unless you're desperate for a good cup of tea,' she says, clamping the mangle back into place and edging in the sheet.

Dibble gives her a weary smile. 'I had an overnight stakeout nearby and, yes, I could do with a decent cuppa.'

'Just let me get this on the line, and we'll get inside out of the cold.'

Dibble carries the basket out, and Hazel quickly pegs the washing and pushes the prop up to its full height. Despite the chill, they pause to watch the sheets dance in the breeze for a moment. It's a perfect drying day, a bright blue winter's morning. By midday every backyard in Surry Hills will have flapping white sheets hoisted high on prop lines, signalling their surrender to Monday wash day.

'Now, let's get that kettle on,' says Hazel. 'I've got some poppy seed cake in the tin.'

She makes the tea and wields the poker inside the range until the embers glow.

Dibble slips off his coat, places his hat on the table and sits down. 'I only half expected to find you here. I heard you'd found a job.'

'Did you now?' asks Hazel, doubting that's what brought him to her door.

He gives a shrug. 'It was in the papers. "Famous Tea Lady Accepts Position"—'

Hazel laughs. She brings the teapot and cups over to the table. 'I believe you bumped into Mrs Dewsnap recently – she's a more likely source. It's big news for me after being out of work for so long. Almost eighteen months.' She pours the tea, puts two slices of cake on a plate and sits down. 'I start next week with the Dockside Workers Union. On top of that, I'll continue my volunteering at the People's Palace. So I'm suddenly very busy.'

'The People's Palace,' repeats Dibble dubiously.

'In the doss and dormitory women's sections.'

Dibble raises an eyebrow. 'Some interesting types there.'

Hazel nods. 'I do meet some troubled souls and hear some very sad stories. Makes me glad to have a roof over my head, even if it is a leaky one. It seems that more and more companies are replacing their tea lady with a machine, so I'm pleased to have found a position.'

'They've actually taken the machine out of police headquarters and the tea lady's back.' With a grin, Dibble adds, 'Important men like to be waited on.'

'Let's hope it's a trend that continues. Now, I'm sure you didn't creep up on me this early in the day to discuss the fortunes of the tea lady.'

Dibble takes a leisurely bite of his seed cake. 'It was partly the prospect of tea and cake, but I'm also interested to hear about your position with the union. Do you mind me asking how that came about?'

'I'm sure you're acquainted with Rex Shepperton, the Dockside Union secretary?'

Dibble nods. 'Highly controversial fellow, especially with all the strike action and union wars on the waterfront.'

'Our families lived next to each other growing up.' Hazel nods up the street. 'Just two blocks from here. He's the youngest of five boys. Sadly, the mother was in and out of hospital with TB, and so the boys were in and out of homes. My family used to help out where we could. I was twelve when Rex came along, and I used to keep an eye out for him – unlike his brothers.'

'Like a big sister?' suggests Dibble.

'Exactly. Anyway, he heard that I'd been out of work for a while and offered me a part-time position.' Hazel pauses. 'Why the interest, Detective?'

'Does the word "Krugerrand" mean anything to you?' he asks.

'I've heard the word bandied about in the news recently with the robbery,' says Hazel. 'It's some sort of commemorative gold coin?'

'It's a 22-carat gold bullion coin issued at the start of last month by the South African government. Something quite unique – 91.67 per cent pure gold and the rest is copper. In Australia, it's illegal to own or trade bars of gold bullion without permission from the Reserve Bank, but the Krugerrand gets around this. It's a legal currency that can be used anywhere in the world. One coin is worth about a hundred and fifty dollars here.'

Hazel nods. 'I see. Hmm . . . I can already imagine it opens the door for money laundering and moving funds around easily.'

'That's what I'm working on.' Dibble pours himself another cup of tea. 'So this was the first shipment of Krugerrand into this country. Brought in on the *Cape Argus* from Port of Durban, imported by an authorised dealer by the name of Charles Beauchamp. As a safeguard against it being stolen, the cargo was listed as "souvenirs" on the bill of lading.'

'Was it really a precaution or was he was trying to avoid import duty?' asks Hazel.

'He claims he planned to declare the goods correctly once the vessel docked in Sydney. The *Cape Argus* off-loaded goods in Darwin and customs officers went on board there, on the lookout for contraband coming in from South Africa. They accepted that the coins were souvenirs and were none the wiser.' He pauses. 'And to be fair, none of us had even heard of Krugerrand until this robbery.'

'So the coins were stolen between here and Darwin?' asks Hazel. 'Did they stop at any other ports down the coast?'

'No, there are only a couple of ports on the east coast suitable for cargo ships. But anyway, when customs boarded the *Cape Argus* in Sydney, the goods had mysteriously disappeared.'

'I read it was around a million,' says Hazel.

'Almost seven thousand coins, all packed in presentation boxes,' confirms Dibble.

'Gosh, that's a lot of coins to hide. So quite small boxes?'

Dibble flips open his notebook and flicks through the pages until he finds what he's looking for. 'Black velvet boxes four inches square, half an inch deep. I suppose the sort of thing a pair of earrings or a pendant would come in. It'd fit in the palm of your hand. Why do you ask?'

'Just trying to picture them. And are the captain and crew the main suspects?'

'They're being questioned. There are a few nationalities on board, so we've had to get interpreters involved, making it more complicated. On the surface, it seems like an inside job, but Beauchamp is adamant that the captain and crew were not aware of the true cargo. He evidently went to some trouble to represent himself as an importer of souvenirs. Something he's done before with more success in the past, so he says.'

'Do you think this recent death on the waterfront had anything to do with it? I was down there when they were taking the poor fellow away,' says Hazel.

'Who knows? From what I understand, that bloke was part of the criminal fraternity down there. I wouldn't waste any time feeling sorry for him.'

'Could the gold have been dropped overboard somewhere along the way? Or smuggled off the boat while it was in the harbour?' suggests Hazel.

'All possibilities we're investigating. Given it was the first ever shipment into the country, if any of the coins go into circulation then we'll have something to track. But it's more likely the thieves want to get them out of the country again.' Dibble sighs. 'It's early days, but right now we have nothing. This is just the sort of mystery case that the public love, and the papers are lapping it up. On top of that, Charles Beauchamp is something of a personality. He and his wife, Angela, are well-known society types with friends in high places.'

'Ah, the Beauchamps,' says Hazel. 'Even I've heard of the annual Beauchamp Ball held at the Wentworth – always covered in great detail in the society pages.'

'Exactly. A diamond-studded event, as they say, opened by the mayor and packed with politicians. So, as you can imagine, the pressure is on to solve the robbery.'

Hazel smiles. 'And that's where the tea lady comes in?'

Dibble gives her an embarrassed smile. 'I just thought you could keep those very sharp eyes of yours open, and put it out to your tea ladies' network.'

'I imagine there are plenty of places to hide things if they got the cargo ashore,' muses Hazel. 'There would have to be a few people involved.'

'There's a lot of skulduggery on the wharves. There'll also be crooks trying to find the stolen goods – we're talking serious villains, like the Toe-Cutters gang. There's no shortage of hard men down there.' He pauses, considering his words. 'Mrs Bates, keep in mind that Rex Shepperton is also a hard man. You don't get into a position like that playing by the rules and being a nice bloke. So watch yourself there.'

Quietly offended, Hazel says, 'Perhaps, but I do believe he's a man of integrity.'

Dibble shrugs. 'Anyway, be careful. You've got my home number if you see anything interesting, but keep your head down.' He gets up and puts his hat and coat on. 'Just pretend you're a tea lady.'

'I won't be putting myself in the way of danger,' says Hazel, as she walks him to the front door. 'Tea ladies are just mere mortals, you know.'

Dibble laughs. '*That* I don't believe.'

Stepping outside, he pulls up the collar of his coat. 'Thanks for the tea, Mrs Bates. Good luck with the job.'

'And let's not forget my job is making tea,' Hazel reminds him. 'Not fighting crime.'

He gives her a grin and raises his hands in mock surrender.

4
BETTY HAS A GLIMPSE OF THE FUTURE

Betty never looks forward to delivering morning and afternoon tea in the haberdashery department of Farley's Frocks. In the factory, the girls are friendly and cheerful. In the office, where they do stock control and process garment orders, the ladies are always pleasant. But the wholesale haberdashery department, which takes up the entire first floor of the building, is the mainstay of the firm, so the staff there tend to think they're better than the rest.

To an outsider, haberdashery might appear chaotic, but it's actually highly organised. Everything has a place. There are long shelving racks that stretch the width of the room with colourful bolts of fabric; hundreds (if not thousands) of boxes of buttons, domes, hooks and eyes; cards of trimmings; boxes of industrial cotton reels; and more bits and bobs than she can possibly name. This department is busy all day long.

The seven women and three men who work in this department are always in too much of a hurry to chat with the tea lady. And on several occasions she's been shouted at by someone loaded up with bolts of fabric or towering boxes of cotton reels to get out of the way. Awfully rude given that she's simply doing her own important job.

The staff have all been here for donkey's years. So it comes as a surprise when Betty arrives with morning tea to find a new staff member. Even more surprising is that the young woman greets her with a warm smile and introduces herself as Lucy. She's pretty, with a delicate face framed by long thick hair in a plait that falls to her waist, like a princess in a storybook.

All the women in this department wear frumpy button-up smocks or a pinny with pockets, but Lucy is oddly dressed in a long cotton frock with a thick jumper over the top. No doubt the supervisor, a crotchety old fellow who's been here thirty years, will be having a word to her about that.

Lucy, who takes her tea black, no sugar, asks, 'We're allowed to take a break, are we?' as if she thinks Betty's in charge of things.

'Yes, I suppose so,' agrees Betty.

That's technically correct but no one in this department ever takes a proper break. They grab their tea or coffee and gulp it on the move, leaving their cup on a shelf somewhere for Betty to hunt down.

A couple of the staff mutter 'thank you', while others ignore Betty altogether as if she's an extension of the trolley. Lucy perches on the edge of the sample table, rolls a cigarette and sips her tea. Smoking in a leisurely manner, she asks Betty all about herself, how long she's worked there, where she lives and so forth. This is the most interest anyone has ever taken in all the years Betty's worked at Farley's.

'You have lovely hands, Mrs Dewsnap.' Lucy leans over for a closer look.

Betty holds her hands up for inspection, noting that the pink pearlescent polish sets them off nicely. 'Oh gosh, they used to be one of my best features but now . . . I don't know.'

'Do let me read your palm,' says Lucy, hopping down off the table.

'Um, all right,' says Betty, taken by surprise. 'I have to collect the cups in a minute.'

Lucy pinches her cigarette out and puts it in an ashtray. 'Be done in a jiffy.' She takes Betty's right hand in hers and gazes intently at her palm. 'Oh, so intriguing,' she murmurs.

'I hope there's no journey across the sea,' says Betty. 'I get terribly seasick. I suppose a tall dark handsome stranger would be all right, but not too tall. Or too handsome.'

Lucy glances up with a knowing smile. 'I can see you're quite emotional,' she says, tracing a line across Betty's palm. 'Your heart is warm but fragile too. Easily broken. Your love line is quite short.' Lucy's fingers gently trace the line on Betty's palm. 'Did you lose someone close to you?'

'My husband died some years ago . . .' Betty stops, afraid of bursting into tears.

'I can see an important journey for you ahead,' Lucy continues. 'Not across the seas – more a personal odyssey, a spiritual journey within yourself. Into your soul, I suppose.'

All this attention is making Betty feel a bit jangly and confused. She says brightly, 'Thank you, dear, but right now I need to go on a journey to find all the cups left around the place.'

Lucy laughs. 'Why don't you come around for tea on Saturday, to my house? I can tell you in more detail what's in store for you. I'd love it if you could come.'

Betty barely knows what to say. While the girl seems genuine enough, it's hard to know if she's serious. No one at Farley's has ever invited Betty home, let alone at their first meeting. 'Um . . . lovely,' says Betty, packing up her trolley.

Lucy claps her hands happily, like a child. 'I'll give you my address tomorrow.'

As Betty wanders around collecting the cups from the various hiding places (only one with a cigarette butt floating in the dregs), she finds herself pleased and puzzled, which is quite a nice feeling, she decides.

Betty's relieved to step out of the cold and into the Hollywood Hotel. Its cosy atmosphere and familiar faces are so welcoming on this otherwise bleak evening.

She and Hazel make their way to the table where Irene sits alone with a shandy – which she must have bought herself!

'Evening, Mrs B, Mrs D,' says Shirley, the publican, delivering two more shandies to the table as they sit down. 'Mrs T's full of surprises, isn't she?'

Irene scowls. 'Yer think I've never paid for me own drink before?'

'Let's just say I'll be running that fiver past the fraud squad when they're in next.' Shirley gives Betty and Hazel a wink and heads back behind the bar.

'What would be shocking,' says Betty, 'is if you bought someone else a drink.'

Irene gives a sly grin. 'Yer never know. I'm very unpre . . . pred . . .'

'Unpredictable?' suggests Betty.

'Cheap,' admits Irene.

Hazel laughs. 'At least you're honest.'

'Hmm, that's a stretch,' says Betty. She glances over at the door. 'Oh goodness, here comes the abominable snowwoman.'

A moment later, Merl looms over them, almost unrecognisable with a hat pulled down over her ears, a thick woollen scarf and heavy coat. 'We're in for a frost,' she announces.

'At least it's cosy in here,' says Hazel. 'Can I get you a drink, Merl dear?'

'Thank you but Shirley's bringing one over,' says Merl. Unwinding her scarf, she drapes her coat over the back of the chair and makes herself comfortable.

When everyone's settled with their drinks, Hazel asks, 'Merl, you mentioned you wanted to bring up something important prior to our Guild meeting?'

'Well, I didn't want to embarrass you in front of the members at the meeting but . . .' Merl hesitates for a moment, then continues. 'The fact is that you have been the Chairlady of the Tea Ladies Guild but, in actual fact, are no longer a tea lady.'

'Lotta facts in there,' says Irene sarcastically.

Merl ignores her. 'But I understand this is soon to be rectified?'

'Yes, I start my new job next week,' says Hazel. 'So I'll be a bona-fide tea lady.'

Merl just sniffs and pulls her knitting out of her bag. 'As I said, I didn't want to bring it up in front of everyone. But I'm glad to hear the situation is resolved.'

Betty gives a start. 'Oh, now I know what you're up to, Merl Perlman! You thought *you* could take Hazel's place as Chairlady by disqualifying her.'

'I'm sure Merl was thinking of the Guild—' begins Hazel.

Bristling with indignation, Betty continues, 'Hazel, you always think the best of people, but I think the reason Merl was trying to push a cleaning job on you was so she could get control of the Guild!'

Merl frowns at her knitting – an admission of guilt as far as Betty is concerned.

'It's the first I've heard of it,' says Hazel, looking to Merl for a response.

'Betty's being dramatic, as usual. It's not some Machiavellian plot—' begins Merl.

'Who's he in his undies?' interrupts Irene.

'There's no need to be coarse, Irene. What I'm saying is it wasn't some cunning plan to dethrone you, Hazel. I was only thinking of your financial situation and offering a possible solution. I was simply trying to be helpful. That's all.'

Betty doesn't believe a word of it. She knows Merl all too well. The woman is given to scheming and certainly *would* like to take the reins of the Guild, which would be disastrous. When the Guild was first established some years ago, it was Merl's prejudices and whispering behind closed doors that caused it to collapse. Last year the Guild had reformed to support tea ladies losing their jobs to automation, and they're now trying to raise funds for the new orphanage at the convent.

'Of course, if I did step down, the position would go to a vote,' says Hazel.

'I might put meself up for election,' says Irene, baring her dreadful dentures in a grin.

'Heaven forbid,' says Merl, looking amused. 'Where are you working, Hazel?'

'I'll be at the Dockside Workers Union in Trades Hall on Sussex Street two days a week and then one day a week on the wharves.'

'Sweetenin' up the reds,' says Irene, getting out a large cigar.

'Please don't smoke that in here, Irene,' says Betty. 'Even your pipe was better than those things. Also, where are you getting them from? They look expensive.' Getting no response, Betty continues. 'Much as I don't like to agree with Irene, they are all communists in those unions. You'll have to watch out they don't brainwash you, Hazel.'

'I can't imagine why they allow the Communist Party to operate here,' adds Merl. 'What's the point in fighting them in Vietnam when we're letting them sprout up here?'

'Free country,' says Irene, lighting her cigar (much to Betty's annoyance).

'Not for long if they take control,' warns Merl.

'I don't really think there's any risk of them taking over,' says Hazel. 'And I'm sure they won't force me to become a party member. I'll just be making the tea. I've known Rex Shepperton since he was a baby—'

'He's a big baby now,' says Irene. 'A big bloody pinko.'

Changing topics, Merl starts harping on about the Guild again. 'The thing is, I feel I need a title that reflects my seniority in the Guild—'

'How about Chief Twit?' suggests Irene, grinning.

Merl doesn't rise to the bait. 'I am one of the founding members and I am solely responsible for fundraising. We still don't have even close to enough funds for all the little orphans' beds, and the orphanage opens in two months.'

Betty raises her hand. 'That's because every time someone has a fundraising idea, you squash it in favour of something you want to do.'

Merl puffs up her chest indignantly. 'I beg your pardon, Betty. That's simply not true. It's my job to weed out the practical from the impractical. I just think I deserve a little more credit and respect than I'm currently receiving.'

'How about Queen of Sheba?' suggests Irene, obviously enjoying herself.

'Will you be quiet, Irene?' snaps Merl.

Hazel holds up her hands for peace. 'You make such a valuable contribution, Merl. No one is questioning that—'

'I am,' interrupts Irene, who can't resist any opportunity to rile Merl.

'I just think we need to be careful we don't become top-heavy with titles. Currently we just have the usual committee titles . . .' At Merl's stubborn and disagreeable expression, Hazel adds, 'But, if it's important to you, perhaps something like "Fundraising Coordinator"?'

Merl purses her lips. 'Chief Fundraising Coordinator.'

Hazel hesitates, obviously thinking through the potential consequences of giving Merl a title with Chief in it, and Betty steps in.

'It's not my decision,' she says, 'but I think the word "chief" is a bit silly, and it's going to get the other ladies' backs up.'

'I've got me back up already,' adds Irene. 'Carrying on like a pork chop over a stupid title.'

'Perhaps start with the simple title and see how we go from there?' suggests Hazel.

Merl gives a stiff nod. She turns her attention to her knitting, but Betty can see from her expression that this is not the end of it.

5
PRETENDING AND FORGETTING

'Ah, Mrs Bates, you are a good volunteer,' says Mrs Babinski when Hazel arrives for her shift at the People's Palace. Turning her attention back to the giant pot on the stove, the cook gives it a stir. 'Always on time. And with the smile.'

Hazel thanks her. She's noticed that Mrs Babinski herself almost never smiles, and imagines she has her reasons. Apart from once revealing that she'd escaped Warsaw during the war, she never discusses her life. Solid and strong, her iron-grey hair always in a tight bun secured by a hairnet, she's probably in her seventies but in some way ageless.

Mrs Babinski points at a sack of potatoes to be peeled and chopped for soup. 'Like us ladies, these have gone to the seed outside but still good inside. Is extra work but praise the Lord, we are thankful for this generous donation.'

Hazel opens the sack to discover they have not only sprouted but there's a terrible rotting smell accompanying them. She glances over at Mrs Babinski.

'You make this bad face, Mrs Bates. Beggars cannot be choosers.'

'Of course,' says Hazel and, putting on an apron, she begins the task.

Not one for idle chat, Mrs Babinski likes to hum quietly, sometimes well-known hymns but often rousing tunes unfamiliar to Hazel, which she finds herself humming along to anyway.

When the potatoes are diced to her satisfaction, Mrs Babinski drops them into the soup pot and leaves it to simmer. 'We have tonight the bread rolls,' she says, pointing to a sack sitting on the floor. 'I bring dripping from my house.'

Hazel sets herself up at the breadboard and, slicing the rolls open, adds a generous layer of fat to each one.

Glancing over, Mrs Babinski says, 'Mrs Bates, we are not the Ritz.'

'This bread is very dry,' Hazel points out, wondering how they will even swallow it.

'We only have this food nobody wants,' says the cook. 'We do not complain. We are grateful to God for every crumb.'

Hazel can't argue with that and agrees to apply the dripping a little less generously.

The People's Palace, in the heart of the city, is run by the Salvation Army. As well as a hotel section, with affordable accommodation for people visiting from out of town or looking for work, there are dormitories where, for a few cents a night, the poor and the homeless can find shelter and a hot meal. The penniless can work for their keep and, in the drunk's ward, can have their souls prayed for by the devoted. No extra charge.

Hazel works in the women's dormitory and the doss section, the latter for women classified as 'fallen and drunken', however she would classify them as victims of poverty, bad luck and, all too often, violence at home. Some have been found sleeping in doorways or are runaway teens picked up for soliciting and brought in by the police.

One of the reasons Hazel first volunteered at the People's Palace was that she'd found it so lonely being at home all day without a job. At Empire Fashionwear she'd served tea and biscuits to thirty staff across four floors, twice a day. She'd been part of the fabric of the place, aware of the politics of the business and involved in the lives of its employees. And almost every lunchtime she met with Betty, Irene and Merl in the laneway. They knew everyone and nothing went on in the lane that they didn't know about.

Then, last year, she'd been unceremoniously sacked. Between one day and the next, she had nowhere to go. No routine. No purpose and no companionship. Now she looks forward to the one afternoon a week when she comes to help Mrs Babinski with food preparation. She also makes new arrivals a hot cup of tea and watches that the biscuits don't get stolen. They may be small things, but a cup of tea and a kind word makes a difference to every single one of them. It brings some to tears.

At the appointed hour, Mrs Babinski carries the heavy vat of leek and potato soup out onto the serving table in the dining room, where the women have already formed a queue. Hazel ladles the soup into bowls and hands each of them a bread roll.

After dinner, while Mrs Babinski washes up, Hazel gives everyone a hot cup of tea with as much sugar as they like. Often someone lingers to chat, which is nice. It must be a lonely and frightening life without a place to call home.

This evening a woman in her fifties with weathered skin and greying hair, her clothes clean enough but well worn, strikes up a conversation, introducing herself as Flo Fletcher. She and Hazel talk about general things, the cold weather and the prospect of spring ahead. As they chat, Hazel mentions in passing that she's about to start a new job after a long period of being unemployed. When she explains that the new position is with the Dockside Union, Mrs Fletcher brings a crumpled black and white photograph out of her bag to show Hazel.

'Can you look out for this boy down there?' she asks. 'Cliff, his name is. I'd be so grateful. I was told he could be working down on the docks. Someone said a lot of the men get jobs there after . . .' She catches herself, seemingly afraid to give too much away. 'If you wouldn't mind keeping an eye out.'

Hazel takes the photo from her. It's a picture of a young man, a big fellow with a cheeky grin, hair that needs a cut and the rough work clothes of a manual worker. Behind him is the wall of a weatherboard house with peeling paint. Hazel gives her back the photo. 'If he's homeless, he could be in the men's dormitory. Have you asked at the office downstairs?'

'Cliff has a home,' says Mrs Fletcher. 'I'm here to bring him back up north where he belongs.'

'Of course,' says Hazel, her curiosity piqued but not wanting to pry.

'He's really a good lad. Ginger curly hair,' Mrs Fletcher says. 'Like a beacon, he is, and a big boy too. Hard worker.'

'I'll look out for him,' Hazel assures her. Even as she says it, she realises the futility of this statement. There are hundreds of men working on the docks, many of them strapping young fellows like Cliff Fletcher.

Mrs Fletcher thanks her and moves away, shoulders drooping despondently.

At the end of her shift, Hazel goes along to the dormitory and finds the woman sitting on her narrow iron cot, silently watching the other women prepare for bed. Hazel asks if she can sit down and Mrs Fletcher nods.

'I wondered how young Cliff ended up coming to Sydney in the first place,' says Hazel. 'Was he looking for work?'

Mrs Fletcher shakes her head. 'The truth is that he and his friend got into a neighbour's shed and stole a couple of rifles. It was a bit of skylarking. They didn't hurt anyone. They got caught and he was sentenced to twelve months in Long Bay.' She sighs. 'He got out three weeks ago and I came down here from Taree to take him home. But I haven't been able to find him. I was staying over in the hotel section, then I ran out of money and came over to the dormitory section. I want to take him home before he gets into more trouble. He has a trade, so he can get work up there.'

'And you've been to the police?' asks Hazel. Her tingling ears tell her that this is either not a true story or not the whole story.

Mrs Fletcher shakes her head. 'I don't want the police involved.' After a moment she adds, 'The boys could have been let off with a warning. The police were too hard on them.'

'I'm here on Thursdays,' says Hazel. 'If you lend me his photo, I could ask around.'

'I have to go back home for a week anyway. Nothing happens when I'm not there.' Mrs Fletcher gets the photo out of her handbag. She stares at it with such longing, it breaks Hazel's heart. But she hands it over. 'I just need to find my boy.'

To Hazel, the lad in the photo is not a boy but a man, old enough to be out of his mother's control. But she says nothing and promises to take good care of it. 'Let's exchange numbers, and I'll call if I hear anything,' she reassures Mrs Fletcher.

Mrs Babinski is sitting in the back room having a cigarette

when Hazel goes to collect her coat. 'Do you know one of the ladies called Flo Fletcher?' Hazel asks.

Mrs Babinski gives an indifferent curl of the lip. 'Skinny worn-out lady?'

This describes most of the women here, but Hazel assumes they're talking about the same person. 'She's looking for her son.'

'I see the picture,' says Mrs Babinski.

'Has anyone checked if he's been here at any point, in the men's doss section?'

Mrs Babinski takes a long drag on her cigarette and exhales a stream of smoke. 'Mrs Bates, all the people, they have a story. Do not believe what you hear. If you look for so many missing and lost . . . you also become lost. Chop the vegetables. Make the tea. Go home. Forget what you hear in these walls. There is much pretending and much forgetting.' She pauses, adding with a shrug, 'The boy is probably dead. The mother does not want to believe it. This is what happens. By the grace of God, we accept this is life.'

Hazel can understand Mrs Babinski's scepticism and gloomy outlook. Added to her own experiences of life, the cook has probably heard too many tall tales over many years working here. Perhaps she had once believed the stories and, over time, became disillusioned. Certainly Mrs Fletcher is not telling the truth, or not the whole truth at least. Nevertheless Hazel will do her best to help find this young fellow to put his mother's mind at rest.

6
PIXIE SUFFERS A SETBACK

Pixie Karp sits down at the desk to double-check the details of the Mark Foy's fashion parade. It's still a couple of days away but it's such an important event for the Mod Frocks brand that everything needs to be perfect. Her eyes blur with tiredness as she runs her pen down the list, ticking each item off. She can feel one of her headaches coming on and realises she forgot to have dinner. It's almost midnight, the building's empty and the factory dark and eerie without the roar of the sewing machines and the transistor on full blast, but at least it's quiet and she can fully concentrate.

At times like this, when she's working late into the night, she sometimes wonders why all this is so important to her. Other girls her age are out dancing and going to parties with friends, seemingly without a care in the world. It always comes back to the fact that Empire Fashionwear has been a part of her life for as long as she can remember. When she was a child, her grandad told her stories about arriving in Australia as a refugee after the war. He started with one sewing machine and built up a business with over thirty employees. He was proud to be one of the first garment factories to employ New Australians: Italian, Greek and Lebanese.

Pixie always knew she was destined to work in the family firm and, as an only child, would eventually inherit the company. The rag trade is in her blood and there's no escaping it. She has never wanted to do anything else.

When she started at Empire Fashionwear the garment industry had been turned upside down by the arrival of the miniskirt worn by British model Jean Shrimpton. Pixie had just turned nineteen and, as far as she was concerned, this was the most exciting thing that had ever happened in fashion. Her father, known to all as Frankie, insisted it was a fad, but Pixie saw an opportunity for something new. Alice, a machinist in the factory (who walks with sticks as a result of childhood polio), showed she had a talent for design. So, working with her and Gloria, the factory supervisor, Pixie had established Mod Frocks and sold mini-dresses by mail order with surprising success.

When Pixie's grandfather (old Mr Karp, as he was known) died last year, her mother, Dottie, joined Empire and began interfering in every aspect of the business including Mod Frocks, immediately toning down the designs, changing the fabrics to be less 'gauche' – one of Dottie's favourite words – and lowering hemlines, which has now begun to affect sales. It's been so frustrating, and Pixie hasn't been able to find a way around it. She feels responsible for the firm and everything her grandad worked for but, right now, she'd do anything to escape her parents' control.

She puts the list aside and goes over to inspect the rack of garments. She starts at one end and carefully checks each item to make sure the hems and facings are neatly finished. She knows shoppers won't notice, but store buyers definitely will. There are twelve mini-dresses in psychedelic pink, blue and red colourways, with matching headscarfs, four pairs of floral bell-bottom hipsters and four pairs of shorts with matching waistcoats.

When she's satisfied every garment is perfect, she checks the accessories: bright plastic bangles, wristbands of fabric flowers, strings of beads and scarves, each item tagged with numbers to match the garments. In the glare of the fluorescent lights, the collection looks like a garden of blooming flowers, bursting with colour and ready to leap onto the runway. Well, not exactly a runway, just a small temporary stage in the middle of the store.

Everyone is wearing these sorts of outfits in London, but not here in Sydney yet and Pixie knows that some shoppers will find the designs shocking. It seems to her that older people love being shocked by the latest fashions. But young ones will be crazy for them, and Pixie secretly hopes this parade will create enough interest for the department store to consider installing a Mod Frocks section on the designer floor.

Satisfied that everything is ready, she gathers her things and leaves through the front entrance. Locking the door behind her, she hurries down the street to where her car is parked. Lisbon is not the safest street for a young woman at night. There are working girls on every street corner, and she's had a few scares in the past with cars pulling up beside her and men asking what she charges for a quickie. She always breathes a sigh of relief when she hops into her little red Hillman Imp and locks the door.

Driving home, she wonders if they should start with the frocks or pants. Go for maximum impact first or build up to it? She's been to a few lunchtime parades to get ideas, but they've been quite boring and not at all what she wants to do. There's probably a knack to it and she's aware of her own inexperience. There's so much to learn . . . she wants to learn everything there is to know and more!

She lets herself into the family home and tiptoes upstairs to her bedroom, wondering for the hundredth time how she will ever escape her parents. She'll soon be twenty-one but working with those two, each difficult in their own way, is making her old before her time.

Pixie arrives in the morning to find Gloria, hair teased up in an old-fashioned beehive, her eyes circled by thick black liner, standing with her hands on her hips.

'Did you move the rack?' she asks.

Confused, Pixie looks around. 'Did it go for pressing?'

'It was all pressed, so why would it? It's all ready to go.'

Pixie feels suddenly sick. 'And where's the box of accessories? Everything was here when I left last night, I checked it all off. It doesn't make any sense. You ask around, I'll go and ask upstairs.'

She takes the lift to the top floor where her parents' offices are side by side. In the outer office, the firm's secretary, Edith Stern, looks up from her typewriter. 'They're not in,' she says, her eyes on Pixie while her fingers continue typing.

Pixie stops with a frown. Her parents had already left the house when she got up. Very unlike them. 'Where are they?' she asks.

Edith stops typing and gives her an odd look, almost guilty. 'They're out.'

Pixie stands in front of her desk. 'Please tell me what you know, Mrs Stern.'

Edith gives the keys of her typewriter a long hard stare. She looks up at Pixie. 'It's not right what they've done. I don't approve or condone it, but who listens to me?'

'What have they done?' asks Pixie, her heart sinking.

'They're at Mark Foy's, meeting about tomorrow's fashion parade—'

'What? Why are they involved?' asks Pixie, struggling to make sense of this.

'I'm sorry, Pixie, but they had your garments sent out to the storage unit first thing this morning . . . They plan to show the La Mode range instead.' Edith gives a huff of disapproval. 'I very much doubt that lunchtime shoppers and office girls have the money for ridiculously expensive cocktail gowns—'

Pixie can't decide if she wants to cry with disappointment or scream with frustration. At the ping of the lift, she manages to push down the urge to do either.

A moment later Dottie appears, hair set like stone, dressed to the nines in a peach-coloured suit with a mink slung across her shoulders. She pauses, tilting her head to one side, her gaze on Pixie. 'Now, before you throw a tantrum . . .'

Pixie takes a deep breath to calm herself. She's never thrown a tantrum in her life; there's too much competition from her parents. Determined not to be distracted, she asks, 'Can you just explain why you stole my range and replaced it with your own?'

'Sweetheart, it's not stealing. We're all part of the same company! We have to do what's best for the firm overall. Frankie and I discussed it last night and decided, with all this brutal weather, the timing was perfect to get *La Mode* on the runway with the samples we already have. It will be wonderfully aspirational for shoppers, reminding them of all the spring and summer parties ahead.'

Pixie grits her teeth. She and Alice never tire of mimicking Dottie's fake French pronunciation of La Mode but today it's not funny.

'Why didn't you discuss it with me?' Pixie asks. Then a terrible thought enters her head. 'What did you tell them at Mark Foy's?'

'We simply explained that the Mod Frocks range wasn't ready – really, Pixie, those shorts are absurd! And the fabrics – garish and tasteless. I don't know what you were thinking. Really, you should have cleared everything with me first, instead of sneaking off and doing things behind my back. Thank goodness we were able to step in at a moment's notice with the *La Mode* range.' Dottie turns to Edith Stern. 'Now, I have a VIP guest coming this afternoon—'

'I set that parade up—' interrupts Pixie, fighting tears.

'I'm sure Mr Fysh would be very disappointed to hear you claiming all the credit. He is the sales manager for the *entire* firm, may I remind you. We're all on the same team here.' Turning back to Edith, Dottie continues. 'As I was saying, Mrs Stern, I have Mrs Beauchamp coming in for a meeting at five. If you could organise some refreshments – champagne – and take her straight to the boardroom.' She pauses in the doorway of her office. 'Please make sure you're there, Pixie – she's an absolutely *vital* contact for the firm.'

But all Pixie can think of is how she's going to break the news to Gloria and Alice.

1
A SIGNIFICANT MEETING

Despite being furious with her mother, Pixie does as she's told, arriving at the top floor boardroom right on five. She's never met the famous Mrs Beauchamp but has certainly seen her in the social pages and heard Dottie talk about her often enough.

The boardroom is nicely furnished with a long, polished table, comfortable chairs and a well-stocked drinks cabinet. To Pixie's surprise, Mrs Beauchamp is already seated at the table. Dottie will probably be late as usual.

Pixie introduces herself and Mrs Beauchamp graciously stands and shakes her hand.

'I know who you are, Pixie. You're the talk of the town, and I've been so interested in watching Mod Frocks' success.'

Mrs Beauchamp is small and elegant, in a pale grey suit with her dark blonde hair in a French twist. Pixie would have expected her to be bristling with jewellery, being in the gold and diamond business. But there's nothing showy, just a pretty necklace and some diamond rings. She's nicely spoken, like an actress, with a lovely warm voice.

With a mischievous smile, Mrs Beauchamp nods towards the champagne in an ice bucket. 'Shall we get started on this?'

'Oh, of course,' says Pixie. She picks up the bottle and stares at it. She's seen her parents uncork hundreds of bottles but never attempted it herself.

'Let me, I'm an expert,' says Mrs Beauchamp with a throaty laugh. She takes the bottle and gently eases the cork out. No explosion, just a soft popping sound.

Sitting at the board table with their drinks, they chat about the fashion business. Mrs Beauchamp talks to Pixie as if she is an adult – not just an adult but an equal.

'I love the simplicity of your designs,' says Mrs Beauchamp. 'Sadly I'm a bit old for them and, in any case, I always have to be more conservative at meetings and charity events. If I were younger, I'd love to have my hair cropped like yours, so cute and fresh. Like Audrey Hepburn in—'

'*Roman Holiday*,' says Pixie, and they both laugh. 'It's called a pixie cut,' she says.

Mrs Beauchamp claps her hands in delight. 'It was made just for you!'

Dottie comes rushing in, all apologies and excuses. Pixie wishes she'd been delayed even longer so she could have more time to bask in the glow of Mrs Beauchamp's approval.

'You've met my daughter, obviously,' says Dottie. 'We're grooming her to take over the firm one day. That's a long way off yet, though.'

Pixie flushes but Mrs Beauchamp says, 'She seems to be doing brilliantly – all the young girls are talking about her frocks. I'm envious of her success. She must be a natural.'

'They're not for everyone, of course,' says Dottie, as she pours herself a glass of champagne. She joins them at the table and raises her glass in a toast. 'Here's to the wonderful Beauchamp Ball. We're so honoured to be involved.'

Mrs Beauchamp raises her glass in response. She takes a sip and lowers her glass gently to the table as if to signal they're about to get down to business.

'As you know, my Cinderella Program sponsors three young women from underprivileged backgrounds, and we provide them with gowns, jewellery and professional make-up and hair styling for the ball. It's a night they'll remember for the rest of their lives.'

'Lucky girls,' says Dottie.

In her velvety voice, Mrs Beauchamp explains she'd like the gowns to be beige silk with a grey silk tulle overskirt, the bodices decorated with gold and pink bugle beads. 'No diamantes, they'll cheapen the real thing,' she insists. 'Stella Cornelius is providing silver fox stoles, although perhaps a tulle wrap would also be nice once they take the stoles off?'

Dottie is silent. It's as if she's hypnotised, hanging on Mrs Beauchamp's every word.

These fussy gowns and old-fashioned fur stoles do not appeal to Pixie but she watches in wonder as Dottie agrees to provide the gowns (which Mrs Beauchamp must approve at every stage) completely free of charge. Dottie pretends to be delighted by the arrangement, but Pixie is quite certain this is not at all the way she saw things going. The meeting has been an education in so many ways, a lesson Pixie won't forget.

On her way home, Pixie finds herself on Hazel's doorstep. Welcomed in, she's taken along the hall to the small cosy kitchen and sits down at the table.

'You look quite frozen, dear. I'm going to make you some hot cocoa,' says Hazel, getting a saucepan from the cupboard. 'Betty's out, so we've got the place to ourselves and all the time in the world to chat.'

Pixie explains how her fashion parade was derailed. 'Gloria was furious, and Alice started crying when I told her. I feel just horrible about the whole thing.'

'It's not your fault. You couldn't know Dottie would pull a dirty trick like that.'

'She even used the models I booked through an agency, then had the cheek to complain the girls weren't "busty" enough to fill out the cocktail frocks. She said they looked more like boys than girls. I picked those girls especially. The agency rang me and complained about the way they were treated.'

Hazel puts a steaming cup of cocoa in front of Pixie. 'I thought your grandad had separated Mod Frocks from the Empire company and that the brand was yours?'

Pixie shakes her head. 'Dottie and Frankie talked him into keeping the company together until I turn twenty-one. Then Mod Frocks will come under my control.'

'But that's only a month away, from memory,' says Hazel, sitting across from her.

'I think they could still make it difficult. I don't really know how that all works.' Pixie takes a sip of warm, sweet cocoa. 'I wish I could get out of that building and start somewhere else, away from Dottie. Somewhere she can't steal stock and sabotage us.'

Hazel, who has always taken an interest in the business, asks about the new range and Pixie finds some pleasure in describing each garment. 'I'll have to get those garments back and try again,' Pixie concludes. 'I hoped this was going to be our breakthrough and we'd get our own boutique in the store.' She finishes her cocoa, dreading the moment she has to leave. 'I suppose I better go. Thanks for listening.'

'Before you go, I'd like to show you something,' says Hazel. 'It's just an idea.'

They put on coats and scarves and step out into the street, Hazel carrying a torch. 'I don't pretend to know anything about starting a business,' she says. 'It's just that I pass this shop so often and always think it would be perfect for a little dress shop.'

They cross Commonwealth into Vine, a narrow street off the main road. A few doors along, Hazel stops in front of a shop, flicks her torch on and shines it through the display window into the empty showroom.

'It was a hat shop, but it's been empty for months. Downstairs would be perfect for a boutique and there's an upstairs area the milliner used as a workroom. Could this be a possibility for you?'

Pixie leans her forehead on the glass, peering into the shop. She's touched that Hazel is taking such an interest, but it seems like an unrealistic idea for Mod Frocks to have its own premises, for now at least. Even though Pixie had brought up the idea, she didn't expect anyone to take it seriously.

'It's a nice thought, Hazel. But how am I going to rent a place? The cost of setting it up, the sewing machines and staff . . . I wouldn't know where to start.'

They discuss the possibilities for a few minutes and then, feeling the cold, walk back towards Glade Street. 'Pixie, perhaps this is not the right time but, from what I've seen, you're a natural businesswoman. Everyone learns as they go, and I'm certain that if you really wanted to do this, you could make it work.'

'Thanks, Hazel. And thanks for your faith in me.'

As she drives away, instead of turning right towards home, Pixie finds herself turning left and arrives back outside the shop. She stops across the road and has a better look at the building. It's an old terrace building in a row of others. There's a good-sized display window and the upstairs has a balcony with double doors. She wonders if she could live upstairs as well as work there. They would probably only need one sewing machine to start – that's what Grandad started with – and Alice is a skilled machinist. It would need the three of them to make it work. Alice would design and sew, and Gloria could manage production; she has all the contacts in the business.

The longer Pixie sits there looking at the building, the more vivid the picture becomes. She sees the bright racks of clothes and accessories, maybe even shoes. Something completely independent from her parents. It's exciting and frightening, and probably crazy. Maybe it's impossible. Maybe not.

8
HAZEL'S FIRST DAY ON THE JOB

Hazel is surprisingly nervous as she walks from the station to Trades Hall on her first day. She's aware that the union staff will be a very different set of people to those at Empire, and wonders how much truth there is in the claim that they're all communists. While she agrees that wealth could be spread more evenly and workers should be treated fairly, she certainly doesn't agree with any group wanting to overthrow an elected government.

She's delighted at the prospect of seeing Rex more often. She had been so fond of him when he was a child, a shy little fellow growing up in difficult circumstances, and she can't help but be proud that he's risen to the position of a well-respected union leader and political figure – controversial or not.

Trades Hall is an old building on the edge of Chinatown with the railway tracks running behind it. In the foyer, a crowd of men dressed in suits talk among themselves as they wait for their turn to board a very small lift. Young women clatter up the stairs in their high heels. Hazel assumes these are secretaries, since the union world is well known to be a male domain.

Looking around for some signage, she notices a timber rack of engraved signs and walks over to look for the Dockside Workers Union's office. She's interested to see the variety of unions in the building: wicker workers, milliners, milk and ice carters, mill employees, boilermakers, bookbinders, slaughtermen and dozens more small unions, as well as the powerful well-known organisations like the Builders Labourers Federation. All together under the one roof.

Locating Dockside's office, she takes the stairs to the 2nd floor. The set-up is exactly like the wharf office with a polished timber counter running the width of the room and offices behind it. At a desk on the other side of the counter, a young woman types furiously. She is perhaps thirty-ish, dark hair worn in a bob framing a sharp face. She glances up enquiringly.

When Hazel introduces herself as the new tea lady, she says, 'Tea lady? First I've heard of it.'

'Mr Shepperton employed me,' explains Hazel.

The secretary picks up the phone and presses buttons until someone answers. 'Did Rex hire a tea lady?' she asks. She listens for a moment, makes a noncommittal sound and hangs up. 'Suits me. I'm sick of making tea for that lot,' she says.

Standing, she lifts a section of the counter to allow Hazel entry. Hazel follows her through a door into the main office, which is a large room with a dozen or so desks in a haphazard arrangement. Rex has his own office in one corner. A regiment of mismatched filing cabinets lines one side of the room, above which a row of dirty windows casts a dull light. Only half the desks are inhabited, all by men. A couple of them glance up uninterestedly as the secretary marches past, leading Hazel into a hallway where she stops and points into a small kitchen.

'Here you go. All yours.'

Hazel glances inside. 'What time do you normally have morning and afternoon tea?'

The secretary shrugs. 'Whenever you like.'

'All right,' says Hazel, trying to appear more cheerful than she feels. 'Sorry, I didn't quite catch your name.'

'Yvonne,' she says and stalks off, heels clicking away into the distance.

The kitchen is smaller than the one in the wharf office but has the basics: a kettle, sink bench and floor-to-ceiling set of cupboards. There's a little natural light through a dusty window that overlooks a busy road and Chinatown beyond. Hazel quickly sets to work wiping out the cupboards, scrubbing the bench, washing the floor, and cleaning the window as best she can. She finds a box of tea, a large tin of Nescafé and a bottle of milk but no biscuits, and pops out to the front office.

'We don't get biscuits because everyone eats them,' explains Yvonne.

Determined to make a good impression on her first day, Hazel gets her handbag, takes the lift downstairs and walks along the street until she finds a corner shop where she buys a packet of Monte Carlos and one of Milk Arrowroot biscuits.

By ten o'clock she has the kitchen cleaned and the trolley ready for the morning service. She pops the photograph of Cliff Fletcher in her pinny pocket, just in case there's an opportunity to ask about him.

There are only four people left in the office now. Undeterred, she pushes the trolley to each of their desks, introduces herself and asks how they like their tea. Two of the men, both thickset with slicked-back hair, are similar enough to be brothers. Both take their tea black with three sugars and help themselves to an equal number of Monte Carlos. Neither man introduces himself and only one says thank you. The third fellow appears to be an SP bookie. His desk is covered in form guides and racing pages. He holds a phone to each ear, discussing odds in a three-way conversation, and accepts his tea with a cursory nod.

The last fellow is a man in his thirties with an explosion of brown curly hair and owlish glasses. He's also on the phone but, seeing Hazel, excuses himself and hangs up. He gets to his feet and shakes her hand, introducing himself as Ted. 'But call me Teddy,' he adds, with a gesture towards his unruly hair. 'Everyone does. I didn't know we were getting a new tea lady. We've been making do for ourselves – unless we can bribe Yvonne. Will there be biscuits every day?' he asks, taking one of each.

'There will,' says Hazel with a smile. She looks around at all the empty desks. 'When will the others be back?'

Teddy shrugs. 'Don't worry. People come and go. They turn up when they turn up.'

When Hazel takes Yvonne a cup of tea and a biscuit, she asks suspiciously, 'Where'd you get those biscuits?'

'I bought them myself for today.'

'All right. White with one. Thanks.'

Hazel recognises Rex's hearty laugh in the hallway outside and a moment later he bursts through the door, hugging a satchel jam-packed with papers to his chest.

'Morning, ladies! Perfect timing!' he says with a grin, heading to his office.

Hazel follows him, delivering a cup of tea and two Monte Carlos to his desk.

'Tremendous,' he says, taking a slurp of tea. 'How's it going, Hazel? Anything you need, just let me know. Your wish is my command.'

'Of course I will, Rex. Really, don't worry about me. I'll be back for your cup.'

'Hah, the royal treatment!' He leans back in his chair, beaming at Hazel. Then an idea occurs to him. He gulps the rest of his tea and gets to his feet. 'There's something I want to show you before I forget.'

Bemused, Hazel returns his cup to the trolley and follows him out of the office and down the stairs to the first floor. Along the corridor, Rex opens a glass-panelled door and ushers Hazel inside. Glass cabinets full of books line the walls and a long, polished timber table and chairs sit in the centre of the room.

'This is the Trades Hall workers' library,' says Rex. He opens one of the cabinets and hands her a book on mechanical engineering and another on electrical circuitry. 'It's a centre for trades education. That's where improving the lives of workers begins.' He suddenly looks embarrassed. 'I'm sorry, Hazel. Have I put my foot in it? I'd quite forgotten the problems you had . . . I didn't think . . .'

'It's absolutely fine, Rex. There's a term for it now: dyslexia. I'm still working on it. Practice makes perfect, as they say.'

'Dyslexia? I didn't realise it was a condition. Well, good for you.'

Hazel hands the books back to him. 'Although mechanical engineering and circuitry might be a stretch for me.'

Rex laughs. 'All at your disposal. I'm sure there's something more to your taste.'

As they walk back up the stairs, Hazel remembers Mrs Fletcher's photograph. She gets it out and asks Rex if he's seen the young man around on the wharves. 'You can't see in this photo, but he has quite distinctive ginger hair,' says Hazel.

Rex takes the photo from her, frowns at it and hands it back. 'Nope, don't know him. There's a lot of young men working on the waterfront, bloody hundreds of 'em – takes more than a carrot top to stand out down there. Even if he's a member of our union, I don't deal with the rank and file on an individual level very often these days.'

Hazel's tingling ears indicate there's a fib in there somewhere. Sifting through his response, she wonders if he might have seen this young fellow but for some reason would rather not say. She wonders why that could be.

As he opens the door to the union office for her, Rex adds, 'As I mentioned, be careful who you talk to down there. A lot goes on under the surface and you might step in something mucky.' The phone in his office starts ringing. He gives Hazel a wave and charges in to pick it up.

9
HAZEL ASKS AROUND

On Wednesday, when Hazel arrives for work at the dock office, the wharves are lined with cargo ships and the whole place is seething with workers unloading and loading goods. Metal drums are lifted in cargo nets into one vessel and large crates lowered from another into waiting trucks. It's heavy work, dangerous and dirty, and, pausing to watch the flurry of industry, she considers herself fortunate only having to wrangle a teapot and hot water.

When she takes the trolley round, Rex's office door is closed, and she can see through the glass panel that he has a visitor. A well-dressed fellow wearing a suit, he leans forward in his chair gesticulating aggressively.

Seemingly unfazed, Rex glances over the man's shoulder. He gives Hazel a beckoning wave. When she opens the door and asks the visitor if he'd like tea or coffee, he turns to stare, his thick black brows knitted in a frown. He has the rugged good looks of a pirate captain, with a curved scar from the corner of his eye to his jawline that makes him look quite dashing. Hazel wonders if it was an accident with a wharfies hook, or perhaps not an accident.

'Coffee. Black with four, sweetheart,' he says.

Rex gives her a nod. 'Just my usual, thanks, Hazel.'

Hazel pours the tea and coffee, adding a couple of Milk Arrowroot to each saucer.

'Biscuits, eh?' says the man.

As she closes the door behind her, she hears him add, 'You couldn't find a fresher bird than that old boiler? Should've asked me.'

Hazel doesn't hear Rex's response but next time this fellow is here she might be tempted to slip some laxative in with all that sugar – one of Betty's old tricks. She smiles at the thought.

'Good morning, Mrs Bates. Nice to see your smiling face,' says Teddy, looking up from his paperwork.

'Who's that in with Rex?' Hazel asks, nodding towards Rex's office.

'Ah, that's Rizzo. Colourful identity, as they say. Holds a lot of sway around here for all the wrong reasons.'

'Not with me,' says Hazel. 'What does he do?'

'He'd call himself a negotiator, but basically he's a fixer.'

'I'm none the wiser,' admits Hazel. 'Now, ready for a cuppa?'

'Always.' Teddy heads over to the filing cabinets and flicks through files, removing one after another and placing them in a pile on the counter.

'Busy day?' she asks, adding a couple of biscuits to his saucer.

'Accident investigations,' he says. He picks up his tea and takes a sip. 'Delicious. We have an ongoing battle with employers who cut back on labour to save costs, which means more accidents and slower progress. They won't take any responsibility for injuries and so it goes on. Round and round.'

Hazel decides it's probably safe to show Teddy the photo. 'I wonder if you've seen this boy around in your travels?' she asks, getting it out of her pinny pocket.

Teddy peers at the photo and gives Hazel a quizzical look. 'What's your interest?'

'His mother's looking for him. He was released from Long Bay a month ago—'

'Ah, there's your answer. Can I give you some advice, Mrs Bates?' Without waiting for a reply, he continues. 'Forget this kid. If he's been in Long Bay, you want to steer clear of the bloke. Forget you ever heard of him.' He finishes his tea, puts the biscuits in his pocket and hands the cup back. 'Stick to your bikkies, that's my advice.' Briskly loading all the files into his briefcase, he heads out onto the wharves.

Hazel watches him go, not knowing what to make of him or his advice or why her ears tell her he's lying. The conversation only confirms her belief that Cliff Fletcher is known around the waterfront. Either they are protecting him, which seems unlikely, or protecting Hazel.

According to Mrs Fletcher, Cliff got himself mixed up in a silly prank and was dealt an overly harsh penalty. There may be more to it than that but it's hard to imagine that a year in Long Bay Gaol has turned him into a hardened criminal. Teddy's advice is probably sound, but Hazel has no plans to stop looking for Cliff until she finds out what's happened to him and can offer the boy's mother some peace of mind.

It's a busy morning in the office, with a mix of people from stevedores to shipping company officials arriving for meetings that in several cases involve a lot of shouting. But Rex seems to have a knack for remaining calm and calming others.

At lunchtime, the SP bookie parks himself at the front counter and a different group of men shuffle in and out, consulting form guides and placing bets. Grimy, weather-beaten men, many wearing black singlets despite the cold, others in heavy jackets. While they discuss the odds in their mother tongues, all seem to know the secret language of placing bets.

After a quick sandwich for lunch, Hazel continues serving tea to whoever wants it, right through to 2 pm when she knocks off for the day. She's tidying up the kitchen when Rex appears in the doorway.

'I just wanted to apologise for that uncouth comment Rizzo made.'

'Well, it's true I'm no spring chicken,' says Hazel, with a smile. 'But I have other more enduring qualities.'

'You make an excellent cuppa for a start. You're doing more good PR for us than the PR people,' he says. 'Keep it up and we'll be attracting a few more members. It's good to have you on the job. I meant what I said the other day. I wouldn't be here today without you.'

'I'm sure you would have survived. You were always very enterprising.'

Rex wanders over to gaze out the window. 'Remember that time you pulled me out of the creek down in Frog Hollow?' he asks, turning to her.

'Ah, yes,' agrees Hazel. 'It was flooded after all the rain and the kids were going down there to play. It was just lucky I saw your brothers walking up Ann Street without you, and there you were, left sitting in the creek, up to your neck in water.'

'I like to think they would have come back for me,' says Rex with a chuckle.

'You all survived. That's a miracle and you've done well for yourself, Rex.'

He nods thoughtfully. 'What do you remember most about those times, Hazel?'

'I remember them as hard. I think we all do. There was never enough to go around, but no one had any more than anyone else – and that was before the Depression. By the time that came along, I was married. John had a trade, so things were better for us than for many people.'

'It's the bugs I remember most. Cockroaches, bed bugs, lice. Never having enough to eat and Mum sick all the time. But plenty of good memories apart from that.'

'You had it tougher than most, Rex. But your dad was a hard worker, didn't drink.'

'Work nearly killed him. That's why I wanted this job. I want to improve the lives of people like us, working people. We're still fighting for decent working hours, so men like my dad aren't working twelve or fourteen hours a day, and so they have basic facilities – toilets, for example. Some things haven't improved at all.'

'It's an admirable aspiration,' says Hazel. 'Something worth fighting for.'

'Capitalism relies on inequality, so the government has a vested interest in keeping workers down,' he continues. 'We have to redress the balance of power, redistribute wealth across the workforce.' He pulls himself up short, and smiles. 'Sorry, Hazel, I'm taking up your time and telling you things you already know.'

'I'm very proud of you, Rex,' she reassures him.

'As I am of you,' he says cheerfully. 'See you Friday, Hazel.'

Hazel steps out to a perfect winter's afternoon, the air chill, the sky crystalline blue and not a whisper of breeze. The pigeon fancier is in his usual spot at the end of the wharf with his baskets and cart, and she goes over to say hello. He gives a start and clutches his chest in fright. 'Where did yer come from? Mrs Jolly, isn't it?'

'Mrs Bates actually. I'm the tea lady at the Dockside Workers Union.'

'Are yer now?' He looks her up and down. 'No place for a lady down here.'

'So everyone tells me, but tea ladies can handle themselves,' says Hazel breezily.

He gives a scoffing laugh and turns his gaze back to the sea, squinting into the afternoon light. She wonders what he's doing exactly – training his pigeons? He's found a spot that's quiet but still close to all the noisy activities of the wharf: the roar of ships' engines, trucks and forklifts, and men shouting over the top of it all. There must be so many better places to do whatever he's doing. It seems odd to that he comes to this exact spot.

It occurs to her that he might be just the person to ask about Cliff Fletcher. She gets the photo out of her handbag. 'You probably get around with your birds. I'm wondering if you might have seen this young man in your travels?' she says, showing him the photo.

He reaches into his coat pocket, brings out a pair of reading glasses held together by sticky tape. He looks at the photo and Hazel sees a glimmer of recognition.

'Why're yer looking for him?' he asks, handing it back.

'His mother's worried about him. She heard he might have found work down here.'

The man shakes his head. 'Never set eyes on him,' he says.

It's no surprise that Hazel's ears begin to tingle but she thanks him and goes on her way.

Walking up to the station, her thoughts turn from puzzling about Cliff's connection with the docks to the continuing mystery of the stolen Krugerrand, which is in the news almost every day. The papers offer various theories as to whether the gold was spirited away during the journey or smuggled off the ship in Sydney and hidden on the waterfront, beneath the noses of the police. Never missing an opportunity to denounce waterfront workers and unions alike, they regularly make the point that seamen and wharfies are famously expert at concealing contraband from the customs officers.

On the way to the station, she's pleasantly surprised to see her neighbour, young Maude Mulligan – looking very smart in her police uniform – standing at a pedestrian crossing holding a stop sign while school children stream across the road.

'Constable Mulligan, what a nice surprise!' says Hazel, standing well back to avoid being trampled by children running off in every direction.

'Probationary Constable,' corrects Maude, ushering the last few kiddies across. 'What are you doing in this neck of the woods, Mrs B?'

'I started my new job. Three days a week, and down at the wharves on Wednesdays,' explains Hazel. 'I thought you'd be out on the beat by now, Maude dear.'

'All graduates have three weeks on traffic. We do point duty at some intersections and they're sending us to monitor some of the dangerous school crossings. Then I have three weeks with the prosecutors and three with the detectives – I can't wait for that!' Maude glances at her watch. 'I'm finishing up now. I'll just pop the sign back and walk with you.'

Hazel waits while Maude takes the sign into the school. It's good to hear her so enthusiastic about policing, especially since her parents are both unhappy about her choice of career. Her mother thinks it will put off any potential suitors and her father, a nightwatchman at Tooheys Brewery, runs a sly grog shop selling pilfered liquor on the side. Apparently Maude has threatened to make him her first arrest.

As they walk together, Maude continues. 'Once we're through this part of the training, I'll likely end up doing office work. I asked my boss about taking the detective exams and he said not to bother. He said I'd be better off learning shorthand, girls can't get into the detectives. There are only fifty-eight females who are regular officers but I'm planning to be the fifty-ninth. Until then, it's typing and filing duties.'

'You'll be learning a lot as you go,' says Hazel. 'According to the papers we're in the midst of a crime wave, so they're going to need more smart young women on board.'

'I'm going to have to prove myself somehow,' muses Maude.

'Well, I might have something for you,' says Hazel. She explains how she met Flo Fletcher and hands Maude the photo of Cliff.

'He might not want to go home,' suggests Maude. 'He could be avoiding her.'

'Well, the plot has thickened. I've asked three people about him. All of them said they'd never seen him, and all three were lying.'

Maude stares at Hazel. 'How can you be sure they're lying?'

Hazel, always reluctant to explain her special gift, says, 'Look, keep this to yourself, Maude dear, but I have a special sort of radar. It's probably high time you knew about it.'

'Go on,' says Maude, looking intrigued.

'I get a sort of tingling along the rims of my ears. It sounds silly, I know, but it's fairly accurate. There are different intensities – sometimes a little light tingle and other times almost like a burning feeling I can't ignore. I've always had it, even as a child.' Hazel pauses. 'You can see why I keep that to myself.'

'Yes, it sounds a bit doolally. But you're the most sensible person I know, so I believe it.' Maude looks at the photo. 'I haven't seen the fellow.' She glances at Hazel. 'Am I lying?'

Hazel shakes her head. 'No. But I noticed the other day that you lied to your mother about where you were on Saturday night.'

Maude gives a shout of laughter. 'All right! Cliff Fletcher. I'll see if I can find out more about him. His poor mother, she must be worried out of her wits. Why doesn't she report him missing to the police?'

'I gather she doesn't trust the police,' says Hazel.

'Hmm . . . I can understand that. There's a lot of dodgy cops around and it's right out in the open as well. That came as a bit of a shock to me.'

'Have you come across Detective Pierce by any chance?' asks Hazel.

'Was he kicked out of Criminal Investigations – went over to Surry Hills?'

Hazel nods. 'He's the son-in-law of one of my tea lady friends, Merl Perlman. She seems to think he's the bee's knees but I know differently. He's definitely one to steer clear of – we've had a few run-ins with him in the past.'

Maude nods. 'Thanks for the tip-off. And I'll pop over if I find anything out.'

10

BETTY OUT OF HER DEPTH

Dressed in her good wool frock and best coat, Betty makes her way to Lucy's house in Rosemont Street for afternoon tea. She had the idea that Lucy came from a wealthy background, not just because of her nice speaking voice, but her apparent self-confidence – so it's a bit disappointing to find she lives in such an unsavoury part of the city. All the houses in her street are in a terrible state of disrepair. They must be rented out to students, because almost every house has a bedsheet painted with anti-war slogans and peace signs hanging from the upstairs balcony. One, written in bright red letters, reads: *FREE LOVE – APPLY WITHIN.* Betty wonders if that's a joke. She passes a young man wearing blue eyeshadow and a shabby tuxedo. His shoes sparkle with sequins glued all over them. Not something she has seen before, but she smiles to let him know she's not shocked (even though she is a bit).

Lucy's house also looks derelict, but Betty gathers her courage and knocks at the front door. It's opened by a young man, tall and slender with a dark fringe falling over his green eyes. He's so startlingly handsome, Betty blushes hotly in his presence.

'Is . . . a . . . Miss Fuller in?' she stammers.

'And who might you be?' he asks in a gentle voice.

'I'm Mrs Dewsnap. Lucy . . . Miss Fuller and I . . . we work together.'

His lips curve in a smile. 'Ah, I thought you might be the landlady.'

Betty splutters. 'Me? Own a house like this? My goodness, what a thought.'

'Come on in, Mrs Dewsnap. Welcome,' he says with a sweeping gesture. 'Take the stairs, and her room is second on the right.'

Still blushing, Betty makes her way up the stairs. She wonders if this is one of those 'mixed' households there's so much talk about lately. According to Merl, having young people of both sexes sharing houses is breaking down family values and allowing immorality to fester behind closed doors. She'd like it banned. Betty doesn't really have an opinion on that. Perhaps she should. She'll have to give the matter more thought.

At the top of the stairs, she falters, wondering if there's still time to turn around and hurry back to the comfortable world of Glade Street. But she's here now, and she knocks at the door. After some delay and several more knocks, Lucy opens the door wearing a long fur coat over a pink silk slip. Her feet are bare.

'Oh, I'm so sorry,' says Betty. 'Is it the wrong day?'

'No, no, of course not . . . Come in,' says Lucy groggily, beckoning her in.

Betty finds herself in a large dark room, the only light leaking through holes in the full-length curtains. As her eyes adjust, she makes out an unmade bed (a double!) and a confusing amount of clutter spread on every surface with clothes flung everywhere, including all over the floor.

Lucy yawns and stretches. 'What time is it?'

Betty doesn't need to look at her watch. 'Just after four pm,' she confirms.

Lucy crosses to the windows and pulls back the heavy curtains. 'I must have slept in. Grab a seat. I'll just go for a pee,' she says, heading out the door.

With the curtains pulled back, dull afternoon light seeps into the high-ceilinged room to reveal walls streaked with water stains, the wallpaper hanging in shreds. There are a couple of old armchairs and a coffee table covered with books and full ashtrays. One armchair is draped in clothes, and the other occupied by two sleeping cats. There's an easel in the corner and a table set under the windows covered in tubes of paint and piles of paper. Dotted around the room are old wine bottles with candles dripping wax (which, in Betty's opinion, presents a serious fire hazard).

When Lucy reappears, she suggests they go downstairs and have tea.

'I can come back another time if it's not convenient,' says Betty, still standing awkwardly in the middle of the room.

Lucy laughs. 'Is anything in this world ever convenient?' Gathering the fur coat around her, she wanders off down the stairs.

Betty follows, wondering what that comment might mean and how soon she can escape this peculiar situation. They walk through a large lounge, sparsely furnished and untidy with empty wine bottles, more candles and someone rolled up in a blanket asleep on the sofa. The kitchen is freezing cold. The benches and dining table are covered in dirty dishes and empty wine flagons. Betty looks around, wondering how people can live in such an untidy muddle.

'We had a bit of a do last night,' explains Lucy. She fills the kettle, puts it on the stove and sits down. Rubbing her face distractedly, she adds, 'Didn't get to bed till dawn.'

'I could help you clear up, if you like,' suggests Betty.

Lucy shrugs. 'It's not really my job but . . . if you want to. What sort of tea?'

Betty wonders what she could possibly mean. 'Just ordinary tea, thank you.'

While Lucy potters about making tea and searching for biscuits and aspirin, Betty locates the rubbish bin and scrapes the plates (a sticky mess of rice with colourful bits of veg in it), fills the sink with hot water and detergent and lowers the dishes into it. By the time the tea's ready, she's cleared the glasses and bottles, and wiped down the table.

'What a treasure you are, Betty Boop,' says Lucy warmly.

Betty's not sure about this Betty Boop nickname, that's something new. She'd suggested Lucy use her first name (everyone at work does), but Betty Boop?

They sit down at the table and Lucy pours the tea (rather anaemic looking, but never mind). The promised biscuits don't appear (disappointing).

Lucy sips her tea and seems more awake. 'They're a funny lot at Farley's, don't you think? It should be called Fuddy Duddy Frocks,' she says, with a tinkling laugh.

Betty hesitates; she's been with the firm for a long time and loyalty is a quality she values highly. But, of course, Lucy is right. They are very old-fashioned and stuck in their ways. 'They haven't quite joined the swinging sixties yet,' she agrees.

'They think there'll be rioting in the streets if a dress is more than four inches above the knee.' Lucy sticks a cigarette paper to her lip and takes a packet of tobacco out of her coat pocket. 'They have a sort of morbid fear of women's bodies.'

Betty's not sure if this is a joke but laughs just in case. 'I think most of the firms are finding the new groovy fashions hard to accept.' Secretly pleased with her first-time use of the word 'groovy', she adds, 'I suppose they're all run by older men.'

'The self-appointed protectors of women's virtue,' agrees Lucy. Deftly rolling a cigarette, she lights it and blows a stream of smoke towards the ceiling, then swings her bare feet (gold rings on her toes!) onto a nearby chair. 'What are your candid thoughts on the patriarchy, Betty?'

Betty thinks hard. She's not sure exactly what the patriarchy is but, if Lucy's tone is anything to go by, it's not good. 'I don't think much of it,' she says decisively.

'That's so great to hear,' says Lucy. 'I can't believe how many women of your generation are completely brainwashed. They can't see how repressive the patriarchy is towards women. So ridiculous when men are making such a mess of everything – this senseless war, for a start.'

Betty's having trouble keeping track of this conversation, but nods firmly. 'We could do better. I'm sure we could.'

Lucy exhales a smoky sigh. 'You're such a free spirit, Betty. Despite a lifetime of repression and discrimination, your rebellious nature is still intact. It's so inspiring.'

Betty gives an embarrassed smile. It's hard to imagine anyone less rebellious (or inspiring) than her and, as if to demonstrate, she takes her cup to the sink and picks up a grubby cloth to wash the dishes.

'Don't do any more!' cries Lucy. 'The boys will finish it. We're re-educating them after so many years of being coddled by their mothers.'

Betty abandons the cloth and sits down. 'It was very nice of you to invite me. I've been at Farley Frocks for nine years, and no one has ever invited me to their home.'

'That's appalling,' says Lucy. 'You're the most fun person there.'

'That's not saying much,' Betty says. 'Especially in haberdashery.'

Lucy laughs. 'True, they're a gloomy lot, aren't they?'

'Well . . . it's more to do with the tight little groups in there,' explains Betty, still feeling disloyal. 'The management keep to themselves, as you'd expect, and the factory girls think the office girls look down on them, and the office girls *do* look down on them—'

'And my department seem to think we're royalty,' adds Lucy.

Betty can't disagree with that. 'All in all, there's not much room for friendships.'

'Just another example of constructed class warfare,' says Lucy, pouring herself more tea. 'But you have those friends you meet in the laneway.'

Betty nods. 'All tea ladies. There used to be more of us, but Mrs Bates lost her job at Empire Fashionwear last year. They replaced her with a tea-making machine.' Emboldened by Lucy's grimace of distaste, Betty continues. 'We had one put in at Farley's but someone sabotaged it and they sent it back.'

'Was that someone you?!' asks Lucy, in mock horror.

Betty smiles modestly. 'I really couldn't comment on that.'

'Ah, the quiet anarchist,' Lucy muses, shaking her head in wonderment. 'Well, it would be nice if we could be friends.' She pauses. 'But actually . . . I did have another reason for inviting you around today.'

Betty remembers there was the promise of having her palm read and her tummy does an anxious flip. But Lucy seems to have forgotten that because she asks, 'I wondered if you would consider letting me paint you?'

'Me?' asks Betty, pointlessly.

'You have the most beautiful, voluptuous, womanly body . . . and such a sweet face to go with it – that's why I call you Betty Boop. I want to capture your Rubenesque beauty for a feminist art exhibition coming up later in the year. What do you think?'

'Oh no, I'm far too . . . too old,' Betty protests, blushing at the mention of her 'womanly' body but flattered at the same time. 'When I was young . . . well, people said I was pretty and, of course, I was quite slender back then, but now . . .'

'Age doesn't diminish beauty,' Lucy reassures her. 'You have the face of an angel, generous breasts and curvy hips—'

Flustered by this last comment, Betty gets up, knocking her chair over backwards. 'Oh goodness . . . I just remembered an appointment . . . at . . . the . . . um . . . dentist. I'd quite forgotten.'

'On a Saturday evening?' asks Lucy, in surprise.

Betty takes a moment to set the chair to rights, wondering why on earth she came up with such a silly excuse, but there's no going back. 'Yes, he's very . . . dedicated. Also, it's an emergency.'

'I didn't mean to paint you now,' says Lucy, with a smile. 'Some other time. Just think about it.'

Nevertheless, Betty picks up her handbag and moves towards the door.

'And before you rush off, let me give you a couple of books you should read.'

Back in the lounge room, Lucy rifles through a pile of books on the floor and thrusts a couple into Betty's hands, insisting she come for dinner the next evening. Thanking her, Betty backs out into the hall, almost colliding with the handsome young man. With furious blushes and mumbled apologies, she dashes out the door and is rewarded by a sharp breeze to soothe her burning cheeks.

On the way to the bus stop, her tummy does flip-flops with the usual explosive accompaniment but fortunately there's no one around to hear. Rubenesque beauty? She wonders what it means. And talking about her bosoms . . . she's just not used to that sort of attention. It's strange to hear from a beautiful young woman.

As soon as she gets home, without even taking her coat off, Betty goes straight to the bookshelf in the front room, locates the appropriate volume of the encyclopaedia and flicks to the back to find 'Rubenesque'. The index sends her to an artist named Peter Paul Rubens and a black and white photo of one of his works, entitled *The Judgement of Paris*. Three pale, fleshy women with angelic faces, surrounded by cherubs, stand about without a stitch on – bosoms and dimpled bottoms on display for all to see.

Betty snaps the book closed and puts it back on the shelf.

At bedtime, she normally slips into her nightie as quickly as she can. Not just because of the cold, but for reasons of modesty. It's a virtue she was raised to believe was important. On her wedding night, her mother's only piece of advice was to never allow her husband to see her 'unclothed'. Evidently her mother had dressed and undressed in the wardrobe all the years of her marriage because, she explained, modesty was not just a virtue but a necessity. She didn't elaborate further, and Betty didn't like to ask. And while she never went as far as retreating to the wardrobe, she did follow her mother's advice and changed her clothes in a modest way. A habit she saw no reason to break.

Undressing this evening, Betty pauses for a moment to look at herself in the wardrobe mirror. In her long-sleeved spencer and high-waisted undies, she looks beige and bulgy, like a badly made sausage. She turns off the overhead light and switches on the more forgiving bedside lamp. Feeling cripplingly self-conscious, she takes off her spencer and brassiere and steps out of her undies. She turns to look at herself again in the mirror. No Rubenesque beauty appears (apart from the dimply bottom), just a short, plump old lady with faded hair.

She puts on her nightie, climbs into bed and turns off the lamp. Lying in the dark, she hugs her hot water bottle tightly to her chest and lets her mind drift back to her younger years. It was a time when being seen as a 'good girl' was all that mattered, and it didn't take much to blacken a girl's reputation. You would be considered cheap if you had pierced ears, plucked eyebrows, wore too much make-up, smoked in public or made a cheeky remark to a man. It seems to Betty that the world is a very different place for young women today. They want to be themselves, free of all that silly nonsense, and wear rings on their toes if they want to. And, although the conversation with Lucy was embarrassing, Betty knows she will go to the house on Rosemont Street again. It was fascinating, like visiting a foreign country, a strange and interesting experience in her otherwise boring life.

As she drifts off to sleep, she thinks again about that handsome young man at Lucy's and wonders what the young Betty would have made of him. She'd probably have been just as tongue-tied and flustered as she was today. Some things never change.

11
IRENE HAS AN OFFER SHE SHOULD REFUSE

'Mrs Turnbuckle, can I have a word, please?'

Irene flinches. Miss Palmer has a way of creeping up on her, and there's no such thing as a friendly chat with this one. But Irene's secretly pleased that her boss has caught her on her knees cleaning the bathroom floor, not enjoying a bubble bath or taking a nap on the four-poster bed, as she does quite regularly.

Gripping the side of the bath, Irene gets to her feet and steps out into the hall.

'Can you give me an extra couple of hours today, Mrs Turnbuckle? The cleaning lady at one of my other establishments is in hospital and I need the place done this afternoon.'

'Could probably manage it . . . It's a Saturday but . . .' Irene leaves it hanging.

'How does ten dollars sound?'

'An hour?' asks Irene. Never hurts to ask.

Miss Palmer sighs. 'I suppose so, provided it doesn't take more than two hours.'

'All righty, what's the address?'

'It's my new place in Chapel Lane, Darlinghurst. Two bedrooms upstairs, living room, kitchen and one bathroom. Smaller than this place.'

'Darlo,' repeats Irene. 'Chapel Lane . . . Dunno, bit dicey down there.'

'You'll be absolutely fine,' says Miss Palmer.

Irene wonders if the cleaner's in hospital suffering from a knife in her ribs. She tries to think of an excuse to get out of it, but Miss Palmer reads her mind.

'Look, my driver can drop you at the door and pick you up – if that addresses your reticence,' she says.

Irene has no idea what an addressed reticence is but she's keen to be driven fairly much anywhere in Miss Palmer's Rolls-Royce.

'It's not that easy to find someone I trust at short notice,' adds Miss Palmer.

It's news to Irene that Miss Palmer trusts her. Goes to show that she's not as smart as she thinks she is.

'One o'clock suit yers?' Irene asks.

Miss Palmer nods and hands her a set of keys. 'The place will be empty. All the cleaning materials are in the kitchen. Just strip the beds, I'll get the girls to make them up.'

It's only when Miss Palmer stalks off down the hall that Irene notices she's wearing black shiny stiletto-heeled boots that come up to her thighs; she might be off on a fishing trip.

With her tight slacks and glamorous looks, Miss Palmer is nothing like the other madams that Irene's met over the years, the first being her gran, Molly Mullins, who dressed in black for as long as Irene could remember. The old girl was wider than she was tall and had a bamboo cane she used like a street fighter. If someone did her wrong, she'd bring that down on the back of their neck and knock them flat on their face. She could throw it like a spear and bring down some poor bugger making a run for it. She'd used it against Irene on more than a few occasions, making Irene work in that brothel from the age of sixteen until she was twenty-one. They were the worst years of her life, and that was saying something. But Miss Palmer's nothing like that old bag. She's a very classy lady.

At one on the dot, the driver turns up in the shiny black Rolls. Irene takes her time wandering down the front stairs in the hope of an audience (Merl would be ideal, but that one never sets foot in Lisbon Street unless she's going to work). She stands beside the car and, when the driver doesn't get out to open the door for her, taps on the front passenger window. 'Where's yer bloody manners, mate?'

The fellow shakes his big bald head like an angry bull, but he gets out of the car and opens the back door for her. He looks her over and stares at her slippers. It crosses Irene's mind that she should have worn her good hat for the occasion.

'Thank you, kind sir,' she says. Her bottom slides in nicely on the smooth leather seat.

Sitting behind the driver, she notices his neck is the same size as his head with only a thick fold of skin between the two. A couple more rolls and he could pass for a squeezebox from behind. Since he hasn't bothered introducing himself, she dubs him the Neck.

She perches on the edge of the seat, keeping an eye out for anyone she knows, planning to give them a queenly wave. But, thinking about it now, ten dollars an hour isn't much for going into the thick of Little Malta. She might not come out alive.

Chapel Lane is right off Woods Lane, which is known locally as the 'doors'. In the afternoon and evenings, a nicely dressed tart stands in every doorway, while blokes wander along the lane to check out the goods. Legally the girls have to stay in the house. If they step out onto the street, they can be arrested for vagrancy.

Irene knows for a fact that the whole area is run by the Maltese mafia. The boss is a fellow called Joe Borg – 'King Borg' they call him – a dangerous crook who owns a good dozen brothels down there. Miss Palmer's got real guts if she's muscling in on his act.

The Rolls pulls up outside a narrow terrace house, not as smart as 555 but decent looking compared to the houses around it. Irene has a good squiz up and down the street.

'Yers waiting here?' she asks the Neck.

'Not on your life. Back in a couple of hours.'

'I'm not waiting outside, mate. Give us a toot when yers get back.'

12

A SURPRISE AWAITS UPSTAIRS

Irene gets out of the Rolls and darts up the front steps. Once inside, she locks the door with all three bolts and the safety chain, then goes into the lounge room and has a look around.

It's much plainer than 555, less luxurious, no chandeliers, but still classy. There's a locked liquor cabinet (she'll deal with that later), a few lounge chairs and a record player with a stack of records beside it. She flips through them to see if there's anything to her taste. Count Basie, Billie Holiday, Ray Charles, Frank Sinatra – not bad. She puts on a Nat King Cole LP and wanders down to the kitchen.

The cleaning cupboard has the same stuff as 555. Mr Sheen (big favourite with Miss P), borax powder, dusters, broom, mop and vacuum cleaner. Irene pulls them all out and breezes around with a feather duster, humming along with Nat King Cole to 'Mona Lisa'.

When the downstairs is done, she drags the vacuum cleaner upstairs. She flings open the first door in the hall to find a linen cupboard. The second door is a bathroom. But opening a third one, she's treated to the sight of a tall, handsome (stark naked!)

Black man leaping out of bed. He looks as shocked as she is and grabs at the sheet to cover his private bits (to Irene's bitter disappointment). With a quick glance around, she notes an American GI uniform folded neatly on a chair and a peroxide blonde asleep in the bed.

'I'll come back later then?' she asks.

'Thank you, ma'am. That would be appreciated,' the man says.

Irene backs out of the room, keeping her eyes on him until the very last second. What a sight for sore eyes! She'd have *paid* ten bucks for that treat. Chuckling to herself, she takes herself off to the other bedroom, but sadly no handsome men in the nuddy.

Stripping the bed, she hears someone creep up behind her and spins around to find the GI now in uniform. 'Well, hello,' she says with a grin.

'Ma'am? Can I ask you to please keep my presence here to yourself?' he asks, a nervous smile showing off two first-class dimples.

It crosses her mind that there could be another ten dollars in it, and they might be American dollars. But she'd rather feast her eyes on his broad shoulders, looking almost as good in his serviceman's uniform as they did in the altogether.

Dimples is waiting for an answer.

'Course,' she says, with a wink. 'Yer can count on me, soldier.'

Flashing a wide grin (nice set of clackers) and a mock salute, he runs off down the stairs. Irene follows. She leans over the railing to catch a glimpse of his rear and is not disappointed. When he's gone, she goes downstairs and locks up again. Nat King Cole's still mooning on in his dreamy way. She moves the stylus back to the first track and sways about the room, dancing with an invisible broad-shouldered partner.

Back upstairs, the blonde is still dead to the world and the roaring vacuum cleaner doesn't even wake her. Must have been quite a night.

Finally, Irene gives her a good shake. 'Oy, Blondie!'

The blonde grunts, rolls over and starts snoring.

Irene takes the top sheet off and pulls out the bottom sheet, rolling the sleeping woman onto the mattress, and throws the sheets on the pile in the hall with the others.

When the place is done, Irene puts Nat King Cole back in his sleeve and slips a pick into the lock of the liquor cabinet. She takes a good couple of swigs of the Glenfiddich, fills her flask, returns the bottle to the same spot and locks the cabinet.

Not game to wait in the street, she stands at the window to watch out for the Neck. From here, she can see a dark blue Ford Falcon with two men sitting in it. The driver's door is painted in pink primer, making it stand out. Where has she seen the car before? Lisbon Street, she's almost sure of it. Could these blokes be watching both Miss Palmer's places? She has a quick tipple from her flask to sharpen her thoughts and decides she needs to get a better look at them.

Armed with a plan, she goes out the kitchen door into the yard. The back wall has a mess of barbed wire and broken glass on the top of it like a prison. Irene finds the gate key on the ring that Miss Palmer gave her and steps out into the laneway. She scouts around for missiles and finds half a brick. There's no one around, but she tucks it under her pinny just in case. She walks along the lane to a pathway, cutting through the houses until she finds an ideal spot, hidden by a wall on the corner and the Falcon within pitching distance.

She does a bit of a warm-up to loosen her arm, eyeballs the target and bowls overarm, aiming for the roof. The moment the brick leaves her hand, she scuttles back along the path as fast as her cranky knees allow, belts in through the back gate and locks it from the other side. Panting, she hurries to the front room just in time to see the Rolls pull up out front.

Irene steps outside, locks the door behind her and quickly gets in the car. As they pass the Falcon, she ducks her head down and spies out the window.

'What're you playing at?' asks the Neck, watching her in the rear-view mirror.

'Mind yer beeswax.'

Irene turns to have a good look at the two men standing beside the car. The driver's door is open and one of the fellas, a short and swarthy bloke with grey hair, stands up on the doorsill, checking the damage to the roof. The other is looking around for the culprit, the half-brick in his hand.

'Yer know them fellas?' Irene asks.

'You don't wanna mess with them. They're Borg's men.'

Irene had heard Borg's minders were old fellas. Not to be messed with, eh? Irene's not to be messed with either. 'I reckon them Malteses are watching the place,' she says. 'Seen 'em before up on Lisbon Street.'

'What's it to you? Aren't you the cleaning lady?' asks the Neck.

'That's just a sideline,' says Irene. 'I'm a tea lady, as a matter a fact.'

The Neck gives a rude grunt. 'Stickybeak then?'

'Say what yer like. Point is, I reckon them blokes are watching Miss Palmer's places.'

'So what?' he asks.

'So what is that I live in the attic at 555. If the place gets blown up in the middle of the bloody night, I'm the one getting toasted, mate.'

He shrugs. 'I wouldn't worry too much about it.'

Irene gives an angry tut. It's clear she's not going to get any help from this bugger. She'll have to go straight to Miss Palmer. Probably not going to get much help there either. Miss P thinks she's untouchable, but Irene's pretty sure she's wrong.

13
HAZEL TO THE RESCUE

Hazel sits at the card table in her front room, sipping rhubarb wine and surveying her jigsaw puzzle. It's very quiet without Betty's chatter. The only sound is the gas fire hissing in the background. Betty's out again this evening visiting this new friend Lucy.

Hazel brings her attention back to the Great Wall of China. It's a compelling scene, with the wall gliding over hills of green like a roller-coaster. The puzzle doesn't offer as much scenic variety as some of the other Wonders of the World jigsaws, but it's still a pleasure to gaze at the scene and imagine taking that walk. She's had so much time on her hands these last months, she could have finished this one ages ago, but she likes to save it for when she needs to ponder problems. There's something about a jigsaw that allows her to nut things out while her hands are busy.

Her thoughts turn again to young Cliff Fletcher. The number of times Hazel's been fobbed off makes her certain that he has been on the docks at some point. All these warnings make her think that he either has dangerous friends or is dangerous himself. Alternatively, and it doesn't bear thinking about, he could be dead and no one wants to admit it. Either outcome will break Mrs Fletcher's heart.

Is it possible he has a connection to the Krugerrand robbery, and that's what is scaring people? She would think that for a heist of that size and complexity, experienced criminals would be enlisted by someone at the top of the game. So it seems unlikely that a young man of Cliff's age and inexperience would be involved. One thing that's still bothering her is how he ended up in prison for what his mother described as a misdemeanour. There's clearly more to that story.

Her thoughts are interrupted by the sound of the front door being closed quietly. Betty normally announces her arrival, but not tonight for some reason.

'I'm in here, Betty dear,' calls Hazel.

Betty wanders into the room and sits down heavily on the sofa, still wearing her coat. Her cheeks are flushed scarlet, either with the cold or something else. 'Hel-lo,' she says in a singsong voice.

Torn between respecting her friend's privacy and concern, Hazel asks, 'Can I get you a glass of rhubarb wine?'

'I better not.' Betty closes her eyes. A fruity burp escapes her lips. 'Pardon me.'

'Are you all right, dear?'

'I think I'm a bit tight,' she says with a snort of laughter.

Hazel smiles. 'That's not like you. Did you have a lovely evening at Lucy's?'

'I hope you're not jealous, Hazel. About Lucy, I mean. You are still my oldest and dearest friend. I think she's a little lonely and . . . needs a mother figure.'

Never, in all their years of friendship, has Hazel caught Betty out in a fib. She's breathtakingly honest, even when it's not in her best interests. Now Hazel's ears are tingling, but it's difficult to know which of those statements are not true.

'I'm delighted you have a new friend,' says Hazel. 'You obviously get on well.'

'She's inter . . . inter . . . she's . . . I better go to bed.' Betty smothers a giggle.

'Good idea. Be careful when you go out to the toilet, the yard is a little icy.'

Betty wanders out, leaving the door wide open. 'I will. Goodnight, Hazel, dear Hazel.'

Since she has to get up to close the door anyway, Hazel decides she'll also go to bed. She switches off the gas fire, turns off the lamps and goes into the kitchen. She has a final tidy up while she waits to get the torch back off Betty.

After fifteen minutes, there's still no sign of her. Hazel opens the back door to find Betty lying flat on her back on the cold bricks of the yard, the torch by her side and her coat fallen open.

Hazel rushes out to help. She picks up the torch and shines it in Betty's face, calling her name several times with no response. She's breathing steadily and there's no head injury, so Hazel goes inside and quickly gathers some blankets. When she gets back, Betty's snoring loudly.

'Betty dear, wake up.' Hazel gives her a shake. 'You're going to freeze to death!'

Betty murmurs contentedly in her sleep and gives a chuckle, as if enjoying a pleasant dream. Hazel piles the blankets on top of her. Deciding against calling an ambulance for the moment, she goes out the back gate and into the Mulligans' house next door.

At this time of evening, the younger Mulligans are usually in bed and the older ones in the kitchen reading aloud to Mrs Mulligan while she cleans up. But the kitchen is empty, and Hazel can hear muffled sounds coming from the front room. She hurries down the hallway, littered as always with shoes, several broken bikes, beer crates and school cases. The lounge door is closed but a telltale blue light flickers under the door. Hazel opens it to find the family sitting in the dark around their new television set watching a Western, all riveted by the sight of a cowboy galloping on his horse and shooting wildly in the air.

'Sorry to intrude. I need help!' Hazel shouts over the gunfire.

The only one who stirs is Maude. Keeping her eyes locked on the telly, she asks, 'What's up, Mrs B?'

'Betty's fallen in the yard. She's too heavy for me to lift.'

Mrs Mulligan springs to life, struggling to get out of her chair. 'Spare me days! Turn that silly thing off,' she cries. 'Hazel needs our help! Come on. Get up, you lot!'

Maude and the two oldest boys reluctantly follow Hazel next door, where Betty's still asleep and seems quite relaxed. Between the four of them, they manage to get her upright and bundle her up the stairs and onto her bed – without her waking! Hazel tucks her up with blankets. She's always been a solid sleeper and hard to wake, but this takes the cake.

When the boys go home, Maude hangs back to ask Hazel exactly what happened.

'I don't really know. She'd been out to a friend's house and had a little too much to drink. She must have slipped . . . I did warn her. It seems odd she hasn't hurt herself at all.'

'Who was the friend?' asks Maude.

'A friend from work. Lucy, her name is,' says Hazel. 'Why?'

'Um . . . I think it's possible Mrs Dewsnap might have taken drugs.'

Hazel stares at Maude. 'What on earth makes you think that?'

'It was part of my training. I recognise the smell of cannabis on her. They call it marijuana or pot – there're a few different names,' says Maude.

'I have no idea what that is, dear. You'll have to enlighten me.'

'They smoke it like tobacco but they get "high" or "stoned" on it. I don't really know what that means either, I haven't come across it before. We're getting training because it's one of the drugs soldiers are bringing in from Vietnam.'

'Drugs? I find it very hard to believe of Betty but . . . of course, I trust what you're telling me.' Hazel pauses. 'You're not going to arrest her, are you?'

Maude shakes her head. 'Of course not, but you might want to find out where she's getting it. Sounds like she's tangled up with a bad crowd.'

'Yes, I agree. Leave it with me,' says Hazel, more puzzled than ever.

'Oh, by the way,' says Maude, 'I did find out that the bloke you're looking for, Cliff Fletcher, has a string of firearm offences and a conviction for assault. Bit of a wild one, and from a young age it seems. The firearm robbery wasn't his first offence – that's how come he ended up in Long Bay.'

'A-ha. That makes more sense, thank you. You've been a great help this evening.' Hazel pauses. She meets Maude's concerned gaze and realises how much the young woman has matured in the last year. 'I think you've found your true calling, Maude dear.'

'Aw, thanks, Mrs B,' Maude says with a shy grin. 'Hope Mrs

Dewsnap's feeling better in the morning,' she adds, closing the door behind her.

'How are you, dear?' asks Hazel, when Betty comes down for breakfast. 'There's porridge in the pot.'

'Very rested.' Betty ladles a generous serving of porridge into a bowl, and then adds milk and golden syrup and a sprinkling of brown sugar.

Not sure how to approach the subject, Hazel begins. 'I was a little concerned last night. You fell asleep in the yard. I had to get the Mulligans over to carry you up to bed.'

Betty pauses, the spoon halfway to her mouth. 'Oh dear. Mr Mulligan too?'

'Mr Mulligan was at work. It was the older boys and Maude.'

'How embarrassing,' says Betty. 'I don't know what came over me.'

'Maude thought you might have been smoking marijuana.'

'Marijuana?' Frowning, Betty puts her spoon down carefully. 'What is that?'

'According to Maude, it's an illegal drug,' explains Hazel.

Betty flushes. 'Lucy said it was a herbal cigarette that helps you relax . . . and, as you know, I haven't smoked for twenty years but I'd like to be more relaxed. Dearie me. Oh Hazel, I promise I won't smoke it again. The thought of the children lugging me upstairs, and Maude . . .' Her mouth turns down at the corners. 'So now the police know about me.'

'I'm sure Maude has already forgotten the incident. The police have many more important things to worry about than a stoned tea lady.'

'I don't know what that means but, anyway, I'm so sorry, Hazel. That must have given you quite a scare.' Betty picks up her spoon again and takes a mouthful of porridge.

Hazel smiles. 'It did, but I'm glad it wasn't something more serious.' She glances at her watch. 'Now, I better get cracking or I'll be late for work.'

On her way to Trades Hall, Hazel ponders why Betty has become so infatuated with this Lucy. And why is this young woman taking so much interest in Betty? From what Hazel can gather, Betty is not just a mother figure but old enough to be her grandmother. She suspects there is more to it than Betty is letting on.

Rex stands in the doorway of his office, consulting the racing guide in his hand as he calls out his bets across the room to the bookie. Each of his picks is the cause of hilarity and ribbing from Teddy and the two grumpy fellows, who are positively cheerful today.

'Dashing Days has got one hoof in the knacker's yard,' comments one.

'Rex's bet will seal her fate and dash all hopes,' says Teddy.

'You know I support the underdog,' says Rex. 'Twenty to win.' He looks up and notices Hazel. 'Good morning, Hazel. Fancy a flutter?'

She shakes her head. 'Not for me, thank you. Life's a gamble enough for me.'

'That's true,' agrees Rex, with a chuckle. 'Always the sensible one.'

Hazel prepares the morning tea and trundles around with her trolley. Teddy thanks her, as always, but the others have gone back to ignoring her. Yvonne's in a sulk about something and accepts her tea and biscuit with a scowl.

Hazel taps on Rex's door and pops her head around. He's talking on the phone in a tone that sounds quietly aggressive and almost threatening. At the sight of Hazel, he quickly terminates the call and drops the phone back into its cradle. Judging by the look on his face, he's tempted to explain himself but then thinks better of it. It strikes Hazel that, despite his jovial persona, he is careful with everything he says and does, just as he was as a child. He was always quietly strategic, but Dibble is also right — there's a hardness in him that wasn't evident in the young Rex.

'How are you finding things here, Hazel?' he asks.

Adding two sugars to his tea, Hazel gives it a good stir. 'I'm just very glad of the work, to be honest,' she says, placing it in front of him.

'Have you wondered how "lil Rex" ended up a union boss?' he asks.

Hazel smiles. 'I don't think of you as "lil Rex" any more — obviously.'

'This is just a step in my career ladder,' he says, taking a sip of his tea. Lowering his voice, he says, 'This is the middle rung, closer to the top than the bottom. Politics is what I've got my eye on for the future.'

Hazel raises her eyebrows. 'The top job?'

He nods his head seriously. 'What do you think?'

'You obviously have the leadership qualities . . .' begins Hazel.

'Holt's done some good things as Prime Minister,' continues Rex. 'Dismantling the White Australia policy, and not before time. The Labor party has a strong contender in the next election with Whitlam. That's what I've got my sights on next. Getting into the thick of politics. Doing some good from the top down, making fair policy for the battlers.'

It occurs to Hazel that he's trying to impress her, and not just her – everyone. He's still trying to keep up with all those older brothers, even though, to the best of her knowledge, he's the only one to achieve an office of any standing. The others all went into the trades as boilermakers and factory workers; one was in prison last time she heard. But here's Rex, the baby of the family, with a respected position and staff, running a powerful union and with his eye on the top job. He has the charm, and the ambition – what more does he need? The approval of the tea lady, apparently.

'You can count on my vote, Rex,' Hazel assures him. 'I think you'd make a terrific Prime Minister.'

'Thanks, Hazel. So would you,' he says, with a grin.

14
RUMBLES IN THE GUILD

A dozen tea ladies are gathered in the upstairs room of the Hollywood Hotel for the monthly meeting of the Tea Ladies Guild. With only a two-bar electric heater to take the chill off, everyone stays rugged up in coats and gloves, hands clamped around their cups of tea for extra warmth.

Betty gets out her notebook and glances over the minutes of last month's meeting.

Disappointingly, they're not getting very far with their fundraising efforts to provide beds and blankets for the Sisters of Hope orphanage, and they still need to raise a further $300, which seems an impossible sum at this point. Worse still, they've recently been informed that the building construction has overrun its budget, and the nuns are counting on the tea ladies for all the bedding.

The fundraising has not been helped by the falling number of attendees. Last year the Guild gained dozens of new members when they joined forces to fight the invasion of the tea machines (with mixed results). But since then, the numbers have gradually fallen off.

The usual stalwarts are here this evening: Hazel, Merl and Irene, as well as Effie Finch from the fire station, Mrs Li, who works at the police station, Violet from Imperial Slacks, the two Italians from the *Herald* office, and three ladies from the Defence Department. Many more tea ladies frequent the downstairs bar but are too comfortable down there to make it upstairs for the meetings.

'The main item of business this evening is fundraising for the orphanage,' says Hazel, after welcoming everyone. 'Would you like to report, Merl?'

Merl frowns. 'I don't know why everything rests on my shoulders.'

Irene (a cigarette tucked behind each ear for some reason) is spoiling for an argument. 'Didn't yers appoint yerself chief fundraiser? Could be it?'

'My role is to manage the fundraising, not do it all myself,' snips Merl.

'Merl, we would all like to make a contribution,' says Hazel diplomatically. 'But it does seem that many of our suggestions don't meet some criteria that we're not aware of.'

One of the Defence tea ladies raises her hand. 'We offered to have a whip-round in the office. That idea was knocked back.'

'That's just begging,' says Merl dismissively.

'I said I'd bake rock cakes for your cake stall,' says Violet. 'And got a "no, thanks".'

'There was a reason for that,' declares Merl. Her head wobbles, making the diamantes on her specs twinkle irritably.

'One bad batch and there's a black mark against me forever,' complains Violet, nodding at the murmurs of commiseration.

'The Guild has to bear the cost of ingredients . . . It's simply a waste,' says Merl. 'We need high quality goods as befits the Guild name.'

'Mate, the Guild hasn't got a bloody name,' says Irene. 'We just need the dough.'

Betty's quite sure that Merl has some hidden motive; she probably imagines she's in competition with the Country Women's Association, who are famous for their baked goods. But it doesn't do to put Merl on the spot; she'll just dig her heels in and make things worse.

'What's the profit margin on a cake anyway?' asks Effie Finch, turning to Mrs Li, the treasurer. 'There's got to be faster ways to raise money.'

'Depends on the cake,' says Mrs Li. 'Scones are low-cost—'

'Apart from the butter,' interrupts Merl. 'Scones don't keep well. Sponge cakes are the most popular and cheap enough to make. But there's also the cost of the greaseproof to take into account, when sold by the slice.'

Hazel nods. 'One of the problems is that to buy a slice of cake, or even a scone, is a luxury for most people around here.'

'There's got be a quicker way to raise funds than baking,' insists Effie.

Betty sighs. This is the same discussion they had last meeting. How can they still be bogged down in problems and no closer to a solution? 'I've heard about people doing walks to raise money,' she suggests.

Irene grins. 'People pay to watch yers walk?'

'They sponsor you for every mile you walk,' explains Betty. 'You obviously can't just walk around the block and expect to get paid for it—'

'Unless you're Marilyn Monroe,' adds Violet.

'Not a very good example, given the woman has passed on,' says Merl, clearly bridling from the earlier discussion. 'That's a waste of shoe leather, in my view.'

'I'm just trying to think creatively,' says Betty, starting to feel tired. 'Hazel, you could sell your wine.'

'Good idea. Save people buying rat poison,' says Irene.

Hazel laughs. 'Thank you, Irene. Selling alcohol without a licence . . .'

'There's a dozen sly grog shops within walking distance of here,' says Effie.

'You'd just need to supply one of them,' says Betty. 'Mr Mulligan, for instance.'

But she can see by Hazel's expression that's not an option and lets the subject drop.

The discussion goes around in circles for another half an hour with suggestions getting more outlandish by the minute. There was a time when Betty had envisioned the grateful little orphans, their sad eyes alight with joy as they gathered around their cosy new beds. She'd planned to propose a brass plaque to commemorate the generosity of the Guild. Now they are faced with the tragic little orphans sleeping on hard floors because the Guild failed miserably in its quest. Never mind the plaque.

'The Sisters are relying on us. If we can't come up with something clever by the next meeting, we're going to have to resort to standing on street corners asking for donations,' concludes Hazel. 'I just can't see any way around it.'

'I will tender my resignation if we have to stoop to begging,' announces Merl.

'One point in its favour then,' says Irene with a grin, getting a cackle from Violet.

'Very amusing,' says Merl, not at all amused.

Hazel does her best to finish on a positive note. 'Let's agree to put on our thinking caps and bring some fresh ideas to the next meeting.'

Betty adds to her notes and reads aloud: 'Butter, greaseproof... cost of... and shoe leather, of course. Sly grog. Begging. Fresh ideas.'

Merl gives an exasperated tut. 'You might as well rip that page out for all the use it is.'

'We ended on the right note with fresh ideas,' says Hazel. 'Thank you, Betty dear.'

Betty gives her a smile. Trust Hazel to find the good in this lacklustre list. What the committee don't seem to grasp is that the next meeting will bring them a month closer to the deadline. She has a sudden vision of the disappointment on the faces of those poor little orphans and shuts her eyes tight to stop the tears.

'What're yer blubbing about now?' asks Irene, lighting both of her cigarettes.

'The orphans!' Betty says in a wobbly voice. 'The poor little orphans.'

Irene lets out a jet of smoke. 'Jesus wept, I need a drink.'

With that, she gets up and leaves, and Violet follows. The Italian women, who have limited English, take that as their cue and the Defence ladies, assuming the meeting is over, wander out as well. Everyone's anxious to get back to the bar downstairs.

Merl picks up her bag. 'Well, I suppose that's meeting adjourned. It's just unfortunate that all formalities have now been dispensed with,' she adds, sailing out the door.

Now only Hazel, Betty, Effie and Mrs Li remain. 'Now it's just us, I'll raise another topic,' says Hazel, reaching for her bag. 'You might recall I volunteer at the People's Palace, and I recently met a woman there, Mrs Fletcher, who is searching for her missing son, Cliff.'

Hazel hands the photo of the lad to Effie, who stares at it for a moment and passes it on to Mrs Li, who also gives it a long hard look.

'Mrs Fletcher is reluctant to go to the police because young Cliff was recently released from Long Bay. She doesn't want to get him in any more trouble,' continues Hazel.

'He would have met some types inside,' says Mrs Li. 'They'd find him work on the outside.'

'How old is he?' asks Effie.

'Mid-twenties,' says Hazel. 'His main distinguishing feature is his ginger hair, and, judging by the photo, he's a big brawny-looking fellow. She thinks he might have found work somewhere on the docks.'

'A lot of blokes do get work on the docks straight out of the clink. No one else wants to hire crims,' says Effie, nodding.

'I can see if there are any files on him at Surry Hills or Darlinghurst police stations,' says Mrs Li.

'Maude has already looked into it and discovered he had a few firearm convictions and an assault, prior to going to Long Bay,' says Hazel.

'If he's got involved with crooks like the Painters and Dockers, the police will have his name on a list,' suggests Mrs Li. 'They keep a close eye on those people. Although, right now, the detectives are all working on this Krugerrand robbery, so I can't see a missing person getting much attention.'

'I know you're keen to get this lad back with his mother, Hazel,' says Effie, 'but he is an adult and just graduated from prison, so likely a career criminal by now.'

Hazel nods. 'It's hard to accept that anyone could be hardened at that tender age, but let's keep our eyes and ears open. He can't have just disappeared.'

'People do,' says Mrs Li gloomily. 'All the time.'

'I've asked a few people down at the port, and I'm almost sure several recognised him but denied any knowledge. So that's made me wonder if there is more to it.' Hazel remembers something else she wanted to ask Mrs Li. 'Have you heard of a fellow called Rizzo, who works down there?'

Mrs Li nods. 'Tony Rizzo. He's quite well-known. There was a time when he was regularly on the front page of the papers. He was a union secretary but got caught taking bribes. They made an example of him and kicked him out. Now I think he's a sort of go-between, making deals between parties. He's a friend of Detective Pierce. I've seen them together drinking coffee at the Coluzzi Bar.'

'Another dodgy type,' adds Effie. 'Be careful, Hazel.'

Betty's more and more concerned about Hazel working at the port, where there's always trouble. She makes a mental note to have a serious conversation about this. There has to be a more suitable job for Hazel somewhere.

Lucy's job in the haberdashery department is serving customers who come to the counter as well as tidying items back on the shelves where they belong. From what Betty has seen, Lucy is not the tidiest of people and perhaps not naturally suited to that role. Hopefully everything is going back in the right place, because, quite honestly, there will be hell to pay if certain people can't find what they're looking for in a hurry. Order is everything in this department, and she would hate to see Lucy get fired (on-the-spot sackings are commonplace) for being a bit lax about that.

She's been off sick the last two days and Betty has missed her cheerful presence. But today, as soon as Betty arrives, she hears Lucy's voice. 'Hello, Betty Boop! Looking lovely as always!'

Betty did make an extra effort with her appearance today. Not that she ever neglects it, but with everything going south, it's sometimes tempting to just give up. Several of the other haberdashery staff glance at Betty and exchange smirks. Everyone's so grumpy in here. They're mostly older people and seem to enjoy complaining more than anything in the world. Betty wonders if they're a bit jealous of Lucy's sunny personality and the many compliments she throws Betty's way.

'Do we ever have herbals here?' asks Lucy, watching Betty pour the tea.

Betty's smile fades as she remembers about the marijuana. 'Ah . . . no,' she says.

'I could bring some from home,' suggests Lucy. 'Mint or sage?'

'Oh, the staff here wouldn't drink that sort of thing,' says Betty, relieved. 'They think coffee is a beatnik drink.'

Lucy laughs. 'You're so funny, Betty.'

'It's true . . . about the coffee, I mean.'

'By the way, we're having a party on Saturday. Can you come? Please say yes. Everyone would love to see you there. You're our good luck charm. Bring a date if you like.'

'A date?' echoes Betty. 'I haven't been on a date since 1932.'

Lucy throws back her head and laughs so loudly people turn to look. 'We'll have to find you one then. Bring a friend. I'm sure you have hundreds.'

'I'll think about it,' says Betty, but she already knows that none of her friends, including Hazel (who is very open-minded), would approve of Lucy's bohemian household.

Rosemont Street is another world but one in which Betty has been made welcome. After only a few visits, she feels she's a different person when she's there. She's wise and witty, and people ask her advice and give her compliments and sometimes even hugs.

In the last year, with Hazel out of work and tea ladies being made redundant left, right and centre, Betty sometimes felt she was just trudging towards the end of her life. Once the work dried up altogether, so would she. But being with these young people has made her see things differently. They don't care about work. They talk about dropping out (which apparently means enjoying not working) and going to live in Kathmandu or Greece, where it's cheap. Lucy even suggested Betty come with them! Now she feels as if there is a whole new path of life opening up ahead – one she could never have dreamed of.

15

HAZEL HAS HER SUSPICIONS

Hazel walks out into the narrow lane beside Trades Hall to find Mr Kovac already there, wearing as usual his duster coat, hair neatly plastered down, shoes polished to a shine. He has his van doors open as he loads up a two-wheeled trolley with boxes of tea and biscuits.

'Mrs Bates!' he cries. 'It is a great pleasure to see your face.' He walks over, hand outstretched, then changes his mind and embraces her warmly. 'I am very happy to see you,' he declares, standing back to look at her.

Hazel smiles. 'I'm delighted to see you too, Mr Kovac. It's been a long time, over a year.'

'In the past, we talk every week. We share our little troubles. I think of you as a friend,' he says earnestly. 'A lost friend.'

Hazel agrees, reminded again of the many people who were once part of her daily life. 'How have you been, Mr Kovac? And your family, are they well?'

'We are all in splendid health. Business has been better. I can admit this. Some of my customers . . . they disappear. But many are very loyal, like yourself and also Mrs Turnbuckle and Mrs Dewsnap.' He gives a chuckle. 'They do not change. But at Empire, the warehouse man has been made in charge of buying supplies. Mrs Karp thinks this is saving money, but they cannot buy in bulk like myself—' He stops himself. 'You do not need to know this story. I am happy you have a new position.'

'As am I,' agrees Hazel. 'Unfortunately, there are two locations, which makes it more complicated. And smaller quantities, I'm afraid.'

Mr Kovac finishes unloading Hazel's order and follows her into the building. Upstairs, they pass Yvonne's desk and Hazel introduces the two of them. Yvonne regards Mr Kovac with suspicion. Hazel takes him to the kitchen and shows him the supplies cupboard. She suggests they go down to the wharf office together in his van, and he agrees.

She can't help but be impressed by the orderliness of the van interior. All the delivery dockets are neatly clipped to the sun visor. Not what you'd expect for a delivery van, but Mr Kovac is efficient and fastidious. He's someone she knows she can always rely on.

As they pull onto the wharves, he says, 'I have never been here, but I read about this place in the newspaper. I know you are not afraid of anything, Mrs Bates—'

Hazel laughs. 'I don't know where you got that idea.'

'You are fearless, it is true, but please be careful. There are more pleasant parts of the city, which are better for a fine tea lady like yourself.'

'I'm sure you're right, but none of them have jobs available right now. They're letting tea ladies go and not rehiring . . . We can park over there,' she says, directing him towards the union office.

Mr Kovac gives a heartfelt sigh. 'The Café-bar machine is popular with the management but not with the staff. There is also not much interest in the tea bag. You can make one cup of tea, it is simple. But the beauty of the teapot is tea for everyone to enjoy together, so people don't care for this lonely little bag. One day, perhaps.'

'It's true, tea is something to be shared,' says Hazel. 'Especially in this weather.'

'I miss our philosophy discussions, Mrs Bates.'

'Well, you know where to find me now,' says Hazel, giving him a smile.

Getting out of the car, she braces herself against the icy wind. As she waits for Mr Kovac to unload the goods, she notices a group of men well-dressed in suits and coats gathered on the wharf, deep in discussion. After a few minutes, they walk off towards the gates, talking among themselves. One of the men hangs back a little, in a furtive way that gets her attention. He pauses beside Goods Shed 3, has a quick glance around and then tucks something behind the downpipe, walking on quickly to re-join the other men.

When Mr Kovac is ready, Hazel takes him a slightly longer way so she can take a peek. There's definitely a piece of paper, or an envelope, folded and wedged in tight behind the downpipe. Her curiosity is piqued; before she leaves she'll check to see if it's been picked up.

In the kitchen, Hazel shows Mr Kovac where the supplies will be kept and gives him a spare key so he can make deliveries at a time that suits his schedule.

'Are you sure I can't give you a lift back, Mrs Bates?' he asks.

'Thank you, no, you have deliveries to make. I'm almost finished for the day now, so I'll get the train,' Hazel tells him.

When he's gone, she spends a few minutes reordering the cupboard, locks up the kitchen and goes on her way. Passing Shed 3 she can see the note behind the downpipe is now gone and the pigeon fancier is back in his usual spot, watching the sky through binoculars.

The wind has picked up and rain clouds tear across the sky. Nevertheless, she makes her way over and says hello. In the distance, buffeted by the wind, the pigeons battle their way towards their master on the wharf.

Seeing Hazel approach, the man says, 'Ah, the tea lady. Still here, are yers?'

'So it would seem,' Hazel replies. 'It's a bitter day to be out. Do you come here every day?' she asks, thinking aloud.

He turns to her, eyes narrowed. 'What's it to yer?'

'Oh, I just noticed we're here on the same day and wondered—'

'I come whenever I fancy it, don't I? Don't need a bloody reason, do I?'

Hazel apologises, taken aback by his aggressive tone. Her ears tingle, warm despite the cold, making her suspect there must be a good reason for him to be here in such weather. Shed 3 is directly in his line of sight, and it crosses her mind that the note may have been for him.

He turns on her angrily. 'Yer a nosy old bird. Gorn, get out of here. Yer the one that don't have no reason to be here. Stick to yer tea. Off yer go. Shoo!'

Hazel wonders if she should apologise again or just leave. She decides on the latter and walks away.

Living in Surry Hills, a suburb with a long history of crime, she's well aware that criminals are attracted to particular locations. Hidden laneways that offer privacy for transactions, violence and sometimes even murders. Racetracks where money openly changes hands. Nightclubs with dark corners for secret meetings. And the waterfront, a place where it seems the rules don't apply. Pillaging is rife. Fights are commonplace. Shadowy corners offer spots for two-up games, and in the evenings, ship girls openly solicit down here. Hazel casts her mind to other nefarious activities apart from gambling, theft and prostitution; the most obvious one is smuggling contraband. Criminals are also attracted to places populated by other criminals, for obvious reasons. This fellow is up to no good, she's sure of it. The pigeons won't be the only ones keeping a beady eye on him in future.

As soon as she gets home, Hazel hurries to the kitchen to add coal to the range and stir up the smouldering embers to warm the room. She makes a pot of tea and sits down to read the paper she bought on the way. It's not something she ever looks forward to – reading is still a struggle for her – but this daily habit has helped. Today, she turns to a section she's never bothered with: the shipping news. She runs her finger down the bewildering list of names, arrival times and places of origin and captains' names. Some are obviously cruise ships, with names starting with 'Princess', and others are cargo vessels. She has no idea what she's looking for, but there must be a reason the pigeon fancier inhabits that spot at various times – and was so annoyed at her question.

'Cooee! I'm home!' comes a cry from the hallway.

'Welcome home, Betty dear,' calls Hazel.

'Oh gosh, I think it was sleeting as I came in.'

Betty peels off her outer clothes, piles them all on a chair and sits down with a sigh. Hazel, sensing there's something on her mind, pours a cup of tea and passes it to her. They talk about their day, and Hazel's meeting with Mr Kovac. Then, out of nowhere, Betty asks, 'Do you ever wish you were young again?'

'I never really think about it,' says Hazel, puzzled. 'A little nostalgia goes a long way. It's easy to forget the not-so-good aspects of the past. What's brought this on?'

'It's just . . . we were such good girls, weren't we? When we worked at the exchange all those years ago. Always doing the right thing.'

Hazel smiles. 'You were a bit naughty eavesdropping on private conversations.'

'That's the only fun a switchboard girl gets. What I'm saying is . . . we didn't expect much from life, did we? That was a boring job, but we didn't question it. We never thought we could be artists instead of switchboard girls.'

'Artists?' asks Hazel, wondering if she's heard correctly.

'Or actresses or dancers.'

'I don't think artists or actresses have very reliable incomes, although go-go dancers seem to be in great demand these days.'

Betty doesn't seem to be listening. 'And also, now there's "free love", and you don't have to be married. Women don't have to be well-behaved all the time because there's the contraceptive pill and people aren't so judgemental.'

As far as Hazel can see, there has been any amount of trumpeting about the collapse of decent society with the advent of the Pill. Young people do want to be freer, but their elders have responded to that idea with furious indignation. However, she doesn't want to pour cold water on Betty's enthusiasm, so takes a neutral stance. 'Is it Lucy who's making you rethink your youthful choices, dear?'

'I know you've probably formed an opinion about her, Hazel. But to me she's a breath of fresh air. Never mind your corsets and suspender belts, she doesn't even wear underwear!' Betty says, with a shocked giggle.

Hazel smiles, slightly bemused by that revelation. 'Betty, you know I would never form an opinion about someone I had never met, but I was concerned about the marijuana—'

'I think that was a mistake. I'd had a bit too much to drink.'

'You don't have to explain to me, dear. It's your life, I'm not trying to interfere or be judgemental, I'm just concerned . . .' but noting Betty's pout, Hazel quickly changes tack. 'I made some nice savoury mince this morning. I'll put it on now.'

'Oh yummy – my favourite!' says Betty, immediately restored to good humour.

While Hazel heats the mince on the stove, she tells Betty all about the pigeon fancier and his sudden aggression, and about the note.

'Oh, I don't like the sound of him,' says Betty. 'How dare he speak to you like that!'

'He'd been civil enough until that moment. I think he's hiding something. It seems too much of a coincidence that he happened to be there when a note was left nearby.'

'You'd need a good reason to hang around outside in this weather,' agrees Betty. 'He does sound dodgy.'

'Seems to go with the territory down there,' says Hazel with a sigh.

'I wish you could find somewhere safer to work, Hazel. And what about Rex? Do you think he's all right?'

'Well, he has his heart set on a career in politics, so you'd think so. Although we do seem to have plenty of dishonest politicians these days.' The telephone rings. 'Just keep an eye on the mince,' Hazel says, as she goes out into the hall to answer it.

'Mrs Bates?' asks the caller. 'It's Mrs Fletcher.'

'Hello, Mrs Fletcher, I'm sorry I don't have anything to report—'

'I had a letter from Cliff. Just short, he's not much of a writer. He said he's fine and to stop asking around after him,' says Mrs Fletcher in her soft voice.

'I see. Well, that's good news, isn't it?'

'I think someone's made him write it,' she says.

'What makes you think that?' asks Hazel.

'For one thing, it's in his very neatest handwriting.'

'But it's definitely his?' confirms Hazel.

'Yes, but when he wrote to me from prison, it was just in his natural hand, a bit scribbly and rough. This is like a school essay.'

'That's an interesting observation. Anything else?'

'It's on a piece of brown wrapping paper and stuffed in a dirty envelope. That's not my Cliff. He's quite fussy about things. Like with his work.'

'What is his work?' asks Hazel, wondering why she had not asked sooner.

'He's a carpenter and cabinet maker. He's only just finished his apprenticeship but he's very skilled. He'd make a good living if he settled down.'

'I'm sure he will eventually,' Hazel reassures her. 'Is there a postmark on the letter?'

'It's postmarked Sydney, so he's still there. Why doesn't he just tell me where he is?'

'I don't know, but at least he's alive and well,' says Hazel.

'Then why hasn't he come home? And why doesn't he want to see me?'

Hazel hesitates and then asks, 'He's been in a bit of trouble over the years, hasn't he?'

Mrs Fletcher's silence hangs on the line. 'How do you know about that?'

'I don't mean to offend you, Mrs Fletcher, it's just—'

'He's easily influenced and not one for thinking about consequences. That's why I'm keen to have him closer to home, where I can find something local for him. Just a shame he got caught up with the wrong crowd.'

Hazel knows that's not strictly true. This young man *is* the wrong crowd, but she says nothing. 'One last thing. Who else is looking for him? Apart from you and me?'

After a long silence, Mrs Fletcher says vaguely, 'I've asked a few people.'

'I see,' says Hazel. 'Well, if I hear anything on the grapevine, I'll be in touch.'

When she hangs up, Hazel stands in the hall gathering her thoughts and wondering if it was someone she spoke to who doesn't want young Cliff found.

16
PIXIE'S DISAPPOINTMENT

By the time Pixie, Gloria and Alice arrive at the shop in Vine Street, it's almost dark. Gloria presses her forehead to the front window and stares inside.

'This is what they call an impossible dream,' she says, stepping back to gaze up at the exterior of the building.

Pixie says nothing. She'd hoped that Gloria would see the possibilities. Having worked in the factory at Empire Fashionwear since she was fifteen, Gloria has more experience than Alice and Pixie put together. If anyone can make this happen, it's her.

Alice leans heavily on her sticks to look inside the shop and Pixie notices how delicate her friend is with her pale complexion, wispy blonde hair and skinny little legs. It had been difficult enough for Alice to get a job in the first place, so why would she take a gamble and leave it?

'It's a good location,' says Alice. 'I can imagine a beautiful boutique, but . . . I don't know the first thing about business, let alone how to start one.'

Gloria lights a cigarette. The tip glows red in the gathering dark. 'If I told my hubby I was leaving Empire to start a shop from scratch, he'd hit the bloody roof and, trust me, if he had a few drinks in him, not just the roof. It's too risky. I'll stay where I am, thank you.'

Pixie doesn't know what to say. It's hard to believe someone as strong as Gloria would put up with that sort of behaviour from her husband.

Reading her mind, Gloria adds, 'Don't judge me, Pixie. This is what marriage is like. You've got to put up with the good and the bad, for better or worse, as they say.'

'That's why I'm never getting married,' says Pixie firmly.

'Me neither,' says Alice, with a shudder.

Gloria coughs up a laugh. 'You'll be a couple of old maids like the Rosenbaums.'

'On the topic of the Rosenbaum sisters, Dottie made me an offer yesterday,' says Alice in a quiet voice.

'Did she now?' says Pixie, her heart sinking. 'It's freezing standing here, let's sit in the car.'

They all get in the car and when everyone's settled, Pixie and Gloria turn towards Alice, sitting in the back seat.

'All right, what was her offer?' Pixie asks.

'She wants to move me upstairs with the Rosenbaums in the design department. I'd be head designer of a "youth wear" range – a promotion with a pay rise,' says Alice.

Gloria gives a dry laugh. 'You've got to hand it to Dottie. She should go into politics.'

'And what did you say?' asks Pixie, knowing this is all Alice has ever wanted.

'That I'd talk it over with you, of course,' says Alice.

'So, you'd be working on the Mod Frocks range?' asks Pixie. 'You're already doing that. You're the sole designer. And next month, that brand will belong to me—'

'I reckon they're going to start an offshoot brand,' interrupts Gloria.

'I think so too,' agrees Alice. 'Dottie's been nosing around in the factory with a man trailing behind her, asking questions.'

'Really?' asks Pixie. 'What sort of questions?'

Alice shrugs. 'Production times for particular garments, that sort of thing.'

Pixie's surprised. 'Do you know who this bloke is?'

'Someone trying to sell her something, probably,' suggests Gloria.

Alice shakes her head. 'I think he's some sort of financial person, maybe from the bank. I overheard her explaining how the business works. Seasons, store contracts, that sort of thing.'

'That's rich,' says Gloria, stubbing out her cigarette in the ashtray. 'As if she has any idea whatsoever.'

Alice turns to gaze out the window at the shopfront. 'What did the real estate agent say about the upstairs? Is that included?'

'Yes. There's a small kitchen downstairs and two rooms upstairs. Outside loo but attached to the house. He can show us around tomorrow... if we're interested.' Pixie glances from Alice to Gloria. '*Are* we interested?'

After a moment, Alice says, 'I'll come and see it with you.'

Gloria shakes her head slowly. 'I'm sorry, Pix. It's taken me so many years to get to supervisor. This would be a step down, and I might never step up again.'

'This would be our own business,' says Pixie. 'We'd be three equal partners.'

'I don't have any money to put into it,' argues Gloria.

'I get some money when I turn twenty-one. We can use that to get started,' says Pixie.

'You could do better than throw your inheritance away on this mad idea,' says Gloria. 'As I said, it's too risky for me.'

To her frustration, Pixie feels tears suddenly brim. 'I can't do it on my own.'

If Hazel is surprised to find Pixie, Alice and Gloria on her doorstep, she doesn't let on. She ushers them into her cosy kitchen and they sit around the table while she pours them glasses of mulberry wine. 'We went around to see the shop in Vine Street,' explains Pixie.

'What did you think?' asks Hazel, looking at Gloria and Alice.

'I don't know,' says Gloria. 'I mean, Dottie and Frankie are a pain in the bum, but we get our pay packets every week and that makes up for a lot. This is dicey.'

Hazel nods and turns to Alice. 'What about you, Alice?'

'If we could create our own designs and do everything the way we want to—'

'Without Dottie interfering and ruining everything,' interrupts Pixie.

Alice nods. 'I think we'd be more radical in our designs without Pixie's parents getting involved. I'm nervous about the financial risk.' She looks over at Pixie with a smile. 'But I have complete faith in Pixie's business sense.'

Hazel nods. 'Well, it's very timely that you popped in this evening. I was going to get in touch with you, Pixie.' She pauses. 'I had a cuppa with Mrs Stern yesterday.'

'Lucky you,' says Gloria sarcastically.

Hazel laughs. 'Her bark is worse than her bite, as they say. I'm not breaking a confidence here. Mrs Stern wanted me to pass on this information to you. Evidently Dottie and Frankie are working out how they can take control of Mod Frocks before you turn twenty-one and stop it passing to you. They've got a lawyer involved.'

'I knew it,' says Pixie, her heart sinking. 'I knew they were up to something.'

Gloria gives an exasperated sigh. 'Old Karp will be turning in his grave.'

'It goes completely against his wishes,' says Pixie angrily. 'He wanted me to have control of Mod Frocks straightaway – they're the ones who talked him into delaying it.'

'They were playing for time,' says Alice.

'I wish I could tell you more, but Mrs Stern's reconnaissance is limited to what she overhears, and they are being particularly secretive about the whole affair – understandably.'

'Typical,' says Gloria. 'Only surprising it took them so long.'

'Do you think this is because I kicked up a stink about the fashion parade?' asks Pixie.

Alice nods. 'They know they won't be able to control you for much longer.'

'Well, that's that then,' says Gloria, pushing her chair back. 'Stuffed before you start.'

'Gloria dear, it's not like you to give in so easily,' says Hazel, sounding surprised.

'I know what you're doing, Hazel. You're goading me,' says Gloria. 'But I can't commit to a hairbrained scheme like this. I've got a lot more to lose than these two. I'm on the wrong side of thirty, they're on the right side.'

'There's no right or wrong side of thirty. Of course, it's your decision, but you're certainly not too old for an adventure,' says Hazel in a firm voice.

'We've got all the designs and samples for next summer season . . . If I can just get the brand name, that's all we need to get started,' says Pixie.

'We can start small – just the three of us,' says Alice. She glances at Gloria. 'Or the two of us, I suppose.'

'Oh brother,' says Gloria. 'Now I'm going to be made to feel guilty for not pitching in and risking my neck on this. There are other ways to get away from your parents, you know.'

Pixie turns to her. 'By going to work for another company, you mean? I don't want to do that.'

'Pixie, why don't you have a word with Mr Levy and see what he has to say?' suggests Hazel. 'As I've mentioned before, he's not just an accountant; he has an excellent head for business and knows the rag trade inside out. I'm sure he'll have some good advice for you. And you can trust him to keep it to himself.'

Hazel tops up their glasses and Pixie feels more relaxed as they discuss possibilities for the shop, and relieved that Alice is clearly keen to be a part of it. They throw around some ideas and discuss paint colours for the showroom. Gloria suggests they could pick up a couple of second-hand sewing machines cheaply from companies upgrading to new ones.

'You're all so talented in your own ways,' says Hazel. 'A good combination.'

Pixie has always taken Hazel's wise counsel for granted and realises with a jolt how much she misses seeing her friendly face every day of the working week. She wants to say so but doesn't know how to without making an idiot of herself.

Seeing them off at the door, Hazel adds, 'There's no need to rush into anything, Pixie. That shop's been empty for months.'

Pixie thanks her and, on an impulse, gives her a hug and gets a warm one in return. She feels a rush of optimism. Not the silly dizzy excitement she felt earlier in the week, with her imagination running wild. This is something more solid, a proper plan forming in her mind. She just needs the courage to see it through.

17
GOING OVER THE EDGE

'What are you sulking about, darling?' asks Dottie, flicking through the Sunday paper at the dining table while she digs into half a grapefruit with a teaspoon.

Pixie doesn't answer. She continues to spread jam on her toast and tells herself not to get into an argument.

'Me?' asks Frankie, glancing up from the racing pages.

'I didn't know you were sulking, dear. One at a time, please.' Dottie chuckles at her own joke. 'Pixie? Is this still over the fashion parade? You know we *had* to do that . . . it was for your own good. The fashion pages would have torn you apart, my love. As it is Empire got a lovely write-up for *La Mode*, so that was good for everyone, wasn't it?' Turning her attention back to the papers, she gives a huff of annoyance. 'Is there a single event in this city that Carla Zampatti doesn't attend? Three years ago, she was some little fashion assistant that no one cared about. Now the woman is launching her own collection and you can't get away from her.' She flicks the paper closed irritably. 'We need to go to the theatre, the opera even, Frankie. When is that blasted Opera House going to be finished?'

'I'm sure if the builders understood the social urgency, they'd be encouraged to finish it promptly,' Frankie says, without looking up.

'I sincerely doubt that,' says Dottie. 'Well, we do have the Beauchamp Ball coming up. It doesn't get any better than that in this town.'

'No, it doesn't,' agrees Frankie.

'Do you still want me to come?' asks Pixie, wondering if there is a different way to go about this.

'Of course. We need a good showing from the firm, and I think Mrs Beauchamp took a shine to you.' Dottie pauses, then continues. 'Frankie, Angela Beauchamp is sponsoring three underprivileged girls to attend the ball and we've been invited to provide their gowns.' Another pause. 'Gratis, obviously.'

Frankie sighs. 'Really? Is that a good idea, Dot?'

'Yes, it is,' she says. 'Not only will it consolidate my relationship with Angela, but *La Mode* will be publicly acknowledged on the night and featured in the society pages. You can't buy that sort of publicity.'

Frankie puts his paper aside. 'You can, actually. For the cost of three La Mode gowns, we could put a full-page ad in the *Herald*.'

Dottie smiles. 'An ad doesn't come close to matching an endorsement by the Beauchamps. And Pixie and I need new gowns. We'll have to go all out with something more stunning than the charity cases.' She turns her attention to Pixie. 'I know you don't like a fuss, Pixie, but we need to make a real splash. It's the perfect opportunity.'

Pixie nods. 'I don't mind,' she lies.

Her mother looks suspicious. 'Why are you cooperating all of a sudden? You didn't attend a single debutante ball and, from memory, claimed these events make you sick.'

'I understand it's a big thing.' Pixie stalls, dreading getting to the point. 'I mean, I'll be a legal shareholder soon and taking over part of the company. I know I need to get more involved.'

Her parents exchange quick glances across the table.

'It won't be that different,' says Frankie. 'Being a shareholder doesn't mean that much. Dottie and I will continue to run the company.'

Pixie slowly takes another slice of toast from the rack, her mouth dry. 'But I'll also fully own the Mod Frocks brand, so that's different, isn't it?'

'We've been thinking about that,' says Dottie in her 'no-nonsense' voice. 'Grandad really didn't want the firm broken up, so we think it's better to keep Mod Frocks incorporated with Empire Fashionwear. It won't make any difference to you. You'll still manage it—'

'Under your supervision,' says Pixie.

'Of course.' Dottie laughs, as if anything else is ridiculous.

'We've all got along together so far,' lies Frankie.

'We have papers being drawn up to retain Mod Frocks within the firm,' says Dottie. 'There'll be benefits to you. You're so young, my darling, you need to learn so much.'

'I could use the two thousand dollars Grandad left me to take you to court,' says Pixie, without raising her voice.

After a moment of shock, Dottie gives a brittle laugh. 'You could try, but you'll be throwing your money away. That's not what Grandad intended, is it?'

Pixie feels a surge of anger. She almost can't speak. It's not just this business, it's a whole lifetime of Dottie getting whatever she wants without any thought for other people. 'And *you're* respecting Grandad's wishes?' Pixie asks.

Alarmed, Frankie holds up his hands for peace. 'We can talk about it.'

Dottie sends him a dagger look. 'We have talked about it endlessly and made the decision. Don't let me down now, please, Frankie.'

Pixie gets up from the table. As she crosses the room, her mother calls, 'We're still your parents, and we know what's best for the firm.'

Pixie keeps on walking, down the hall and up the stairs to her room. She closes the door and locks it. She sits on her bed for a long time. Finally, she makes a decision.

Pixie has arranged to meet Mr Levy, Empire Fashionwear's accountant of many years, at the Delphi Milk Bar, one place she's confident her parents would never set foot in. She orders a pot of tea and some sandwiches and, right on time, Mr Levy slips into the booth to sit opposite her. He always looks so smart, today in a charcoal suit, white shirt, silver cufflinks and bright blue tie. With his tortoise-shell glasses and his silver hair slicked back from a high forehead, he looks like a well-dressed professor.

He gives her a little smile. 'I think I know what this is about, and I have to admit my loyalties are divided. Having worked for your grandfather for two decades, I naturally feel a sense of loyalty to the firm. On the other hand, I know exactly how he wanted this to work. We talked about it many times. In trying to divest you of the Mod Frocks business, your parents are definitely going against his wishes.'

Mrs Angelos brings their tea and sandwiches, and Pixie thanks her with a smile.

'I know he would have been happy for me to take it over earlier,' says Pixie. 'Mr Levy, I want to run that business on my own, without those two involved. Dottie thinks she knows it all, but she doesn't understand our customers. She's too . . .' Pixie stops herself.

Mr Levy raises his eyebrows in mock surprise. 'Old?'

'Sorry. She's just a different generation, and she doesn't get it.'

'Your grandfather had a lot of faith in your abilities. He compromised under pressure to maintain family harmony, not because he didn't think you were capable.' He picks up a sandwich and examines the contents. Egg and lettuce seems to meet with his approval and he takes a small bite.

'Could I take them to court and fight for it?' she asks.

Mr Levy gives a chuckle. 'I admire your chutzpah, Pixie, but my advice would be to channel your enthusiasm into your business. Taking your parents to court will burn up any money you have and, more importantly, drain you of your youthful energy. It will cause bad blood in the family, and that's not what your grandfather would have wanted.' He pauses. 'And, to be frank, if it got that far, they could portray you as incompetent, and a court may well decide in their favour. A parent's authority over a child would carry weight in this situation.'

'I'm not a child,' says Pixie, with a sigh of frustration.

'I believe your grandfather took out an annuity for you that matures at twenty-one.'

Pixie nods. 'A thousand pounds in the old money.'

'Two thousand dollars,' he muses. 'It's a substantial amount.'

'It's not much help if I can't get my label,' says Pixie.

Mr Levy picks up the teapot and tops up his cup. 'Pixie, I want to tell you something, but it must be in absolute confidence.'

Pixie nods. 'Of course, cross my heart.'

'The reason they want to hold on to Mod Frocks is that it's generating the firm's main cash flow right now and propping up the losses of the other less-profitable labels – La Mode, for example. If they were to lose your brand, the company could potentially collapse in a matter of months. To be honest, if they don't change direction that may still happen. Mod Frocks is not doing as well as it was—'

'That's because of Dottie's interference,' interrupts Pixie.

'Maybe, but it's also possible it's run its course, and customers are looking for the next new thing,' says Mr Levy.

'I'd hate people to lose their jobs, but I don't have any control there anyway.' Pixie pauses. 'I can't stay working at Empire with them. It's killing me.'

Mr Levy nods. 'There is an alternative that could work for everyone. Things have changed in the last couple of years. A brand name is important for the prestige market because traditional customers are loyal to those brands, but the younger market is more . . . fickle, let's say. They embrace novelty, so a fresh brand name may have advantages for you. In fact, it may be essential for future expansion.' He pauses. 'I want to be clear that I'm not suggesting this option to save our jobs – it's my honest observation of the market.'

'So you're saying forget about Mod Frocks and start with a new brand?'

Mr Levy nods. 'It's a clean and simple way to do it. If you're determined to go it alone anyway, why not? You're young and smart, and a tremendously hard worker, and you'd still have your shareholding in Empire.'

Pixie instantly feels a weight lift off her shoulders. She's been dreading fighting with her parents, not to mention facing the possibility of losing that battle. The idea of creating something fresh is exciting and, if Mr Levy believes she can do it, he stands above all others in her eyes.

'I would be fired on the spot if they knew I was giving you this advice,' he adds.

'Of course. It's our secret.' She pauses, suddenly shy. 'I saw a shop for rent.'

Mr Levy laughs. 'I love the flexible thinking of the young mind.'

Pixie slides the document from the real estate agent across to him and waits while he examines it. He finishes his sandwich and wipes his hands carefully on the paper napkin.

'Would you like me to suggest what sort of deal to go after to lessen your risk?'

Pixie gets out her notebook. 'Go ahead,' she says. 'I'm listening.'

18

HAZEL ON THE SPOT

Hazel arrives at the wharves to find a cluster of police standing around on the main dock. It must be something serious because Detective Dibble is there, which means Special Branch is involved. Rex and several staff are gathered outside the office watching the proceedings.

'It was just a matter of time,' says the bookmaker. 'Had it coming to him.'

'Cooper, the birdman,' Rex explains to Hazel. 'Found in the water early this morning, rolled up in a cargo net. They thought it was a trapped shark at first. Turned out to be a body.'

'Cooper?' repeats Hazel, realising she never knew his name. 'Oh dear, poor fellow.' She hasn't spoken to the man since their run-in last week. She would have forgiven him for his outburst, but the next time she saw him he'd scowled furiously at her, so she walked on.

'Wouldn't waste any tears over a cockatoo,' says Teddy.

Noticing Hazel's confusion, Rex says, 'A cockatoo is a lookout – keeps an eye out for someone while they're up to no good, usually.'

Sometimes these blokes see things they shouldn't, and know too much. So they get the old heave-ho.'

The bookie turns to Hazel. 'You better watch yourself. We don't want to find the tea lady floating out there,' he says with a guffaw.

'No, especially since I can't swim,' says Hazel. 'Anyway, there's nothing to fear from a tea lady. Speaking of which, I better get that Zip on. Seems everyone could do with a strong cup of tea.'

In the kitchen, she has time to think. It had crossed her mind previously that this fellow, Cooper, was not exactly a loved local identity. He must have been considered a bit of a nuisance in a working port but was obviously tolerated for whatever reason. She wonders who he could have been working for, and doing what exactly?

It's become increasingly clear that there are competing interests on the docks, parties working around each other for reasons of their own. She wonders if Cooper could have found out something about the missing gold. And why did Hazel's question enrage him? She obviously touched a nerve. But, despite her curiosity, she won't risk sticking her neck out again. She definitely doesn't want to end up in the harbour.

'How dreadful,' says Betty, when Hazel tells her the story of Cooper's demise. 'I know he was rude to you, Hazel, but he didn't deserve to die like that. His birds will miss him.'

Hazel looks up from her dinner. 'Betty dear, you're making it sound as if I'm a suspect. I hope the police don't interview you.'

'Oh Hazel, I wouldn't tell them about that argument you had, obviously.'

'It wasn't an argument, it was a simple question that rattled him. Which has left me wondering why . . .' Hazel trails off, noticing the kitchen door handle twisting back and forth. She gets up and opens the door.

'Why's the bloody door locked?' Irene asks, brushing past her and heading for the range to warm her hands.

'It's called security, Irene,' says Betty. 'Were we expecting you?'

Irene gives her a filthy look. 'Who do yer think yers are, the Queen?'

'Never mind the Queen,' says Betty. 'I doubt anyone would appreciate you barging in like that, especially in a bad temper.'

Ignoring her, Irene asks, 'Anything to drink?'

'We're having mulled plum wine, dear, very hearty and warming,' says Hazel.

'If there's nothing else, I suppose,' grumbles Irene. She tips up the lid of the range, spits into the coals and drops it closed with a clang.

Hazel pours her a cup of the wine keeping warm in a thermos.

Irene takes a sip and screws her face up. 'Hot wine. What's the bloody world coming to?' Knocking it back, she sits down at the table. 'Got a bit of a problem. Yer know that Miss Palmer's a bit of a shady lady.'

'Hence the name,' quips Betty. 'Miss Palm—'

'Mate, me bloody life's in danger, it's no joking matter.'

'She's a madam, so we can assume a degree of shadiness,' says Hazel. 'Go on, Irene.'

'She's opened up a place down in Darlo, right near Woods Lane,' begins Irene.

Betty gasps. 'Oh goodness, that lane is notorious!'

'Yes. As I was saying,' continues Irene crossly, 'it's overrun with

Malteses down there, and she asked me to go down and clean the place—'

Betty holds up one hand. 'Wait. Irene, do you mean the little chocolate—'

Irene gives an exasperated sigh. 'Mafia is what I'm talking about, yer nitwit. Anyhow, I saw these two blokes sitting in a car watching the place. So I go round the back and chuck a brick at them—'

'Irene dear, was that a good idea?' asks Hazel. 'Tell me you didn't hit anyone.'

'Nah, chucked it at the car. Nuthin' wrong with me aim. Hit the roof.'

'Couldn't you have just—' begins Betty.

'No, I couldn't,' growls Irene.

'So did you see who was in the car?' asks Hazel.

'These two old blokes, Malteses. That's what I'm tellin' yers. Joe Borg's blokes. He's got a dozen tart shops down there in Woods Lane. He's always in the papers. I don't know what Miss Palmer's thinkin', cutting in on him.' Irene shakes her head in disbelief.

It occurs to Hazel that the politics of the brothel business are as complex and mysterious as the politics of unions, and she can see there's a common thread of power and monopoly woven into both. She hardly knows what to suggest, especially since Irene has probably inflamed the situation by throwing that brick at these men. 'Have you talked to Miss Palmer about it?' she asks.

'Tried to. Told me to mind me own business. But the thing is, I reckon these blokes have been watching 555 as well. Now she's about to go off gallivanting round the Far East, and I'll be there on me ownsome when they firebomb the bloody place. That's when they'll do it. When she's away.'

'Is there somewhere you could stay in the meantime?' asks Hazel. 'Just until you see what happens? I'm not sure what else you can do.'

'I don't wanna lose me home. Apart from here, it's the nicest place I've ever lived.' Frowning, Irene pulls a large cigar out of her coat pocket and lights it, billowing smoke.

Hazel and Betty exchange glances, silently agreeing they won't begrudge her this one little comfort.

19
A MEETING IN THE DARK

'Madam Reliable,' says Mrs Babinski when Hazel arrives at the People's Palace. 'Volunteers think they can come any time that is suiting them. This is not suiting me.'

'Reliability is important, I agree,' says Hazel, tying on an apron.

Mrs Babinski hands her a paring knife and directs her to a bucket of carrots, washed and ready to chop. 'When you do that, you can start this.' Mrs Babinski nudges over a tin bucket full of celery with her foot. 'Is a bit old but we don't mind. Look in the pot, Mrs Bates. We have nice surprise.'

Hazel looks in the pot to see a chicken carcass simmering. 'Very nice and nutritious.'

'The butcher give me. Expensive butcher. He sells different parts of the chicken. Rich people, they want leg and breast. The best meat only. Such waste for the chicken life.'

Mrs Babinski brings her knife down hard on a head of cauliflower. Splitting it in half, she chops it into chunks with a few deft and violent strokes and throws them into the pot. 'Why you stand here, Mrs Bates?' she asks, without looking up.

'Very good question.' Hazel turns her attention to the carrots and celery.

Mrs Babinski opens a sack of stale bread donated by the nearby bakery. She takes each loaf out and examines it. She diligently scrapes off the mould, explaining that the ladies will get mould on their insides if it's not removed. Then she slices the loaves and spreads them with dripping. 'What a feast we make this night,' she says, with a rare smile.

'I'm sure they will be delighted,' says Hazel.

'Some person will complain,' says Mrs Babinski. 'I know this.' She shrugs.

Twenty minutes later, with the carrots and celery chopped, Hazel moves on to the next task, filling the large double-handled teapot and carrying it out to the table, where she then sets out the cups and saucers, milk and sugar. The place is full as usual, and women form an orderly queue. Hazel has a smile and a kind word for each of them. She adds the milk and sugar herself and gives the tea a good stir. No one looks after these women, so it's nice to be able to offer a little service of care.

The last woman in the line is a similar age to Hazel. Her clothes are good quality but lost their sheen long ago, the collar of her blouse frayed, the elbows of her woollen coat worn. Hazel tries to engage her in conversation but doesn't get much out of her. She drinks her tea in silence, then wanders away, a hunched and lonely figure. Hazel feels desperately sorry for all the women here. She is reminded over and over that poverty and homelessness can happen to anyone at any time, and the formerly wealthy are even less equipped to deal with it than those who have suffered poverty all their lives.

The woman's plight is still on Hazel's mind as she steps out into the dark street at the end of her shift. She feels a sense of disquiet, as if she's glimpsed a possible future for herself in different circumstances. Eager for the comforting security of her own cosy kitchen, she reminds herself that while the union is not her ideal workplace it does provide some income.

'Mrs Bates,' says a voice behind her. 'Good evening.'

She turns to see Detective Dibble, his fedora pulled low, coat collar high as if he's playing a detective in a film. 'You seem to take delight in creeping up on me these days,' says Hazel. 'Is this a coincidence, or were you waiting for me?'

'The latter,' he admits. 'May I walk with you?'

'Of course,' says Hazel. 'I'm headed to the train. I noticed you down on the wharves the other day. Sad for that fellow Cooper.'

'He was a crook by all accounts, record as long as your arm. There's not going to be a lot of time spent on the case. He's a casualty of his chosen profession.'

'Which was?' asks Hazel.

'Acting as a lookout for other crooks. To complicate matters, and something more worthy of police attention, the gold trader, Charles Beauchamp, was found dead in his home last night.'

'Murdered?' asks Hazel.

Dibble nods. 'Shot at close range. Presumably related to the Krugerrand robbery, but how and why, we don't know. The wife was asleep and woken by a window breaking. She came downstairs to find him dead.'

'Obviously not a coincidence,' says Hazel, wondering if Cooper's death is connected.

She glances around for somewhere private and warmer to talk. Across the road is a sandstone church and she suggests they step inside for a minute. The doors are unlocked and the church empty. It's much grander than she would have imagined, with a high curved ceiling of golden sandstone and an enormous pipe organ.

'Let's hope the organist doesn't practise this evening,' says Dibble, as they slide into a pew at the back of the church.

'I don't really know anything about Mr Beauchamp,' says Hazel. 'But I had been keeping an eye on Mr Cooper. At first I thought he was just a local colourful character. Then I had a bit of a run-in with him and started to wonder why he chose that area of the wharves to train his birds. There are many more pleasant and peaceful parts of the harbour.'

'What sort of run-in?' asks Dibble.

'Annoyed at a perfectly innocent enquiry. I just asked if he came there every day, but he chased me off and was quite hostile after that. It aroused my suspicions, and that's when I began to look at the shipping news.'

'Did you now? And?'

'I didn't have time to establish a pattern before he was murdered, but I thought there might be a link between ships coming in and his presence. It crossed my mind that his pigeons could have been meeting particular ships—'

'Before the ship berths,' interrupts Dibble. 'Or, more importantly, before customs officers go on board.'

'Perhaps his pigeons have a story to tell?' suggests Hazel.

'We haven't found his pigeons. They've disappeared.'

'Bird-napping and murder. It gets more interesting by the minute,' says Hazel. 'There's something else. I noticed a group of men on the dock last week. One of them hid a note behind a downpipe on one of the goods sheds, before leaving the wharf.'

Dibble frowns. 'A note for whom?'

'I don't know, but it was the same day as my trouble with

Mr Cooper. The note was picked up quite quickly. I wondered if it was for him, and that's why he was so touchy.'

'Describe the chap who left the note,' says Dibble, getting out a notebook and pen.

'Quite tall, over six foot. Solidly built with greying hair. Expensive coat with a fur collar. He'd be quite a presence in a room, I would imagine.'

'That's Charles Beauchamp himself,' says Dibble. 'Interesting. The trader was above board as far as we know and, as I mentioned, moved in "esteemed" circles. Cooper was a small-time crook. Any connection between them would be unusual, to say the least.'

Hazel agrees. 'Any other clues about the robbery come to light?'

'We know the ship docked in Darwin and there was one change of crew, so we have people up there looking into it, but nothing of interest so far. As I mentioned to you, right now we're in a race with those keen to relieve the robbers of that loot. Stand-over men and the Toe-Cutters gang specialise in exactly this.'

'Rob the robbers? You don't need to be a mastermind for that,' says Hazel.

'No, just be tougher than the tough guys. Watch yourself, Mrs Bates, but keep your eye out for anything unusual. You're on the spot, and I say this with all respect, almost invisible, which we are not.'

Hazel smiles. 'I'll do my best.' She looks around the church, so peaceful and quiet. 'On another topic, does the name Joe Borg ring a bell?'

'An alarm bell,' says Dibble, turning to her. 'Very dangerous man.'

'Irene's boss at 555 has recently opened up a place near Woods Lane, in direct competition with him. Irene's noticed some men watching Miss Palmer's places, and she seems to think he could be planning to do something nasty.'

'She could be right. Firebombing is Borg's calling card. I thought Miss Palmer was smarter than that. The Maltese mafia have a tight hold on that area – she's going to come to grief if she tangles with them.'

'Miss Palmer's going overseas and Irene's worried it'll happen while she's away.'

'I can pass that info on to Vice. They might have some bright ideas. Turf wars always make them look bad, especially in the current political climate.'

'Should we say a quick prayer while we're here?' asks Hazel.

Dibble gives a dry laugh. 'Probably.'

Picking up the paper from her doorstep the next morning, Hazel's not surprised to see the headline reads '*TRADER FOUND MURDERED*', followed by the story of Beauchamp's unfortunate demise, but no new information beyond what Dibble had told her.

Below the main story is another in large type: '*DEATH AND DEFIANCE DOCKSIDE*'. She takes the paper inside and settles down to the task of reading the full story.

> In parliament this week, there were calls for the government to do something drastic to curb Sydney's unfettered crime spree, which largely covers three locations: Darlinghurst, Kings Cross and the port wharves. A member of the Opposition described the docks as a 'fortress for rabid communists and dangerous criminal gangs where the law of the jungle rules'.

Despite the level of crime, violence and pillaging, not a single arrest has been made on the docks this year. And it's common knowledge that the police can often be found drinking with the criminal fraternity in a pub known to locals as the 'bloodhouse'.

And what does Commissioner Allan have to say about this state of affairs? Very little, it seems. Apart from involving Special Branch in the latest debacle, the Commissioner seems unfazed by an unprecedented level of crime that is keeping Sydneysiders awake at night.

When Hazel arrives at Trades Hall, Yvonne is arguing with someone on the phone and ignores her. Teddy and the other two fellows are frantically sifting through piles of paperwork in preparation for a government meeting. But Rex has his feet up on his desk, reading the newspaper.

'Morning, Hazel.' He drops his feet to the floor and takes his cup of tea. 'See the front page? Beauchamp murdered in his own home, poor bloke. No coincidence that the next story is about the rabid commies on the docks – implying it's one of us.'

'I'm not sure how they define "rabid",' she says. 'Seems an odd choice of word.'

Rex laughs. 'Frothing at the mouth, that's me. They're not wrong about the crime down here, but we're all being tarred with the same brush. The pillaging and the murders have nothing to do with each other. Any opportunity to pin something on the unions.'

'I don't understand why they're so biased,' says Hazel.

'Corruption at the top end of town, basically. Workers' rights threaten wealth and power – same old story throughout history.'

Rex gets to his feet and begins to gather files, stuffing them in his briefcase. He pushes a magazine across the desk towards Hazel. 'Look at this. We're about to face the biggest challenge in our history. Currently, when a good size cargo ship is in port, there are weeks of work for hundreds of men, humping loose cargo and sacks – grain, fertiliser. You've seen it. But before long, that could be a thing of the past.'

Hazel picks up the magazine. There's an article and several photographs of ships loaded with boxes the size of large rooms, all stacked high on the decks.

'Containerisation, they call it,' continues Rex. 'It's coming and it'll decimate our work force.' He picks up loose papers, stares at them and puts them down. He closes his briefcase. 'Off to change the world,' he says with a grin, and strides out the door.

In Rex's wake, the office empties quickly, everyone following him. As Hazel collects the cups and saucers, it occurs to her that she doesn't really understand what each person's role is here. Every day there's paperwork, phone calls and the constant organising of meetings in what seems to be a chaotic flurry. In the garment industry every role is specific, and in her former job, Hazel understood exactly who did what. But what she misses most is working in a community of women. While she is grateful for the job, being a union tea lady is lonely.

20
IRENE TAKES A JOB

Irene arrives at the Thatched Pig to see the old soak from a boarding house where she used to live, hunched over his drink at the bar.

'You're back.' Irene leans on the bar beside him. 'Thought you'd gone for good.'

Arthur Smith gives her a stony look. 'Am I not permitted to avail myself of a warming beverage? Or did you back an outsider and purchase this pub, Mrs Turnbuckle?'

Irene nods at the barmaid for her usual and turns back to Arthur. 'Not yet I didn't. Could still happen. Thought yer'd gone bush permni . . . permmin . . .'

'Is "permanently" the adverb you're attempting to conquer?' he asks.

'Thought yers was up there in the Blue Mountains forever.'

'Forever is an illusionary concept, Mrs Turnbuckle.' He turns back to his drink.

Irene slips her coins across the bar and takes a sip of her shandy. 'Good to hear yer still talkin' in bloody riddles, mate. Some things never change.'

'Suffice to say that the current temperature in the mountains is below zero, and a caravan is not the ideal abode. I am temporarily residing back in the boarding house we both previously inhabited.'

'Long as yer can yer pay rent, s'pose yers can live anywhere yer want.' Irene gives him a good look-over. 'Yer seem a bit healthier. Off the turps, then?'

'I have embraced the joys of nature rambles and dabbled in a little birdwatching. There's nothing so bracing as the cry of the kookaburras at dawn.'

'Never mind the kookaburras, they'd have some nasty snakes up there.'

'All God's creatures. I live at one with nature these days.'

'Lordy,' says Irene. 'Turned into a God botherer, have we?'

'I can't speak for you, but I do consult a higher being on occasion. I try not to make a nuisance of myself. Unlike your good self.'

'Mate, I'm a Catholic,' says Irene.

He gives an annoyed huff. 'Much as I enjoy an existential debate, this conversation has got away from me. Will that be all, Mrs Turnbuckle?'

'Thought yers might like some company?'

'Thank you but no,' he says, turning away.

Irene shrugs and heads over to talk to Big G, sitting alone at his corner table. 'Any luck with me telly?' she asks.

'Doing the rounds, are you, Mrs Turnbuckle?' asks Big G. 'Who's your mate at the bar? Was he a copper way back when?'

'Nah, legal eagle. Judge. Down on his luck.'

'Ah, thought he looked familiar,' says Big G.

Irene's keen to get back to the subject of the telly, then remembers the other thing bothering her. She gestures towards an empty chair at his table. He gives a slight nod, and she sits down. 'Yer know anything about Malteses?'

Big G frowns. 'Not really. Prefer a barley sugar meself.'

'What? Darlinghurst . . . you know, them brothels in Woods Lane.'

'What's it to you?' asks Big G suspiciously.

'I'm not asking if yer visit 'em. Do yer know them old Mafia men?'

'Joe Borg's blokes, you mean?'

'Yeah, him. I think this bloke's tryna put Miss Palmer out of business.'

Big G shrugs. 'Expanding her operation in his patch. What do you expect?'

Irene sighs. 'Dunno what to expect any more. What about me telly, then?'

'Yeah, I gotta little telly. Cost you a ton.'

'A hundred! Where am I gonna get that kind of money?'

'Keep your voice down, will you?' Big G glances around the bar. 'That's a bloody bargain. So, you want it or not?'

'I had fifty last week . . .' she says, thinking aloud, then remembers she put that on 'Lucky Day' twenty to one in the three o'clock at Randwick and lost the lot. 'I'll have to save up for it, unless yers can gimme a discount. Help a little old lady out.'

Big G lights a cigarette, takes a drag and stares into the distance. Irene hopes he's thinking about her discount, but eventually he says, 'You could do a little job for me if you want. Worth a hundred.'

'Is it going to get me shot?' asks Irene, being practical.

'No, it'll get you arrested.'

'How am I gonna watch me telly if I'm in the clink?' asks Irene, wondering just how smart this bloke really is.

'It'll only take an hour or so and you'll be out on bail.'

'Who's paying me bail?'

'I'll pay it,' he says. 'You don't have to worry about that.'

'Then what? Do I have to go to court?'

'Yeah, you'll get a $200 fine and I'll sort that out.'

'Coppers are not gonna belt me around with the Yellow Pages, are they?'

'Course not, it's a minor infraction. You don't have any priors, do you?'

'No convictions. Lack of evidence,' she says with a wink.

'Okay then. It's up to you. It's just the bloke s'posed to do the job has the measles.'

Irene thinks about that little telly and how nice it would be to watch it in bed on a cold night. She'd have to keep the singing down, but it'd be worth a couple of hours down the cop shop. She gives Big G the nod.

'All right,' he says. 'Here's how it works.'

21

IRENE FOILS A PLOT

On Friday it's raining, and Merl and Betty decide to meet at the Delphi Milk Bar at lunchtime. Irene agrees to go along. She doesn't mind the place; it's a bit comfier than sitting on the wall in the laneway. Mrs Angelos lets them eat their own sandwiches, and Merl always buys them a pot of tea.

Irene slides into the booth beside Betty. Normally she'd sit opposite because Betty's rear end can be a problem. But today Merl's going flat stick with her knitting, and it wouldn't be the first time someone got jabbed.

They're having a friendly chat, all going well, then bloody Betty starts on about the Tea Ladies Guild fundraiser again. She loves banging on about those little no-hopers. Irene's not interested, and Merl couldn't care less about them either, not really. That one's in it for the glory.

'Can't we wait for the meeting to discuss this?' asks Merl, peering over her glasses.

'I thought we could come up with some ideas before the next meeting,' says Betty.

'Give up now. Merl doesn't want to hear anyone's ideas,' advises Irene.

Merl puffs herself up like an old rooster. 'I beg your pardon, Irene. I take strong exception to these accusations. I'm doing my best—'

'To run the bloody show,' interrupts Irene. 'Not to raise money for the little no-hopers. Yer like a bloody politician, Merl Perlman. All yer want to do is get up the top of the tree and throw pineapples down for yer mates to feed on.'

Merl makes a scoffing sound. 'I have no idea what you're talking about. And I will remind you this is a tea ladies guild, not the city council.'

'What do you mean, pineapples?' asks Betty.

'Not real pineapples, yer dope. It's a . . . yer know . . . it's a . . .'

'A metaphor?' asks Merl coldly.

'Oh, I see,' Betty says. 'Well, maybe now is not the time to discuss it, since it's obviously a sore point.'

They eat their sandwiches in silence for a few minutes, then Irene can't resist boasting, 'I'm getting me own telly.'

'Planning a break-in at Gibson's, are you?' asks Merl, raising an eyebrow.

'Merl, that's a bit harsh.' Betty turns to Irene. 'You're not, are you?'

'D'yer think I'd tell yers if I was?' says Irene.

'Probably not,' agrees Betty.

Irene gets out a cigar and gives it a sniff. She's got a taste for these expensive Cuban cigars now. They're kept in a fancy wooden box on the bar at 555 and she's been helping herself, replacing them with cheapos. The punters won't know the difference.

'I've got a record player on lay-by at Gibson's,' says Betty. 'I'll have it paid off next month. Don't tell Hazel, I'm planning to surprise her.'

'A record player, eh?' says Irene. It crosses her mind that if this job for Big G works out, she could do another one and get a record player as well. 'What sort of records are yer thinking of getting?'

'Well, my bohemian friends—'

'Your what?' asks Merl, looking up from her knitting.

Betty goes pink and ignores her. 'My bohemian friends listen to Bob Dylan and—'

'That long-haired layabout,' scoffs Merl.

'Pull yer head in, will yer, Merl? Let the woman finish,' says Irene.

'I haven't decided what to buy yet. Something Hazel would like.'

'What about some jazz?' asks Irene, lighting her cigar.

'I think Hazel prefers classical. Mozart or Vivaldi,' says Betty.

'Let me know when you've got it,' says Irene. 'I'll come around and have a squiz and yers can come and look at me telly.'

Betty purses her lips. 'Thank you, Irene, but I have no desire to set foot in a brothel.'

Irene grins and takes a puff of her cigar. 'Yer don't know what yer missing.'

On Saturday morning, while Irene's cleaning, Miss Palmer turns up again, smartly dressed in a pink suit with a skirt so tight she'd have no hope of running for the bus in it. 'I'm leaving now. I'll be gone ten days,' she says. 'Can you clean Chapel Lane again today and next week as well?'

Irene considers this offer. 'Yer man gonna drive me?'

'I suppose so.' Miss Palmer gets an envelope out of her handbag. 'This is the money for last week and today.'

Irene takes it from her. 'So, what about them Malteses?'

'I have no idea what you're talking about, Mrs Turnbuckle.'

'I told yers, they're up to something, watching the place.'

Miss Palmer makes an annoyed tut. 'Please just stick to cleaning and leave business matters to me. There's really nothing to worry about. I've got a flight to catch.'

Irene wants to argue the point, but the other party walks off. Miss Palmer thinks her protection money is enough, but it's not going to stop a Molotov cocktail in the dead of night.

Upstairs in her room, Irene counts the money, holding each note up to the light to inspect it thoroughly. There'll be dodgy money come through here. It all seems fine, so she tucks it away in her savings sock under the mattress. While she's on her knees, she pulls a metal box out from under the bed. Opening it up, she looks through the contents: a small pinch-bar, knuckle-dusters, lock-picking tools, various screwdrivers. Nothing that might help in this situation.

At the usual time, she goes downstairs and waits out the front of the house, glancing up and down for anyone who might be watching the place. The Neck pulls up in an old Holden. He leans over and throws the front passenger door open for her.

Irene reluctantly gets in. 'Where's me Rolls?'

They're halfway down the street before he answers. 'Less conspicuous.'

'Yeah, well, used to a certain standard now, aren't I?'

He gives a snort but says nothing.

'Yer worried about them Malteses?' she asks. 'Cos I am.'

He also tells her not to worry but then, when he drops her at the end of Chapel Lane, she's barely stepped out before he takes off with a squeal of tyres.

She unlocks the front door, gets inside and slams those bolts shut, then throws her bag on a chair and heads straight upstairs to see if Dimples is here. Ideally in the nuddy. But the crafty Yank is one step ahead of her, fully dressed in his uniform and quietly letting himself out of the bedroom. He and Irene stare at each other for a moment.

'Fancy a drink?' asks Irene, the quicker thinker.

'Sure . . .' he says, as if he's trying to work out if he has a choice.

He follows her downstairs and she opens the drinks cabinet with a pick. 'Whiskey?'

'Bourbon for me,' he says.

Irene pours them both a generous tipple and hands him one. She doesn't bother asking his name since it's on his uniform: Watts.

'I'm Mrs Turnbuckle,' she says. 'I normally work over at 555 but I'm on special detail here for the next couple of weeks. So, what's the story?'

He sits down on the edge of a chair and sips his drink. 'I don't understand,' he says eventually.

Before Irene can explain, the blonde comes wandering down the stairs, dressed in short frilly bits and pieces with a long see-through thing over the top, nipples the size of wing-nuts poking through it all. She looks at Irene with surprise. 'Hello. Who are you?'

'Mrs Turnbuckle. And yerself?'

'I'm Bunny.' She offers a tiny paw, and Irene shakes it.

'What are you doing here?' asks Bunny.

'Miss Palmer sent me to clean the place. I'm normally at 555. I'll be back next week.'

Bunny glances over at Dimples, who had leapt to his feet when she arrived.

'We'd so appreciate it if you didn't mention this situation to Miss Palmer—'

Irene raises an eyebrow. 'Yer moonlightin'?'

Bunny gives Dimples a soppy look. 'We're engaged.'

'We're waiting for permission to marry,' explains Dimples. 'Army paperwork.'

'Very nice,' says Irene. 'Congratulations.'

'Thank you so much,' says Bunny. She goes to Dimples and lifts her face to his, like a little bird after a worm. They kiss (for way too long, in Irene's opinion), then Bunny announces she's going to take a bath and drifts back upstairs.

'Well, I better go,' says Dimples. 'I'll see you next week. Thanks for keeping our little secret, Mrs Turnbuckle.'

Irene smiles, enjoying having him to herself now Bunny's hopped off. She watches him place his empty glass on the hall table. What a magnificent fellow he is.

'I'll let you out,' she says, getting a grip on herself.

She walks over to the front door and slides each bolt out slowly, then opens it and has a good look outside. In that moment, a man dashes out of the laneway opposite and a split second later, something flies towards her. She puts her hands up to protect herself and somehow manages to catch the missile mid-air. To her horror, it's a bottle with a burning rag stuffed in the neck. She hurls the thing outside with all her might. It spins across the narrow street, smashes on a neighbour's wall and explodes in flames.

Dimples stands with his cap in hand, looking stunned. 'Ah . . . what just happened?'

'Bloody brazen,' says Irene, shaken. 'I was too quick for 'em.'

She steps outside and has another look around. Even with the explosion there's not a soul in sight. She beckons him to come out. 'Just watch yerself around here, soldier. There's a bloody war on. Dangerous Malteses everywhere. And I'm not talking chocolate, by the way.'

'Thank you, ma'am, much appreciated,' he says. Tipping his hat, he gives her a thousand-watt smile that cranks up parts of her body she'd almost forgotten existed.

She closes the door with a sigh, puts some calming music on the record player. Pouring herself a stiff drink, she finds herself chuckling – it's not everyone can catch a bloody Molotov cocktail in flight. If it had hit something solid . . . doesn't bear thinking about. She knocks back her drink and heads for the cleaning cupboard.

22
STRUGGLES IN THE GUILD

Hazel is delighted to see at least fifteen tea ladies clustered at tables in the Hollywood Hotel this evening. It's the Tea Ladies Guild that has brought these women together in friendship. It's just a shame more don't make it upstairs to the meeting.

Turning her attention back to Merl, Betty and Irene, she remarks, 'I think we need to make more effort to get all the ladies upstairs for the meeting and get this fundraiser moving.'

Merl huffs. 'If they can't be bothered walking up a few stairs . . .'

'Well, it is very cosy and convivial down here,' says Hazel. 'I'm going to have a friendly chat with them.' She gets the key to the upstairs rooms out of her bag and hands it to Betty. 'Would you mind popping up and getting the heaters going, Betty dear?'

'Of course. I'll get the kettle on and the cups out,' says Betty.

Merl decides to follow Betty while Irene and Hazel go into the main bar.

Irene makes a beeline for Violet and the ladies from the Defence Department. She stands over the unsuspecting group. 'Yers should be ashamed of yerselves, grogging while the little no-hopers have no bloody beds to sleep in.'

'What are you talking about?' asks Violet, annoyed.

Hazel decides it's too late to intervene there and quickly approaches another table before Irene can get to them. 'Evening, ladies. I hope we'll have the pleasure of your company at the Guild meeting upstairs this evening? The heaters are going and the kettle's on the boil.'

The three ladies nod and smile, but Hazel has the feeling they're happy where they are. Nothing more she can say. She looks around for other likely candidates and sees Effie Finch come striding in, wearing an army greatcoat. She gives Hazel a brisk salute and goes to the bar to order her usual pint of beer.

Joining her, Hazel explains the problem.

Effie gives a grunt of amusement. 'They've discovered the bar and forgotten the reason for meeting here.'

Turning to face the room, Effie puts her fingers in her mouth and delivers a shrill whistle that has people flinching and clutching their ears. 'Meeting commences at nineteen hundred hours. All tea ladies to report upstairs immediately,' she bellows.

Entire tables of women rise obediently from their seats and gather their things.

'Thank you, Effie. I'll see you up there,' says Hazel.

Upstairs, everyone gets settled and Hazel thanks them for coming. Violet calls out, 'Did we have a choice?' which causes a ripple of good-natured laughter.

Betty reads the minutes, which barely change month to month, and then Hazel stands to address the Guild members.

'Here we are, the most capable women you'll ever meet,' she begins. 'We have so many contacts and friends. The orphanage fundraiser should be a breeze for us, but for some reason we can't seem to get it off the ground. It's now only a couple of months until the orphanage opens, and we're less than halfway with the funds needed for the children's beds.'

There are murmurs of agreement, and the group falls silent like a scolded class.

Hazel continues. 'Now, last night, Betty and I came up with an idea. I'd like to explain it to you, get your thoughts and put it to a vote.'

'Do I know about this idea?' asks Merl, looking annoyed.

Expecting this hiccup, Hazel assures her, 'It's just the seed of an idea, Merl. We will need your help to make it work.'

Everyone waits in anticipation, and she continues. 'Imagine an auction where there are all sorts of items to bid on. It could be a service – for example, cleaning or baking. It could be actual items. I'm sure we all have pieces in our china cabinets – a silver teapot or a nice ornament – that we'd be prepared to part with for a good cause.' Hazel glances at Violet, who has enough ornaments in her house to open a shop. 'If you don't have something yourself, you could ask a business owner to make a donation. A butcher could donate some meat, for instance. We'd auction items of any value, from a dollar or two upwards. Lots of contributions for all sorts of buyers.'

'And where would this proposed auction take place?' asks Merl.

'I'm sure St Vincent's would let us have the church hall, since it's for their benefit.' Hazel looks around the room. 'We're hoping each of you can commit to delivering at least one item for the auction. Can we have a show of hands? Who can make that commitment for the Guild?'

There's a buzz of discussion. One by one, every hand is raised in the air.

'Shall we take that to a vote?' Hazel asks.

Everyone agrees, including a clearly reluctant Merl, and the motion is passed.

'Can you each give your name and phone number, and some idea of what you might be able to contribute, to Mrs Dewsnap, please? If you don't know, just write TBA.'

'That's "to be advised",' adds Betty, getting out her clipboard and pen.

As Betty collects names, the room is full of chatter. Merl sits in stony silence.

'Merl dear, I hope you're on board with this,' says Hazel. 'It seems to have met with enthusiasm.'

'It's been taken out of my hands,' says Merl. 'I thought I could make a contribution here, but obviously not. I've been deliberately kept out of the discussions and sidelined—'

'That was never the intention,' interrupts Hazel, also knowing that, given the opportunity, Merl would have poured cold water on the idea.

'Well, it's clear you don't need my help,' says Merl. 'I hereby tender my resignation from the Guild. Effective immediately.'

'Oh Merl, please don't do that,' says Hazel.

But Merl picks up her bag and walks out the door, head held high.

Watching her leave, Hazel realises this was probably unavoidable, but hopefully she'll come around. In the meantime, they will have to make do without the Chief Fundraising Coordinator.

23

HAZEL MAKES A SHOCKING DISCOVERY

As she enters the busy foyer of Trades Hall, Hazel has a wistful moment, wishing she was back at Empire Fashionwear in the soft world of colourful dresses, frothy chiffons, slick satins, beads and lace, diamantes and sequins. All so vivid and glamorous in contrast to the dreary functionality and dark doings of this place. But she pushes those thoughts aside and heads upstairs.

When she delivers Rex's tea, he's in a chatty mood as usual. Picking up his cup, he leans back in his chair. 'How are you liking union life, Hazel?'

Feeling a pang of guilt, Hazel scrambles for a diplomatic answer. 'The people seem nice enough, although I haven't got to know them very well as yet.'

'Bit different from the fashion business,' he says, with a chuckle.

'It's not just that. I was at Empire for ten years, so I knew everyone.' Hazel pauses. 'I still find it surprising to see workers stealing cargo with little or no attempt to hide it.'

Rex nods. 'Unfortunately there's an entrenched idea down here that employers are fair game. The workers see it as a way to redress the imbalance. It probably happens in the garment industry, it's just better concealed.' He stops. 'It sounds like I'm making excuses for stealing, but we have to look at the root cause to solve it. I'm hoping when conditions improve, so will the pilfering. We need to clean up the reputation of the wharves.'

'And something like the Krugerrand robbery isn't helping . . .'

'Exactly. A robbery of that magnitude is worldwide news and not helpful to our reputation as a port.' He smiles. 'Every time you bring me a cup of tea, you get a lecture.'

Hazel laughs. 'I'm interested, so it's a fair exchange. Another cup while I'm here?'

'That would be lovely,' he says, holding out his cup for a refill. 'Now, next Wednesday, you better stay up here at Trades Hall. There'll be a Painters and Dockers meeting down at the docks. Has been known to get ugly. So best play it safe.'

'They have quite a reputation, could they be involved in Cooper's murder, or even Mr Beauchamp's murder?'

Rex shakes his head. 'I don't know about the Beauchamp case, and just forget Cooper, Hazel. And the photo you were flashing around of the lad? I hope you've got rid of that. The place is a tinderbox right now with the gold robbery – police crawling all over the joint and not a single clue. How is that possible? That much gold can't just vanish into thin air. Anyway, it's putting everyone on edge. So keep yourself to yourself.'

Hazel agrees but the conversation leaves her more despondent than when she arrived this morning. Cleaning up the kitchen at the end of the day, she wonders if she has an alternative. Perhaps when the roof repairs are paid for, she'll look for another position. She just needs to be stoic for the moment until that project is out of the way. She feels another pang at the idea of abandoning Rex, but he will find someone else. There are plenty of tea ladies looking for work.

As she puts the cups away, she notices something on the highest shelf of the tall cupboards. She doesn't recall seeing anything there before. She drags a chair over to stand on and reaches up to grab the item. Pulling it out, she steps down and puts it on the table.

It's a black hold-all, the sort of thing that workers bring their thermos and sandwiches in. Inside is a rolled-up towel. Concealed within is a handgun.

Hazel glances towards the door. She's almost sure this bag wasn't here last week. The fact that she noticed it today could mean it was shoved up there hurriedly. Had it been pushed further back on the shelf, she would never have seen it. After a moment's consideration, she returns the bag to exactly where she found it, then stands in the middle of the kitchen, paralysed with indecision. She decides it's better not to involve Rex, just in case it implicates him in some way. There's a phone in the hallway outside the kitchen where she won't be overheard, and she goes immediately to report the finding to Detective Dibble.

24

BETTY HAS AN EXISTENTIAL CRISIS

It's late and Betty knows she should go home, but she can't bring herself to leave the crackling fire and venture out into the cold night. She's at Rosemont Street often now, always warmly welcomed and treated like one of the household. She sometimes cooks for everyone (they're all pretty hopeless) and also fills the tins with baking. No one has asked her to do it – she offered – and now there's an expectation. She doesn't mind. She's become the house mum and has even wondered what it would be like to live here. But she couldn't do that to Hazel.

This evening she's cosy in an armchair close to the fire, while others sprawl on the sofa and big cushions on the floor – deep in discussion as always. The coffee table, an old dining table with the legs sawn off, is covered in the remains of dinner, empty red wine flagons, candles melted down to stubs and overflowing ashtrays.

They love to talk in this house, long and often argumentative conversations covering topics Betty has never thought about before. Young people are so political and serious minded these days, able to discuss high-flown subjects quite naturally. Most of

Lucy's friends are at university or art school and all have a lot of opinions. Betty doesn't dare to open her mouth for fear of revealing her ignorance. She struggled with the books Lucy lent her (very heavy going) and is still looking up terms she's never heard of in the dictionary.

Lucy, the handsome boy and a loud woman called Amelia all live here permanently, but others come and go, bunking down on the sofa, or even on the floor. This evening there are a few people Betty hasn't met before. Not one of the young men has a short back and sides (one has a long thin ponytail). Everyone seems to wear jeans and duffel coats or old army jackets, apart from Lucy, who prefers long flowing cheesecloth frocks.

Betty rouses herself and tries to focus on what Lucy is saying.

'What about something more neutral? Like the Movement for Future Independence?'

'MFI isn't exactly catchy,' says a bearded fellow, shaking the dregs of a wine flagon into his glass. 'Anyway, an acronym is better than initialisation.'

'It doesn't really mean anything,' says Amelia.

'How about Australians for Free Thought?' suggests another fellow. 'AFT?'

'Too nationalistic and nautical,' says Lucy dismissively. 'It sounds like one of those McCarthy-era committees that are the opposite of free thought.'

'We should push the feminist cause and be obvious about it,' says Amelia. 'We should stick with Women Opposing War. That appeals to all women. That's who we are.'

Lucy nods. 'I agree. And you can't beat WOW for an acronym.'

'It doesn't really cover our other equality campaigns, but the war is our main focus,' continues Amelia.

'How about Women Against the World?' suggests a woman with long tangled hair who sits cross-legged on the floor.

'Where do these leave us blokes?' asks the bearded fellow. 'Tagging along?'

'Why not?' asks Lucy. 'We've been tagging along for thousands of years. It speaks well of any man who supports a women's cause.'

'Just seems weak to me,' grumbles the beard.

Amelia leans forward to focus her gaze on him. 'Men thinking that compromise is an indication of weakness is why we're in this war. More women are against this war than men. Their sons are being conscripted. Not what they had in mind for their little lad.'

Another man with a head of greasy curls adds in a slurred voice, 'Little lads who can't wait to exterminate other little lads.'

Amelia sighs. 'Can we ever stop men fighting?'

'The patriarchal structure is built on one-upmanship – it would collapse without it,' says Lucy. 'It's the only thing that keeps it going.'

Confusing as these conversations are, it seems to Betty that these youngsters understand the world much better than her generation ever did. They talk about foreign powers and government cover-ups. The fact that they are so strongly opposed to the war in Vietnam came as some surprise to her. According to the papers, there are hordes of communists determined to advance on Australia, and it is vital to turn back the tide. But apparently that's a load of twaddle; it's all to do with governments conspiring together.

When the term 'feminism' was first bandied about in women's magazines, Betty hadn't taken much notice, imagining it was something to do with being feminine – which she was all for. There's nothing nicer than putting on something pretty and a bit of make-up. But she's now gleaned that it's something quite different. Feminists believe men and women are equal and should be treated equally. It's a nice idea but, in practice, clearly not the case. As they say, it's a man's world. And men are not about to give that up in a hurry.

Evidently these patriarchy people are the enemy. Betty spent some time in the library reading up on it all so she doesn't seem like a complete dill saying the wrong thing. But she can hardly keep up with the growing list in her notebook: women's liberation, female oppression, male supremacists (often referred to as male chauvinist pigs), white supremacists, and on it goes. It's a lot to take in.

While her thoughts drift, the conversation changes tack and now she's suddenly the centre of attention.

'The term "tea lady" reeks of oppression,' observes Amelia. 'Genteel domesticity.'

'She doesn't know any different,' says the Beard, shaking his head.

Betty senses now is the time to speak up. 'I wasn't always a tea lady, you know.' Everyone looks interested so she continues more confidently. 'I worked on the switchboard at the General Post Office for many years.'

'Women servicing men. Connecting "important" men to other "important" men,' says Amelia, in world-weary tone.

Betty frowns. She's not that keen on Amelia and unhappy at being turned into a victim, when it was a difficult and important job. 'We connected all sorts of calls, not just men's,' she explains. 'We were invaluable. Especially during the war. Everything came through the switchboard.'

Staring into his glass and nodding thoughtfully, the Beard looks up at her. 'Did you ever get asked to do, you know . . . *dirty* things when you worked on the switchboard?'

For a moment Betty thinks he's referring to mopping up, then she realises and turns scarlet with embarrassment. Fortunately, in the low light, no one can tell how mortified she is by this question. It was a daily occurrence, but she did nothing wrong. She pulled the plug on every single one of those men. Everyone waits breathlessly, but she's not about to reveal any titillating tales of her switchboard days.

'Sometimes,' she admits. 'One man asked if I could come around to his house and do a week's worth of dishes before his wife came home from her mother's.'

The room explodes with laughter.

'You're kidding, aren't you?' says Lucy.

Betty assures her it's quite true and is relieved when the topic abruptly shifts away from oppression to something that doesn't involve her.

She must have dozed off, because she's woken by the shrill twang of an electric guitar and Jimi Hendrix (a big favourite around here) playing full blast. The lights are off, but Betty can see by the light of the fire that everyone is now half-naked and dancing crazily.

She hardly knows where to look. Lucy has a boyish figure and a modest bosom, so it's not quite so . . . *rude*. But Amelia, with her full bosoms swinging free, arms flung in the air and hair flying, is quite a spectacle. It crosses Betty's mind how utterly shocked her own friends would be to see her now. She's shocked herself, but feels strangely worldly at the same time.

The Beard moves his muscled torso and hips from side to side as he moves closer to Lucy. Then they're dancing together, hips writhing against each other in time to the music as they gaze at each other in a sort of trance.

Betty decides it's time to go.

She struggles out of the armchair, still half asleep, head swimming with too much wine. On her feet, she edges out of the room. Her coat is hanging in the hallway. After a terrible struggle, she manages to get it on and find her handbag. She opens the front door and steps outside. Closing the door, she hears shrieks of laughter and peeks back inside to see the Beard chasing Lucy up the stairs.

Betty shuts the door quickly and stands for a moment to recover, the night air like an icy veil sobering her up. She walks down the street (keeping an eye out for muggers), thinking how helpful it would be to discuss this evening's antics with a friend and make sense of it all. But even broad-minded Hazel would raise an eyebrow at the extraordinary doings of this household. Irene wouldn't care less but would make some off-colour joke about it. Betty will just have to keep it to herself.

At breakfast, Betty's head throbs with pain. The whistling kettle sounds like a fire alarm. Hazel spreading jam on her toast sounds like a yard broom scraping on concrete. She dreads Hazel biting into the piece of toast.

Hazel pauses, the toast mid-air. 'What is it, Betty dear? There's a terrible look of dread on your face.'

'Just a bit of a headache,' says Betty, feeling sorry for herself. 'It's as if my head is trapped in a vice and being squeezed very tight.'

'It's not like you to have a hangover, let alone one every few days,' says Hazel, putting her toast down. 'At least it's Saturday. You can get some rest.'

'I suppose I'll get used to red wine.' Betty takes a sip of tea, but it tastes sour.

'Are you in training for something?' asks Hazel, with a half smile.

'Not exactly . . . I just wish I'd drunk more when I was young.'

'So, it's more making up for lost time?' Hazel takes a bite of her toast (not quite as bad as Betty imagined).

Betty leans her heavy head on one hand. 'That time is gone forever. Our youth flew away while we were chained to the switchboard by the patriarchy people.'

Hazel doesn't seem surprised by this revelation, and Betty wonders if she already knew about this business.

'Perhaps this is a bigger conversation for a time when you're feeling a bit more yourself,' suggests Hazel, topping up the teapot with boiling water.

'Probably,' agrees Betty, gloomy at the thought of this entire day being sacrificed to feeling dreadful and disillusioned with the world.

'I assume you'd prefer I didn't vacuum this morning?' asks Hazel.

Betty nods glumly. 'I'll have a lie-down and hopefully be better after that.'

She leaves Hazel reading the morning papers and tiptoes up the stairs to her room. She sits down tentatively on the bed. Moving makes her head throb. She lowers herself carefully into a lying position. Staring at the ceiling, she thinks about last night. Not for the first time, she asks herself why they invite her. Betty loves becoming a younger, more interesting, version of herself – but what do they see in her?

She wonders if she's part of some sort of social experiment. The word 'proletariat' is often tossed around in discussions, and she learned this is a communist term for the 'working classes'. She only recently discovered she's a member of this class. Is she Lucy's working-class friend? Are they studying her and discussing her like a specimen behind her back? Her head's too fuzzy to think about it.

The fact is that when Betty's there, she forgets all her ailments. She feels young and alive. Everything is exciting, as if she's at the hub of things, instead of watching from a safe distance. But now, as she lies on her bed, all her tedious ailments gather to taunt her. Not only is her head throbbing, but her lumpy varicose veins as well. Her tummy is churned up, and that ache in her right shoulder is back. (Frozen shoulder? She'll look the symptoms up at the library.) They've returned to remind her she's old, and it's too late for her. That time has come and gone, and she didn't even notice it. She wasted it. Now there's nothing to look forward to.

Her throat closes over as tears bubble up inside her. In a moment she's sobbing her heart out, mourning for her youth, so carelessly left behind.

25

HAZEL HEARS BETTY OUT

Reading the papers downstairs, Hazel hears an odd noise coming from the bedroom above. At first it sounds as though Betty's laughing, but then it becomes clear that's not the case. Betty can be prone to tears, and perhaps a little overemotional at times, but Hazel hasn't heard her cry like this in years – not since her husband's funeral.

Hazel goes upstairs and knocks gently on the door. She opens it a crack and peeks inside. Betty lies curled up on her bed in a state of misery.

Without waiting to be invited, Hazel goes in and sits down beside her. 'Betty dear, what on earth is the matter?'

Rolling onto her back, Betty pulls the sheet up to her face and dabs her tears. 'I wish I knew . . . I just feel . . .' She sighs and gives up.

Hazel notices a book on the bedside table called *The Intelligent Woman's Guide to Socialism and Capitalism* by George Bernard Shaw. Normally Betty's reading tastes run to *True Confessions* and *Modern Romance* magazines, so presumably this book came from Lucy. But surely Mr Shaw can't have upset Betty to this degree.

Hazel gets an ironed handkerchief from the dresser and passes it to her. 'What's upset you so much, Betty dear?' she asks. 'How can I help?'

Betty wriggles into a half-seated position. 'I'm just angry with myself because . . . I don't know. Because life has passed me by, and I haven't done anything with it. Nothing worthwhile, anyway. All I ever wanted to do was get married and have children. It never crossed my mind there were other possibilities. But look at me now. I don't have a husband or children, or a career, or anything to look forward to . . .' She blows her nose and gives a wet sniff. 'I feel a terrible sadness and sort of longing to be . . . well, young again. I want to feel free to do whatever I want and not worry so much about people thinking that I'm . . . common, or cheap. I want to get my ears pierced. I want to say words like "breast" instead of "bust" without blushing. I want to swear – just a bit – and burn my bra!'

While Hazel is sympathetic to Betty's struggles, this last comment makes it hard to keep a straight face. 'There's nothing stopping you getting your ears pierced, but brassieres are quite expensive,' says Hazel. 'You wouldn't want to make a habit of burning them.'

'It's the gesture, Hazel.' Betty shakes her head slowly. 'I think it's all too late. We're old now. It's too late for us to be free.'

Hazel struggles to find words of comfort. 'I know what you're saying. People do seem to have very firm ideas of how women should behave—'

'Keeping us in line,' interrupts Betty bitterly.

'Yes, I suppose that's it. There are different rules for men and women, and I can't see that changing anytime soon.' Hazel pauses.

'We all feel nostalgia for our youth sometimes. We all have regrets, large or small – I certainly do. But dwelling on the past can be a little disheartening. Perhaps there's something you could change now and in the future? Our lives are not over yet. It's not too late to enjoy some freedom.'

'I see these young people so full of promise. They talk about waiting for their lives to begin,' says Betty. 'But the next thing you know, it's over, the end is in sight and nothing much happened in between.' She looks at Hazel, tears filling her eyes. 'Where did the time go?' she whispers.

Hazel doesn't have the answer. It's a question she's asked herself in recent years. Sometimes the sight of a little girl skipping on the street will bring back vivid memories of Norma as a child and spark a sense of longing for the past. No one tells you that life will be littered with last times. Like the last time Norma sat on her lap, hung around her neck and pressed her cheek to Hazel's. There were times when Hazel had hurried the girl along because they were going to be late. The destination and urgency are long forgotten, and she'd give anything to feel Norma's hot little cheek pressed against hers one more time. The hours and days roll into years, and it's all swept away so quickly.

Hazel looks at her dear friend in a state of sodden misery and wishes there was something more she could do to help. 'Why don't you have a nap, Betty dear, and we can have a proper discussion about it all later. We could certainly have a ceremonial bra burning this evening,' she adds. 'And you can swear a bit too, if you like. It's a start, at least.'

Betty manages a wan smile. 'Thank you, Hazel. I would like that.'

26

A TERRIBLE INCIDENT

Hazel walks into Trades Hall on Monday morning with some trepidation. Dibble had sent a plain clothes officer an hour or so after she called him on Friday. There were only a couple of people in the office and the fellow came and went without drawing any attention to himself, taking the hold-all with him.

She hasn't heard anything since but is concerned that if Rex finds out, he will want to know why she didn't tell him and how she has connections at Special Branch. She would risk him losing trust in her. Or seeming like she didn't trust him.

Around here, there seems to be more going on under the surface than on top of it. Unseen forces constantly push and pull against each other, and the threat of violence is ever present. Could one of the union staff have got the gun to protect himself? The bookie, for example. It's probably not difficult to get a gun on the docks, where anything is available, both legal and illegal. But why hide it in the kitchen? And she can't quite shake the idea that she was meant to find it. But why?

Yvonne glances up from her typewriter briefly and mutters a

good morning as Hazel passes. The charm of the Monte Carlo has well and truly worn off. Hazel continues through the office, greeting the three men seated at their desks. Only Teddy looks up with a smile and a cheerful good morning.

In the kitchen, Hazel puts on the kettle and stands looking out the window lost in thought. She's so worried about Betty. She's never seen her friend so confused and unstable. Hazel still hasn't met this Lucy and has serious reservations about her, given her influence. Perhaps the next thing is to suggest Betty invite Lucy around to get a better sense of her.

The window looks across a busy street that borders Chinatown. Rex parks his car in the back streets there, so it's no surprise to see him emerge from one of the laneways.

Waiting to cross the street, he checks his watch and glances at the traffic lights with an air of impatience, no doubt late for a meeting. It seems he's notorious for being late. He often gets caught up on the phone coaxing, charming or strongarming someone. Every call seems to end with him telling them that he'll get back to them. He's constantly negotiating with a dozen different factions from the top levels of government and employers, as well as affiliated unions, the arbitration commission and Dockside's executive committee – building a tower of blocks only to have one pulled out and all negotiations collapse.

As he's about to cross the street, Rex is approached by a man wearing a dark grey overcoat, a trilby shadowing his face. There's something in Rex's stance that makes Hazel think this is not a welcome approach. He seems taken aback, annoyed.

She startles at the shrill whistle of the kettle and walks over to switch it off. When she returns to the window, both men have disappeared, and she turns her attention to morning tea.

When she wheels the trolley into the office, Teddy is part-way through dialling a number but puts down the phone and asks Hazel if she had a nice weekend.

'I did, thank you,' she says. 'And you?'

'Yes, but I've got three boys, so I come to the office to rest after the weekend.'

Hazel laughs, handing him his tea – white with one. 'I can imagine. I only have the one daughter but twin grandsons.'

Teddy blows on his tea, settling in for a chat. 'So I hear you were Rex's neighbour growing up. That's how you know each other?'

'That's right. I was twelve when he came along.' Hazel almost mentions what a sweet little lad he was but stops herself just in time. 'He was like a younger brother to me.'

'But you kept in touch?' asks Teddy. 'Over the years?'

Hazel wonders why he's so interested. 'Not especially, but Surry Hills is a small place, we all know people in common. So everyone is kept in touch, whether they like it or not.'

'I'm curious why you'd take a job on the wharves. Not the most hospitable of places for a lady such as yourself,' he says.

'I'm not sure what a lady "such as myself" is exactly,' says Hazel, starting to feel uncomfortable. 'I'd been out of work for a while. Rex offered me a job and I accepted. It's really quite simple.'

'Nothing's ever simple, is it?' he says, turning back to his work. 'Thanks for the tea.'

Hazel has no idea what he's implying but she moves on, taking Yvonne's tea to the outer office. 'Rex hasn't come in yet?' Hazel asks, realising a good ten minutes has elapsed.

Yvonne shakes her head and continues typing.

Rex can't be far away and so Hazel leaves his tea and biscuits on his desk.

Back in the kitchen, she checks out the window but there's no sign of him. He should be here by now. All at once, she's seized by the thought that something is terribly wrong.

Grabbing her coat, she takes the stairs to the ground floor. She glances into some of the other union offices in case he's got caught up, and then goes out onto the street. He's nowhere to be seen. She crosses the road, wondering if the man who approached Rex worked in Trades Hall. In which case they would have crossed over together. Could he have gone back to his car?

Hazel steps into the laneway she saw Rex emerge from. It's dark and damp; she has to watch her step on the slippery cobblestones. Numerous restaurants back onto the lane. It's lined with stacks of crates and bins and populated by stray cats. There's a terrible stench of rotting food in the air.

Almost at the other end of the lane, she spots a dark shape on the ground. Half expecting it to be a rough sleeper, she leans down to take a closer look. It's Rex.

She checks his pulse and is relieved to find there is one. A dark patch of blood seeps from a wound on his temple. Looking around, she pulls open the nearest door and steps into the back of a restaurant where two men in a tiny kitchen turn to stare at her in surprise. She asks them to call an ambulance, but neither speaks English. She walks through to the restaurant, finds a phone and calls triple zero, taking care to explain the location accurately.

She hurries back to Rex's side. Taking off her coat to cover him, she folds up her pinny and uses it to apply pressure to the head wound. She talks to him while they wait, urging him to wake up and reassuring him that help is on the way.

Looking closely, she sees a flickering movement beneath his eyelids. She keeps up her commentary in a calm voice until she hears a siren coming their way. A few minutes later, an ambulance edges into the narrow lane. Two men get out and lift Rex onto a stretcher.

Determined not to leave his side until he's safe, Hazel gets in the ambulance with him. On the way to the hospital, she holds his hand and tells stories about the old days.

'Do you remember when your Jimmy got his head stuck in the railing outside Central Station?' she asks. 'It took the fire brigade an hour to free him. How he got his head in there in the first place I'll never know.'

Hazel barely listens to her own anecdotes. She sees Rex again as a tough little three-year-old, tagging along behind his older brothers. They often played cricket in the street, occasionally smashing a window and getting a thrashing from their father.

At the hospital there are forms to complete – always a struggle for Hazel and especially without all the information. She does know his birthday and where he lives, but not the street number. She asks the nurse if she can use a phone book and looks up Rex's phone number, but it must be unlisted. When the forms are as complete as she can make them, she calls the exchange and asks to be put through to Detective Dibble at Special Branch.

'Mrs Bates,' says a familiar voice. 'Nice to hear from you.'

'Rex Shepperton was attacked this morning. I'm at the hospital with him now.'

After a moment of silence, Dibble asks which hospital, and she tells him.

'I'll be there soon,' says Dibble. 'Stay put.'

He arrives in the waiting room fifteen minutes later.

'He's in Intensive Care,' says Hazel. 'They say he's stable, whatever that means.'

Dibble sits down beside her. 'You'll need to go and make a statement at the local station later on today.'

Hazel tries to assemble all the information in a coherent order. 'I apologise for involving you . . . I know you have important cases on right now. I saw a man approach Rex in the street, but not his face unfortunately. It seemed he was threatening Rex. I think his life is in danger, but I don't know why.'

Dibble looks uncomfortable. 'I'm sorry to have to tell you this, Mrs Bates, but the hold-all has been identified as belonging to Mr Shepperton.' At Hazel's dubious expression, he adds, 'There was a break-in a couple of years ago, and the staff fingerprints are on record. The gun had been wiped clean of prints but is the same calibre as the weapon that killed Mr Beauchamp. There was a search warrant issued on his home yesterday and carried out last night. I understand there's more incriminating evidence but I haven't heard the details.'

'I don't believe it!' Hazel stops herself. She needs to offer a logical argument. 'What possible motivation would Rex have to murder Mr Beauchamp? And why hide the murder weapon in such an obvious place? On top of that, it would not have been difficult to plant the gun in a bag Rex had left around the office. That doesn't make any sense to me.'

'I know what you're saying,' says Dibble. 'But they suspect he was involved with the robbery and Beauchamp got on to him. Shepperton is a clever fellow with an axe to grind. Perhaps he wants to distribute the gold coins to the poor – even things out. That's something he's always banging on about.'

Hazel can't help but smile at the ridiculousness of this theory. 'Rex has his eye on becoming Prime Minister, not Robin Hood. It's obviously a set-up, and not a very clever one at that. I'm surprised they didn't pop one of Rex's business cards in the hold-all, just to make it crystal clear it was his. The gun was left there for me to find, and Rex was left for dead – unable to defend himself and provide an explanation. What does that tell you?'

Dibble nods grudgingly. 'It is all a bit convenient.' He pauses, thinking. 'Look, I trust your assessment of the man, but the fact is that Comrade Shepperton is up to his neck in trouble. He'll be held in custody and under police protection until we know more.'

Hazel is relieved that at least Rex will be under protection. What's worrying her is that, if the police think they have their man, they'll stop looking for the real culprits.

27

PIXIE GETS CAUGHT OUT

Pixie closes all the blinds in the stockroom before turning the light on. She's been in the Empire building after dark many times, but tonight she feels like a thief. Yesterday she signed the lease on the Vine Street shop. She'd tried to talk to her mother several times about the situation but had been talked over and brushed off. So she's moving on with her plans. It's probably better that her parents don't know what she's doing until it's all in place.

Tonight Pixie's taking dozens of sketches, designs and fabric samples she and Alice have put together. She packed everything into three boxes over the past few days but wants to take them out after hours in case Dottie makes a scene in front of the staff.

She carries the first two boxes out to her car, which she's parked in the back laneway – a bit dark and scary at night. She puts them in the boot and closes it just in case. As she walks back into the building, she has the uncomfortable feeling of being watched, but it's probably just her guilty conscience playing tricks.

She picks up the last box and looks around the stockroom, remembering so many happy hours spent working here alongside

Alice and Gloria, Hazel in and out, fuelling them with tea and treating them to 'upstairs' biscuits. It seems to Pixie that life can change quickly, and it's only later you realise how precious that time was. With a last look around, she switches off the light and locks the door behind her.

Out in the laneway she finds two uniformed policemen waiting for her.

'Evening, young lady. Can I ask what you're doing here at this time of night?' asks the taller one in a friendly tone.

Pixie gives a nervous laugh. 'I'm Pixie Karp. This is my family's company.'

'Some identification on you?' he asks.

'Well, no . . . but I have a key. I didn't break in. You can speak to my . . .' Pixie suddenly realises the police calling her parents is the last thing she wants.

The second officer's tone is less friendly. 'Do you have authority to remove company property after hours?'

After a moment of confusion, Pixie realises that the police being here is no accident. Dottie must have found out what she's up to. Did someone at Empire tip her off?

'This is my material,' says Pixie, hearing the uncertainty in her own voice.

'We'll get you to come to the station,' he says. 'We can sort it out down there.'

To her dismay, the unfriendly officer decides to accompany her, and they drive down to the police station in Pixie's car. She sits in the waiting area while the officer calls her home number. The telephone is on Dottie's bedside table. No answer. Pixie is on her own.

'Unless you can find someone to confirm your identity, we're going to have to hold you in a cell overnight,' says the tall officer.

This has gone so wrong so quickly, Pixie can hardly think straight. She tries to think of who would be willing to come out on a cold night to do this for her. Apart from Alice, only one person comes to mind.

Hazel arrives fifteen minutes later, a little out of breath. Her flannelette pyjamas can be seen peeking out from beneath her coat. 'Pixie dear, you're the last person I expected to have to bail out.'

'No charges have been laid,' says the officer. 'We need someone to confirm this young lady's identity.'

Hazel confirms it, but the trouble-making officer reappears and insists Hazel confirm her own identity. Pixie wonders if this is normal or if he's just making things difficult.

'We obviously can't just accept the word of some old lady who wanders in off the street. You could be anyone,' he says. 'What's your relationship to this person?'

Not intimidated in the slightest, Hazel says calmly, 'I'm Mrs Hazel Bates of 5 Glade Street. I worked at Empire Fashionwear for more than a decade, and I've known Miss Karp since she was ten years old. I can't imagine what more you need to know.' She looks suspiciously from one officer to the other. 'What exactly is going on here?'

'That's fine,' says the friendly cop. 'Off you go, ladies.'

As Pixie drives Hazel home, she explains what happened. 'Could Dottie have bribed the cops to come and give me a scare?' asks Pixie. 'Seemed like they were trying to make it difficult for me for no reason.'

'It's possible. That police station is notorious for its crooked cops.'

'It's very difficult to outwit my mother,' says Pixie, pulling up outside Hazel's house.

'I didn't realise this shop business was all going ahead so quickly,' says Hazel.

'Mr Levy helped me with the lease. I signed up yesterday. I've got my suitcase in the back and I'm going to sleep at the shop tonight. Make a clean break.'

'I see. Well, congratulations.' Hazel pauses. 'But without a bed or heating?'

Pixie feels suddenly embarrassed at her lack of organisation. It's not an experience she's looking forward to. But Hazel's not having it anyway. Half an hour later, Pixie's tucked up with a hot water bottle on Hazel's front room sofa and falls asleep in minutes.

28

TEA LADIES GET ON BOARD

Preparing porridge for Pixie's breakfast, Hazel's thoughts are on Rex. She knows him as a man of ideals and principles. It doesn't make any sense for him to get involved with the likes of Beauchamp, let alone a gold robbery. In fact, Pixie's experience last night makes her wonder if the police themselves have framed Rex. They have been under enormous pressure to solve the robbery and murder.

The kitchen door opens. Pixie comes in and sits down at the table. 'Morning.'

'Good morning. Did you sleep well, dear?' asks Hazel. 'There's tea in the pot.'

'Really well apart from a lot of crazy dreams.' Pixie pours herself a cup of tea.

Hazel gets a bowl down from the cupboard and ladles porridge into it. 'This will set you up for the day,' she says. 'There's golden syrup, milk and sugar. Help yourself.'

'Thank you, Hazel. And thank you for taking me in. I would have probably ended up sleeping in my car last night.'

'That's not a safe thing to do around here. Even little kiddies know how to get into cars with nothing more than a bent coathanger.' Hazel serves herself porridge and sits down with Pixie. 'You're very welcome to continue sleeping on the sofa – and I think you should – but if you're determined to go it alone, I have a little mattress upstairs that my grandsons sleep on when they stay. You could take that in the meantime. I'll give you some warm blankets too – you're going to need them. It's my day off today. I can help get you organised.'

Pixie agrees and, after breakfast, Hazel packs several boxes of necessities and Pixie loads them into her car. They squash the mattress into the back seat and drive around the corner to Vine Street.

Parking outside the shop, Pixie says, 'I'm scared, Hazel. Is this a bad idea?'

Hazel gives a chuckle. 'It's not a proper adventure unless you're a bit scared. I'm quite certain that one day you'll look back on this moment with great nostalgia as the start of something big.'

Pixie laughs. 'When I tell my grandchildren how I built my empire?'

'You might not have to wait quite that long,' says Hazel. 'But yes.'

'I did love hearing stories about how Grandad started the company,' says Pixie. 'If only he were still around to advise me what to do. I don't know what he'd think of all this.'

'He had a lot of faith in you, dear. And he was a very canny man.'

They get out of the car. Pixie opens the front door of the shop, and they step into the showroom. Sun streams through the front windows and the empty space is bright with promise. Hazel can see its potential and imagine it full of colourful frocks.

Pixie brings in the three cartons that caused all the trouble. She opens one of them to show Hazel the sketches. Sorting through the box, she falls quiet.

'What is it?' asks Hazel, coming closer to look inside the carton.

Pixie gives a wail. 'No!' She pulls out handfuls of fabric scraps and tangles of discarded thread. Dropping to her knees, she digs deeper into the box with desperation.

'Are these the right boxes?' Hazel asks.

Pixie nods slowly as if she's trying to make sense of what's happened. She opens the other two cartons. 'She's stolen everything,' she says finally. 'All Alice's designs.'

'So Dottie guessed what you were up to and swapped the boxes,' says Hazel.

Pixie closes her eyes. 'I hate her. I hate her so much. She was never going to use them! She just wants me to fail!'

The irony of Pixie being left with scraps does not escape Hazel as she casts around for something comforting to say without sounding trite. 'Or perhaps it's more that she desperately wants to succeed,' she says, finally.

'You don't know her, Hazel. You don't know how spiteful she is. What am I going to do now? We've got nothing! An empty shop. Rent to pay. Three boxes of rubbish.' She looks at Hazel, tears filling her eyes. 'How am I going to tell Alice? All her sketches gone, dozens of them.' Pixie wipes her nose with her sleeve. 'I've made a complete mess of this. I honestly don't know what to do now. Should I beg my parents for help? What do you think?'

'Absolutely not. You would regret that for many years to come, perhaps for the rest of your life,' says Hazel with conviction. 'Let's bring your mattress in and get things set up. I'm sure there's a solution. It just hasn't appeared yet.'

Pixie gives a shuddering sigh and nods grimly. They pull the mattress out of the car and with some effort manage to haul it up the steep stairs to the top floor.

Hazel's pleased to see that these rooms are also pleasant, painted white with decorative high ceilings. The morning sun makes a bright pattern on the timber floors. The rooms are cold and empty, and not at all clean, but anyone could see the potential is there.

'I was going to live in the back room and have a couple of machines and stock in this front room.' Pixie opens the balcony doors and sunlight washes into the room. 'I could see it all in my mind so clearly.'

'Paint the picture for me, dear,' says Hazel encouragingly.

Pixie pauses for a moment and then turns back to the room. 'Two sewing machines, back-to-back, over there by the fireplace. Cutting table in the centre. Alice would have to work downstairs, of course.' She points to the dividing wall between the two rooms. 'Pressing there against the wall, an ironing table – until we can afford an industrial presser. Stock racks along that wall.' She stops and bites her lip. 'I don't really know the exact cost of all those things. I'm such an idiot rushing into this.'

'This is just a setback, and most likely one of many ahead,' says Hazel. 'Your grandad often used to say, "Good things come together slowly, it's bad things that happen quickly." This will be a good thing for you, but it will take time.'

Hazel can't help but feel partly responsible, having shown Pixie the shop in the first place, starting this whole endeavour in motion. 'I'm going to duck home and get some cleaning materials. Why don't you break the bad news to Alice and get that conversation out of the way?'

Pixie nods miserably. She closes the balcony doors, and they make their way downstairs, where she gives Hazel the spare key.

Walking home, Hazel wishes she could make this difficult transition easier. But perhaps the struggle will make Pixie's success all the sweeter. No one can take that from her.

Betty is up and about, making tea and toast, singing happily to herself. Hazel's pleased to see her in such a good frame of mind and not hungover. When she recounts Pixie's dramas of last night, Betty cries, 'Oh my goodness! That Dottie Karp is a piece of work! How could you do that to your own daughter? I've got a spare half-hour before work. Let me quickly get dressed and help you.'

While Betty gets ready, Hazel pulls out the vacuum cleaner and cleaning materials. Between the two of them, they carry everything around to the shop.

'Effie Finch lives in this street, I seem to recall,' says Betty when they arrive.

'Do you remember which house?' asks Hazel.

'I think it's that grey one further down on the other side,' says Betty.

While Betty goes off to see if Effie has a ladder for the cobwebs, Hazel lets herself into the shop and sets about cleaning. Within minutes, Betty and Effie appear carrying a wooden painter's ladder.

'My old man was a painter and paperhanger,' explains Effie. 'I've got to go to work, but I can give you a quick hand.' With that, she sets up the ladder and tackles the cobwebs with a feather duster. Hazel vacuums and Betty wipes down the grubby walls. Effie fetches some methylated spirits and cleans the front windows. By the time Betty and Effie leave for work, the place is in much better shape.

Pixie's little red car pulls up in front of the shop. She gets out and gives Alice a hand to navigate the low step into the shop. Hazel makes them tea and brings a couple of wooden crates from the yard for them to sit on.

When she returns, Alice is saying, 'Look, I've lost drawings before. I always think of it as a sign I can do better. They can have all that stuff, Pix, I'll do more – and better.'

'It's bad enough having to walk away from the Mod Frocks brand, without losing everything we could use for the next season,' says Pixie. 'It's just not fair.'

The two young women sit in the showroom, sipping their tea and talking it through, and it occurs to Hazel that Alice is an ideal business partner for Pixie. Alice's life has clearly been a struggle. There were the years of treatment and managing with callipers on her legs. Every single day she faces difficulties doing things most people take for granted. It's these struggles that have made her a level-headed and thoughtful young woman.

Hazel could have guessed that Dottie would not give up such a talented designer without a fight but, for the moment, it seems Alice's loyalty lies with Pixie.

29

A RUDE SHOCK FOR HAZEL

Hazel arrives home to find Detective Dibble's car parked outside her house. He comes to the front door and holds the vacuum cleaner while she unlocks it.

'I have a feeling you're not here with good news,' says Hazel, putting the vacuum away in the understairs cupboard. 'Come on through.'

She puts the kettle on, while Dibble stands with his back to the range. 'Look, I know you're very fond of Mr Shepperton—'

Hazel turns to him with dread. 'Oh no,' she murmurs.

'Sorry, let me start again. He's doing fine, but forensics came back last night and confirmed that the pistol you found in the cupboard was the same weapon that killed Beauchamp.'

'Rex would not murder anyone. As I said last time we spoke, this has to be a set-up. I don't know by whom or why, but it's all too convenient. And why has someone made an attempt on his life, if not to stop him talking?'

'There was also ammunition found in his home—'

'Who got the search warrant for that?' asks Hazel.

'I'm not sure who exactly, but the warrant was issued at Shepperton's local station.'

'Surry Hills?' Hazel fixes him with a steely gaze. 'So possibly Detective Pierce?'

'Possibly,' admits Dibble. 'But now, with Shepperton's connection to the murder of Beauchamp, he has become the prime suspect in the Krugerrand robbery as well. He's perfectly positioned to know about shipments—'

Hazel shakes her head. 'I guarantee that Rex was not involved. I'd stake my life on it. Whoever committed the crime wants him out of the way.'

'Mrs Bates, you knew him as a little boy—'

'With a kind and fair nature. That hasn't changed.'

'But people do change.' Dibble pulls out a chair and sits down. 'Look, the police force is rife with corruption from the bottom to the top. I'd wager that not one of those men joined the force thinking they'd be on the make. *They* were lovely little boys once. They start with the best intentions and find themselves in a system where it's much harder, and more dangerous, to be honest and do the right thing. The culture within unions, and particularly on the wharves, is not just similar to the cops, it's worse.'

'And he was trying to change that,' says Hazel. 'It's a passion for him. So, this doesn't make any sense at all. I'm sure that once you conduct a thorough investigation, it will become clear. I just hope he's under a proper police guard in hospital, because whoever framed him will benefit from getting rid of him permanently and having the case closed.'

Dibble nods. 'He'll be guarded around the clock . . . but I don't have any control over the officers on shift. I wish I could do more.' After a moment he adds, 'Um . . . would you like me to make that tea?'

Hazel manages a smile. 'Sorry, it slipped my mind.' She gives her attention to the tea preparation. 'I do appreciate you coming round to tell me in person.'

'If I ask you to stay out of it, will it make any difference? This is a highly volatile situation and extremely dangerous. I don't want you taking any risks.'

Hazel pours the boiling water into the pot and pretends she hasn't heard him. 'Have you had breakfast? I expect you'd like a bowl of porridge to go with this.'

Dibble sighs. 'That would be very nice, thank you.'

'In return, do you think you could pull some strings to allow me to visit him in hospital, even for a few minutes?'

Dibble grimaces. 'Bribery by porridge. All right, I'll see what I can do, Mrs Bates.'

On the bus to the hospital, Hazel wonders if it is possible that she has been blinded by her long relationship with Rex. As Dibble said, she knew the boy, but does she really know the man? She ponders those comments about corruption. Certainly the wheeling and dealing involved in Rex's role would have its temptations. But is it possible that he's taken bribes, or been involved in criminal activities? Could he be playing the role of 'man of the people' while at the same time colluding with criminals? Apart from his denial about seeing Cliff Fletcher and the odd PR fib, her ears have not detected any lies from him.

Across the aisle of the bus, a man reads a newspaper with the headline: *'COMMIE CHAOS –WHARFIES UNION BOSS MURDER SUSPECT'*.

Hazel can't read the smaller print, but it's clear to her that Rex is a prime target and the forces working against him have seized the opportunity to undo all his good work.

Rex has been moved to a private hospital room with two police officers guarding the door. Hazel identifies herself, and one of the officers searches her handbag and makes her empty out her coat pockets. He unlocks the door and follows her inside, where she pulls up a chair beside Rex's bed. He's sleeping, and if it wasn't for the drip feed and the bandaging around his head, he could be having a peaceful afternoon nap.

His face and neck are swollen with bruising. The assailant must have tried to strangle him. Watching over him, she feels a rush of fondness. She knows that the dint in his nose happened when one of his brothers pushed him too high on a swing and he came a cropper. The tiny scar upwards from his brow he got crawling under a barbed wire fence. She sees the face of a good man.

The fact is that any man with high ideals will have enemies, people for whom those ideals could mean personal financial losses. People whose livelihoods depend on keeping workers poor and desperate. Seeing him so vulnerable reinforces to Hazel that, even though he's a grown man, Rex needs her help again. She places her hand on his and gives it a reassuring squeeze.

His eyes snap open and he stares at her. He tries to speak, coughs and clears his throat. He tries again and flinches with pain.

Hazel pats his hand. 'You need to rest, Rex.'

He shakes his head, agitated. 'The boy,' he whispers hoarsely. 'The boy.'

The police officer tells her it's time to go. She leans closer to Rex, hoping for more information. His eyes are closed but she's quite sure he's feigning sleep.

30

IRENE HAS A SPOT OF BOTHER

Since the firebomb incident at Chapel Lane, Irene's spent a lot of time scouting the nearby streets on the lookout for Malteses. She's done that much walking, it's a shame no one is paying her to do it. There are plenty of shady-looking blokes hanging around in their cars, most of them perves but no threat to her, or Miss Palmer. Irene hasn't seen the Ford Falcon, the one she threw the brick at, but that doesn't mean those Malteses have given up.

Even the cops can't stop a firebomb like the other day. It can happen in a minute. If she hadn't caught the thing, it would have hit her or the floor. She'd have been covered in petrol and set alight, Dimples would have likely gone up in flames and Bunny barbecued. Just lucky she can think on her feet.

Now she's off to the Tilbury Hotel in Woolloomooloo to get arrested. She hasn't been down to the 'loo' in years. She gets the wrong bus and ends up having to walk a good mile or so. When she finally gets there, the place is rolling in sailors, street girls and deros – rough as it gets.

She tries to remember the exact arrangement. It was simple the way Big G described it. Turn up at six o'clock (it's now twenty past), hold up a yellow pamphlet and get arrested. She gets the pamphlet out of her pinny pocket and looks it over. Confusingly, it's about some new headache tablets. She might need them if this doesn't go well.

She stands in the main bar, holds it up and looks around, feeling like a bloody idiot.

'Hey, lady!' calls the barman. 'He's looking for yers upstairs.' He flaps a tea towel in the direction of the staircase.

Halfway up, Irene meets a young copper in uniform coming down.

'You're late,' he says, glancing at the pamphlet. 'I've been upstairs twice.'

'I got on the wrong bloody bus. Not the easiest place to get to,' says Irene.

He gives a dry laugh. 'Ask your boss to send you somewhere more convenient next time.'

Irene glances at the pamphlet in her hand. 'What's these pills got to do with it?'

'Nothing,' he says. 'It's anything yellow. Come on then. Let's get this over with.'

Irene follows him downstairs and down the driveway at the side of the pub. An older cop is asleep in the passenger seat of a cop car with his mouth wide open. The young bloke puts her in the back seat and slams the door shut, waking his mate. The cops are friendly enough, but Irene would much prefer to be chauffeured in the Rolls by the Neck (who she trusts a lot more than these blokes).

They drop her at the local cop shop, where the duty officer gets her details (raising an eyebrow at her address), then fingerprints her and charges her with illegal bookmaking.

'You'll get a notice to appear at the Court of Petty Sessions sometime. The bail is fifty,' he tells her. 'Sign here.' He shoves a piece of paper in front of her.

'Fifty? I thought it was twenty. That's all he gave me.'

The cop shrugs. 'It's gone up. I can't change it. If you can't post bail, you'll have to spend the night until someone comes and bails you out.'

Irene gives a huff. 'Mate, I've got other things to do. For one thing, those Malteses are tryna blow the place up, and what are yers doing about that?'

'You've lost me. It's pay up or lock up. Make your mind up.'

'I'll take me legal phone call, thanks. And a phone book, if yer don't mind.'

Reaching under the counter, he drops the phone book on the desk with a threatening thump and glances at his watch. 'Don't go anywhere,' he says, and walks out the door.

Irene looks through the phone book and finds the number of the Thatched Pig. She calls and asks for Big G. After a long delay, the barmaid says he's not there. Grumbling under her breath, Irene thinks again and asks for Arthur Smith. The barmaid calls out his name, and Irene can hear him asking who wants him.

'Who's calling?' asks the barmaid.

'Gina Lollobrigida,' says Irene.

She hears this relayed back and then Arthur himself comes on the line. 'Who is this?'

'Arthur, mate—'

'Very inventive, Mrs Turnbuckle—'

'Yer didn't really think it was her, did yer?'

'I am inundated with calls from glamorous starlets, so it's always possible. Now, what do you want?'

'Can yers come down to Woolloomooloo cop shop and post thirty bucks bail for me?'

'What crime have you committed?' he asks. 'Thirty seems cheap.'

'Nuthin', just a stooge job for Big G, playing stand-in for a bookie.'

'Why isn't Mr Big G taking care of this situation? Or the bookie himself?'

'Look, the bloody bail's gone up. I got short-changed. Do us a favour, mate?'

'On the proviso that you refrain from calling me "mate" from now until eternity.'

'Fine,' says Irene, regretting not calling Hazel, who would have been easier to deal with than this galah. 'I can pay yers back when I get the money from Big G.'

'There'll be an additional fee for my time and taxi,' says Arthur.

'Look, maa . . .' begins Irene, stopping herself just in time. 'I've got more things to worry about than this. I got to get the hell outta here.'

'I appreciate your sense of urgency but am utterly indifferent to it,' he says. 'I plan to finish my drink in a leisurely manner and wend my way down to you in the fullness of time.'

Irene forces herself to thank him. As she puts the receiver down, the cop comes back, bringing the smell of hot meat pie with him. 'Done?' he asks.

Irene nods. 'Me lawyer's on his way.'

The cop gives a snort of laughter.

'That pie smells all right,' says Irene, realising she's hungry.

'Chunky beef.' He sits down at his desk and starts eating the meat pie out of the bag.

'Don't prisoners get dinner here?' asks Irene.

'You're not a prisoner, you're a nuisance,' he says, blowing on the steaming pie.

Irene feels in her coat pocket for a Scotch Finger and finds it empty. She gives a sigh. She's got to either train herself to use the other pocket, or get the hole mended.

She walks around the reception area, glancing out into the dark street for any sign of Arthur. How long can a drink take? She does another lap of the room. There's a board on one wall with 'Wanted' posters. To pass the time, she examines these blokes, ugly mugs the lot of them. There are rewards for a couple of them, and those she takes a *really* good look at.

Her examination is interrupted by the arrival of a taxi outside.

Ignoring her, Arthur strides past to the counter. 'Good evening, sir,' he says, placing three ten-dollar notes on the counter. 'Is that all?'

The copper writes a receipt. Arthur takes it and starts heading straight out the door.

'Thanks,' says Irene, following him. 'Can I get a lift—'

'Lady, sign here and you can go,' calls the copper.

She does as she's told and gets outside in time to see Arthur's taxi disappearing. She looks up and down the street, wondering where the nearest bus stop could be. She doesn't want to ask the unhelpful cop, but notices a man in a grey overcoat standing across the street.

'Where's the nearest bus stop, mister?' Irene asks, crossing over to his side.

Closer now, she can see the coat is stiff with dirt. The lower half of his face is buried in a filthy nest of beard. He turns glittering eyes on her. 'I wandered lonely as a cloud!' he shouts.

'Not surprised, yer stink to high heaven,' Irene points out.

'That floats on high o'er vales and hills!' he bellows, rocking with the effort. He drops to a normal volume. 'When all at once I saw a crowd.'

Confused, Irene glances up and down the empty street. 'Oh, I get it – rhymes with cloud.' He seems to be working himself up for a big finish, so she gets in quick. 'Oi! Shakespeare! Where's the bloody bus stop?'

'A host of golden daffodils!' he roars, staggering backwards.

'Yer stuffed it at the end. Five out of ten for rhyming, mate.'

Irene wonders if the silly coot is deaf, not surprising with all that shouting. He holds out a filthy-looking hat and Irene looks inside to see a few coins in there.

'I'm skint. Now, where's the bus stop?'

To her annoyance, he wanders off, mumbling to himself. She takes a swig from the flask in her pinny and sets off up the street. It's been one bloody thing after another tonight.

31

IRENE MAKES A PACT

Irene comes in the back door of 555 to find the Neck sitting at the kitchen table. He's a big lug, and the chair looks about ready to break under his weight.

'Where've you been?' he asks.

Irene's had more than enough for today. 'What's it to youse?'

'Sit down,' he says, pulling out a chair.

'I'm bushed. Been a hell of a day. Bloody poets. Had to walk miles.'

'Sit down,' he repeats.

Irene sits down, gets out her flask and drains the last of the contents. 'Whaddayah want?'

'I had a conversation with Bunny today,' he says.

Irene snorts. 'That what they're calling it now?'

'She reckons someone threw a Molotov cocktail into the Chapel Lane house—'

'Yeah. Listen, that's what I've been telling yers, and her nibs.' Irene nods in the general direction of Miss Palmer's office. 'I reckon those Malteses are gonna burn down her places. Teach her a lesson.

She should've stuck to this side of town, not gone down the swamp. If I hadn't been there, Bunny and . . .' Irene stops herself. 'Well, Bunny—'

'I know about the Yank,' says the Neck.

'Goodo. So, if I wasn't there to catch the flamin' thing and chuck it out the door, those two would be looking down on us right now,' says Irene, raising her eyes to the heavens. 'Not sure I'd be up there but.'

'She told me.' The Neck pauses. 'Quick thinking, Mrs Turnbuckle. And very brave.'

Irene hears a new note of respect in his voice. 'Anyway, yer gonna do something about it now?'

The Neck slides his hand inside his suit jacket. Irene half expects him to bring out a gun, but instead he gets out two cigars and offers her one. Taking it, she gives it a sniff to make sure it's one of the good ones, not the cheapos she's been popping into the box.

He leans over and lights her cigar before lighting his own. They sit in silence for a moment, puffing up a comforting cloud of smoke.

'Why open a place on someone else's patch?' asks Irene. 'She's doing fine here. Doesn't make any sense to me.'

The Neck shrugs as much as his neck allows. 'Now that Sydney's the official R&R locale for the Yanks, they'll be coming in from Vietnam in their thousands. Vice want to keep them all around Darlinghurst and the Cross, not spilling out to other areas causing trouble and getting complaints from decent citizens. That's why the location.'

'Yeah, well, that place won't last till the middle of next week if somethink's not done about them Malteses.'

'Apart from killing them all off, what's going to stop them?' he says. 'And from what I understand, there's a fair number of them.'

'What about hiring a hit man and knocking off the boss, this Borg character?'

The Neck shakes his head. 'Plenty have tried. None succeeded, so far.'

'We could set a couple of their places on fire,' says Irene, starting to enjoy throwing ideas around. 'Or send them a tart with leprosy.'

The Neck nods thoughtfully as he considers these ideas. 'Not sure how easy that would be to organise. Besides, you don't want to do something that affects the girls themselves. We need to get to the boss or his henchmen. We need to make them reconsider their current strategy and give a hint of the possible consequences – in case they're planning something bigger.' He gets up and puts the kettle on. 'Tea?'

'Reckon,' says Irene. 'Yer don't happen to have a Scotch Finger on yer?'

He shakes his head. He opens the fridge and glances inside. 'I can make you an omelette if you're hungry.'

'A whatlette?' asks Irene.

He looks amused. 'Have you never heard of an omelette?'

'Nah. Just a cup of tea will do me.'

He gives a shrug and busies himself scalding the pot, adding tea leaves and pouring in boiling water. 'Milk?' he asks, glancing over his shoulder.

'Just a touch. Yer could get yerself a job as a tea lady, mate.'

'High praise,' he says, setting down the teapot, two cups and sugar bowl on the table.

'I reckon we've gotta be smarter than them,' says Irene. 'They've got the numbers, but we got the brains.' She pours the tea, helps herself to three spoonfuls of sugar and gives it a good stir.

'I had an idea while I was making the tea,' says the Neck. 'I know a few Maltese people – they're not all mafia, most of them are good, decent people, and hard workers too – and they're very superstitious. They believe in all sorts of ghosts – the evil eye, bogeymen, that sort of thing.'

Irene frowns. 'Who doesn't?'

'What if bad things started to happen in Woods Lane?'

'A firebomb is already a bad thing,' Irene points out.

'Unexplainable bad things,' he continues. 'Supernatural things that seem to happen by magic. Things that spook them. You know, like a hex.'

Irene wonders if this bloke is all there, wafting on about getting rid of the Malteses with a fairy wand. 'Like what?'

He sits quietly, drinking his tea and thinking, as if there's no one here but him. His bald head glows pink under the dull kitchen bulb. His face is all dreamy and soft, like an overgrown baby in a blue three-piece suit.

Finally, he gives himself a nod of approval. 'I've got a better plan. There's this product they developed during the war that a mate of a mate has started importing. Actually, there was an article in the *New Scientist* about it recently. It's quite amazing.'

Irene's expecting him to tell her about a new type of grenade or gun, so it comes as a disappointment when he asks, 'Ever heard of super glue?'

32
HAZEL FINDS SOMETHING OF INTEREST

On the way to work, Hazel realises with a jolt that she missed the Guild meeting last night. It couldn't be helped. She was awake half the night trying to work out the connection between the deaths of Cooper and Beauchamp and the robbery, and who might have had the opportunity to frame Rex. Likely someone close to him, or at least working on the docks.

She's almost certain that 'the boy' Rex mentioned is Cliff Fletcher. Rex seemed certain she'd know who he was talking about. She'd shown him the photo but not told him the young man's name. She phoned Dibble last night with this new piece of information and he said he'd look into it but didn't seem as convinced as she was about its importance. It's obvious to Hazel that if it was Cliff who bashed Rex and possibly tried to kill him, he was working for someone else. Someone powerful who wants Rex out of the way.

She wonders now if the only way to clear Rex is to find the missing Krugerrand – something that has proved an impossible task for the police. If it came ashore, the wharves and goods sheds offer a thousand nooks and crannies to hide stolen goods, and the police have turned up nothing so far, despite an extensive search. She remembers Dibble telling her that the Krugerrand were in thousands of individual presentation boxes. She tries to imagine how much space they would take up but it's difficult to picture.

At the wharf office, Yvonne is sitting at Rex's desk, going through his diary to cancel his appointments.

'You must have got a terrible shock to hear about Rex, and all these accusations against him,' Hazel ventures, bringing her a cup of tea.

'Yeah, I was surprised,' says Yvonne. 'But you can't trust anyone these days. Everyone's up to something.' Turning her attention back to the diary, she crosses out an entry and flicks the page over.

'Do you know anyone who might have wanted Rex out of the way?'

Yvonne looks up quickly. 'Are you working for the cops now?'

'Hardly.' Hazel gives an insincere chuckle. 'Just a nosy tea lady.'

'There's plenty of people who hate him. The union rank and file love him. All those New Australians. They think he's a hero.' She shrugs. 'But he's probably just in it to line his own pockets, like the rest of them.'

'Do you really think that?' asks Hazel.

'Don't you? Oh, I forgot you babysat him when he was a little kid.' She stares at Hazel with a flat gaze. 'He's not a little kid any more. He's a big bad man.'

Her comment hits Hazel like a slap. She doesn't believe a word of it and her ears tell her that Yvonne doesn't either.

Until now her impression of Yvonne has been that she's a clock-on, clock-off worker, with little interest in the ideals of the union. She's often flirtatious with Rex, calling him 'Boss' in a way that's more teasing than deferential. Now she seems to be parroting what the newspapers are saying, even though she doesn't really believe it herself. Perhaps she had also thought Rex was a hero and this is disappointment talking. An attempt at cynicism.

It's a busy morning with the full contingent of staff down at the wharf office. Workers arrive in droves to ask after Rex, and then stand around debating his innocence or guilt. Many of the men who come in are Italians and Greeks, and Hazel knows he's particularly popular with these men for his initiative of distributing fliers in their languages and bringing in translators for worker meetings. All the men are indignant at the accusations.

Hazel finds herself assessing every single person. Any one of them could be involved and sniffing around for more information.

At the end of the day, Teddy comes into the kitchen while she's washing up. 'Any news on how Rex is doing?' he asks.

'He's under police guard, but I understand he's recovering,' says Hazel. She dries her hands and turns to look at him. 'Do you think he's involved in this robbery and murder?'

'No, I don't.' He gives a sigh. 'But then what do you really know about someone? In real life, villains don't walk around twirling their moustaches and laughing their evil laughs. For every career criminal there's a couple more blokes who are opportunists and one with a dark secret.' He shrugs. 'Rex is a hard man to get to know well. Plenty of folk think his ideas are radical and dangerous—'

'Who, for example?' interrupts Hazel.

'Where do I start? The government's threatened by his communist ideology and anti-war views – Rex has a lot of power in that area. His demands for decent working hours and fair pay threaten the profits of the shipping companies. And our own executive is threatened by his campaign for members to have the right to vote on matters that concern them – democracy, in other words. On top of all that, he's working to have another union deregistered.'

'So there's practically an army of people with incentives,' says Hazel.

'Absolutely, and powerful people too,' says Teddy. 'It's a complicated way to go about getting rid of him, so you can probably eliminate employers. Shipping companies use politics, not fists – usually. That said, there is a lot of wheeling and dealing behind closed doors around here. But no doubt they'll uncover the truth and justice will prevail.'

Hazel agrees, but she has no intention of waiting for that to happen.

There are very few ships in port and the wharves are quite empty when Hazel leaves for the day. Rows of empty handcarts and piles of pallets sit idle against the walls of the goods sheds. With the place to herself, she takes the opportunity to walk along to the spot where Cooper always stood, waiting for his pigeons. Perhaps he was just a man of habit, or perhaps there was another reason for choosing this particular spot.

It's a still afternoon, not a breath of wind. The sun is low in the sky, giving the water a coppery sheen. The spot where he stood is not difficult to find. Over time, pigeon droppings have been washed into the cracks of the timber deck, encrusted in the worn planks.

When cargo ships are in port, they're moored by ropes lashed to bollards running parallel to the wharf. She hadn't noticed before but in this section there are no bollards, and the view would remain open with clear sightlines across the harbour to Pyrmont, to Cockle Bay and, in the other direction, the harbour entry to the docks.

It's a prime spot for viewing incoming vessels. If he was a lookout, what was he looking out for? And who paid him for information? She can't help but think all these elements are tied together.

As she turns away, a sparkle of light catches her eye. Bending down, she notices something buried in a crack in the board but then loses sight of it. She moves around until the sun glints on it again. Getting out her house keys, she scratches at the droppings cemented into the timber to uncover a tiny stone sparkling in the light. She picks it up, folds her hankie carefully around it and slips it into the pocket of her pinny.

33

HAZEL LOOKS FOR ALLIES

Betty has made shepherd's pie for dinner and Hazel couldn't be more grateful for the warm, nourishing meal. She goes to the pantry, finds a bottle of last summer's blackberry wine and pours them each a small glass.

'Everyone was a bit surprised that you didn't come to the meeting last night,' says Betty. 'I didn't know where you were. Anyway, I added your apologies in the minutes.'

'Thank you, Betty dear. I wouldn't want them to think I'd lost interest,' says Hazel. 'This is delicious, by the way.'

'Cheers,' says Betty, tipping her glass to Hazel's. Taking a sip, she continues. 'Anyway, the meeting went quite well. There were fourteen of us, and almost everyone had some ideas for the auction.'

'Was Merl one of them?' asks Hazel.

Betty shakes her head. 'No, she didn't come, but I think people spoke up more because old Bossy Boots wasn't there. We've set a date for the auction in three weeks' time. Do you want me to confirm the church hall with Sister Ruth?'

'That would be very helpful. We need to start publicising it as well,' says Hazel.

'One of the ladies from the Education Department can roneo copies of a flyer, and we'll take them round the shops and businesses.'

Hazel smiles. 'Sounds as though it's all under control.'

Betty finishes her meal and sits back with a sigh of satisfaction. 'And how is Rex? Is he still in the hospital? I know you're worried about him.'

Hazel explains the chain of events of the last couple of days, as well as her suspicions.

'Oh dear, the whole thing sounds terribly dangerous, Hazel. Perhaps you should leave it to Detective Dibble. Not all the police are crooked, and he knows what he's doing.'

In the past, Betty would have leapt out of her chair to be involved. There was nothing she loved more than playing detective. But it seems to Hazel that since Lucy came on the scene, Betty's become less interested in things she once adored and now worries about things she never worried about before – her lost youth, for example.

The mention of the police gives Hazel an idea. 'Leave the dishes for me, dear. I'm just going to pop next door.'

Not bothering with a coat, she ducks next door to the Mulligans'. Again, the family are crowded into the front room, surrounded by the piles of ironing and bathed in blue light.

'Maude, dear,' says Hazel, standing in the doorway. 'Sorry to disturb. Could I have a quick word?'

Maude doesn't seem to hear, and Mrs Mulligan shouts over the blaring television, 'Maudie! Have you gone deaf, child? Hazel's wanting a word, off you go.'

Maude comes into the hallway. 'How can I help, Mrs B?'

'Shut the door, girl, you're letting all the heat out!' shouts Mrs Mulligan.

Hazel pulls the door shut. It's cold in the hall. Maude looks warm with her dressing-gown on over her clothes, and Hazel regrets not throwing on her coat. Maude suggests they go into the kitchen. She puts the kettle on, and they sit down at the table.

'Have you heard that Rex Shepperton is being charged with murder and robbery?' asks Hazel.

Maude nods. 'Are you investigating that, Mrs B?' she asks seriously.

'I've known Rex all his life. I'm certain he's been set up, and I wondered if you could help me with something.'

'Maybe. I just started my three weeks with the detectives. I suppose I might be able to find out something . . .' Maude says, not sounding confident.

'The police got a search warrant for Rex's home very quickly. I thought they needed to apply to the court and present their evidence.'

'I can explain that. There's an ex-cop who runs a sandwich shop. He's a justice of the peace. He'll issue a search warrant for twenty bucks. I've already been sent there to get a couple this week. They can basically search anywhere they want.'

'Would that stand up in court?' asks Hazel.

Maude shrugs. 'I suppose so. He's legally allowed to issue them.'

'Do you think you could find out which officer applied for that warrant?'

'I don't know. Aren't you friends with Detective Dibble up in Special Branch? He could find out,' says Maude.

'I don't want to involve him at this point,' says Hazel. She pauses and decides to confide in Maude. 'I think the murder of

Mr Beauchamp, the gold trader, and the murder of this other fellow, Mr Cooper, are linked. And quite likely related to the robbery of the Krugerrand. The evidence implicating Rex Shepperton is flimsy and I'm certain he's not involved.' She pauses. 'Someone has framed him, and the identity of that person, or persons, could be the key to everything.'

Maude nods. 'All right, I'll see what I can find out.'

34

BETTY GETS IT ALL HORRIBLY WRONG

Betty's legs are wobbly as jelly as she walks from the bus stop to Rosemont Street. She'd spent forever deciding what to wear and doing her hair and make-up to look her best. But now she's beset with nerves.

When Lucy had first suggested painting her portrait, Betty was taken by surprise. Now she knows that Lucy is a talented artist (which makes it even more flattering) and Betty has agreed to pose for her. But, somewhere along the way, other artist friends have got involved as well – how many, she's not sure.

Lucy answers the door straightaway. Welcoming Betty with a big smile, she plants a kiss on each of her cheeks (something they do around here). 'Oh, your little face is frozen,' she says. 'Come in, we've made the room all toasty for you. I do so appreciate you doing this. Everyone's so thrilled to have you here.'

The lounge room is positively tropical with a blazing fire and the curtains all drawn. It's been transformed into an art studio with a forest of easels set up around the room. A dozen or so young men and women stand chatting in groups.

'Here's our beautiful model, Betty Dewsnap!' cries Lucy.

A hush falls as everyone turns to look at Betty. Some people give a friendly wave; others turn back to their conversation.

'Is this outfit all right?' Betty asks Lucy. 'It's my best dress.'

Lucy looks confused. 'Yes, lovely. You can get changed over here.'

Now Betty's confused as she follows Lucy to the corner, where a folding screen has been erected. Behind the screen is a chair with a pink silk robe draped over it.

'You can put the robe on and just slip it off when you're feeling comfortable.'

Betty looks down at her best blue wool dress with its lace-covered buttons and white piping around the collar and cuffs. 'Should I have worn something different?'

Lucy wears an uncomfortable smile. 'Betty, this is a life drawing class.'

Betty nods vigorously. 'Like a "still life" but with a person instead of fruit.'

'Yes, but unclothed,' Lucy says quietly. 'I thought you understood that.'

'Unclothed?' asks Betty. 'You don't mean . . .'

'Naked,' says Lucy, with a nod.

Betty feels a hot blush seize her entire body. Her face is on fire. 'Nude?' she asks, just to clarify. Her hands move involuntarily in front of her body. 'Without anything on . . . at all?'

'Yes.' Lucy laughs. 'I'll leave you to it. No rush. Just come and lie on the sofa in a pose that's comfortable. You need to be very still. Still life,' she adds with a laugh. 'Keep the robe on until you're ready to take it off. I'll get you a little Dutch courage.'

She disappears for a minute and returns with a glass of wine, handing it to Betty with a nod and an encouraging smile.

Left alone behind the screen, Betty is not thinking about taking her clothes off; she's calculating the distance between her and the door, and working out how to get out of there. Could she crawl out on hands and knees in the hope that no one notices? She'd have to get another job. She wouldn't be able to face Lucy, having let her down in front of all her friends. She could never show her face in this house again.

Hot shame washes over her. She's damned either way. She could kick herself for being so stupid. A quick peek around the screen reveals everyone is still chatting, the air thick with cigarette smoke. They're waiting for their subject to emerge.

Betty looks down at her fully clothed body, envisaging what's beneath these layers: lumpy varicose legs, droopy bosoms, a floppy tummy like an unbaked scone and a shapeless, dimpled bottom. The idea of anyone seeing her naked when she was young was impossible enough, but to have this wonky old body examined and recorded is unthinkable.

'Everything all right, Betty?' calls Lucy.

'Yes. Thank you!' Her voice comes out as a squeak.

She downs the glass of wine in one gulp. The new plan is to either make a run for the door or stage a fainting fit. (She actually does feel a bit faint.) But both options involve her making a spectacle of herself.

With a growing sense of dread, she realises she has no choice.

She takes off her dress, stockings and corset (donned especially for this occasion), followed by her spencer, brassiere and undies. She quickly slips on the robe, horribly embarrassed at the thought of being naked in a room full of people even though she's hidden behind a screen.

Now she's trembling from head to foot, her whole body shaking violently. She reaches for her underwear and hurriedly dresses herself. She's about to slip out from behind the screen when Lucy appears, blocking her way.

'All right?' she asks, clearly noting that Betty is dressed.

Betty shakes her head. No words come.

'I'm sorry about that little misunderstanding, Betty. It's really not as difficult as you think. It's the most natural thing in the world. And no one is looking at you in a sexual way. This is art. They're looking at form and curve and muscle—'

'I don't have any muscles,' Betty whispers, as if this might get her off the hook.

'Why don't you wear the robe and then slip it off when you're comfortable?'

'What if I'm never comfortable?' whispers Betty.

Lucy hesitates. 'That's fine, I suppose,' she says reluctantly.

Lucy steps back to give her privacy, but Betty can see her feet below the screen. There's no escape. She peels off her clothes and wraps the robe tightly around her.

As she comes out from behind the screen, the artists move to their easels with hushed anticipation, gazing at her as if having spotted an exotic animal in the wild.

Lucy leads her to the sofa. Betty sits down on the edge of it, clutching the gown in front of her. From this position, the backs of the easels look like shields. As if they're protected from her. But who is protecting *her*?

'You get comfortable, Betty,' says Lucy cheerfully. 'We'll do two fifteen-minute poses and then take a break and do thirty minutes.'

She demonstrates how Betty could lie on her side with one arm draped along the back of the sofa. It looks like the sort of saucy pose the actress Mae West would adopt while murmuring, 'Come up and see me sometime.'

Betty numbly follows the instructions and finds a fairly comfortable position with the gown pulled and belted tightly around her.

Once she's settled, the artists begin to work, glancing back and forth between paper and the subject. They stare through her somehow with a practised gaze. They could be drawing a tree or landscape.

Fifteen minutes turns out to be a long time to keep still. Every second is painfully slow. The trembling has lessened, but Betty's nose, head and neck all take turns at itching. She fixes what she imagines to be a Mona Lisa smile on her face, though it's probably more pained than the Mona Lisa, who was fully clothed after all.

For the second pose, under Lucy's instruction, Betty sits with her back against the armrest at one end of the sofa, her feet stretched out in front of her, half turning on her hip to be drawn in three-quarter profile, which quickly makes her neck ache horribly.

Eventually there's a break and everyone puts down their tools. They pick up glasses of wine and chat among themselves. Betty sits on the edge of the sofa, feeling marooned and alone in a room full of people, but also relieved at being ignored after so much attention. Lucy brings her a glass of red wine and she gulps it down, searing her throat.

Lucy sits down beside her. 'Could you take your robe off for the last pose, Betty?'

Betty shakes her head vehemently.

'What are you afraid of, exactly?' Her tone is gentle but firm.

Betty considers the question. Is she afraid of being judged? Or of looking ugly? It's not a beauty contest, and she's a bit long in the tooth to be considered cheap. Is it just modesty, or is she ashamed of her body? The thought of this makes her feel strange, as if she's betraying this body, which, apart from a few niggles (quite a lot of niggles), has carried her around capably all these years. On top of that, the last thing she wants to do is let Lucy down and embarrass her in front of her friends – or be thought prudish.

'Could I have another glass of wine?' Betty asks.

Lucy fetches a full glass. Betty knocks it back, spilling some down her front. She takes a deep breath. 'I don't know . . .' she says helplessly.

Lucy seizes on her indecision. 'I'll help you find a modest pose.'

Consumed with dread, Betty allows Lucy to loosen the robe and position her on the sofa, lying on her tummy and leaning on her forearms. Her knees are bent, feet dangling in the air, like a child reading a storybook.

'Don't worry,' says Lucy. 'Your arms are hiding your breasts, and I'll tuck the robe in beside you for extra cover.'

Betty blushes at the word 'breast' but nods. Goosebumps rise all over her as Lucy slides the robe off and her bare skin is exposed.

'Can you hold that pose for thirty minutes?' asks Lucy, tucking the robe in under Betty's armpit.

'I'll do my best,' says Betty. She can't decide if Lucy is being kind or cruel, and suddenly feels tears welling up. The only thing worse than lying here in her birthday suit would be crying at the same time. She grits her teeth and forces a neutral expression.

The wine has made her a little drowsy, and her mind wanders to imagining what the other tea ladies would think if they could see her now. At the thought of Merl's face, she has to push down a giggle. It makes her feel more adventurous and daring.

The time passes in a dream and, the next thing she knows, it's over and Lucy is covering her up.

'Let's have a round of applause for Brave Betty,' cries Lucy, and everyone claps.

Lucy then insists that Betty tour the room to look at each artwork, to which she reluctantly agrees, the robe secured tightly around her. She can't believe the ordeal is over.

Each drawing, some in pencil, others in charcoal, is quite different. Betty barely recognises herself; apart from the curly hair, she looks like any woman. Some are quite flattering. One is *very* flattering. With three glasses of wine under her belt, Betty starts to feel quite good about the whole business. Brave and bohemian – even Rubenesque.

One tall lanky fellow is putting the finishing touches to his drawing and steps aside for her to view. Drawn in black ink, Betty is depicted as a cartoon figure, fat and disfigured with squashy bosoms like jam doughnuts and a face like an old bulldog, jowls drooping above half-a-dozen chins. She wears a prudish expression, her lips pursed as she drinks a cup of tea with her little finger extended. A speech bubble above her head reads: 'Hot and strong. That's how I like it.'

For a moment she can't take her eyes from the horror of it. Then, without a word, she scurries back behind the screen. Tears of humiliation drip off her chin as she struggles back into her clothes. Pulling on her coat, she comes out from behind the screen to see three men standing around this ugly caricature, laughing uproariously. Without saying goodbye to anyone, she heads straight out the front door, slamming it behind her.

In need of fresh air, she walks all the way home. The feelings of shame and humiliation gradually give way to indignation and then a sense of betrayal at the realisation Lucy had not just coaxed her into it, she pressured Betty against her will.

Hazel's gone to bed without leaving a light on, most unlike her, and it makes Betty feel abandoned. She braves the backyard lav and traipses up to bed, weeping softly so as not to disturb Hazel. It's only when she gets to the upstairs landing and sees the bedroom door open that she realises Hazel's not here. Where on earth could she be at this time of night?

35

HAZEL TAKES A DANGEROUS RISK

When Hazel finishes for the day at Trades Hall, she makes her way down to the dock office, empty in the late afternoon. There was some discussion earlier today about the fact that the harbourmaster has released the *Cape Argus* from the layby berth where it was under police guard. It is docked at the main wharf overnight. Tomorrow it will go to nearby Cockatoo Island for repairs, after which it will leave the country. As she listened to the men in the office debate whether or not it should have been released, given the Krugerrand still hadn't been found, Hazel quietly decided to conduct her own research before it was too late.

She waits in the kitchen until the docks are dark and empty. Wearing her brown woollen coat, both warm and invisible, she walks out through the office, keeping her torch low to the ground. The front door is deadlocked; she lets herself out and locks it behind her.

Staying in the shadows of the buildings, her footsteps scattering the swarms of rats feeding on spilt grain, she quickly makes her way to the finger wharf where the ship has been docked.

The *Cape Argus* is much smaller than the other cargo ships that come into port, but still a huge vessel that looms above her as she stands on the dock. No gangplank, but a ladder attached to the side of the ship. Pushing the torch deep into her coat pocket, she reaches up and manages to hoist herself onto the bottom rung. She climbs slowly, step by step, securing both feet on each rail before attempting the next.

When she reaches the top, she faces a difficult manoeuvre to clamber from the ladder onto the deck. Slowly does it, and finally both feet are on the solid steel deck. Keeping her torch low, she wanders around the top deck, into the bridge, taking care where she walks to avoid tripping on any number of coiled ropes, hatches and chains.

She goes down the narrow stairs to the lower level, which has some basic living quarters, two cabins with narrow bunks, two single cabins, a bathroom and a galley. Next to the galley is a dining room with table and chairs. On a sideboard are packs of playing cards and a few well-worn paperbacks. Everything is utilitarian and grubby looking. Not surprising on a working ship.

At the end of the passageway is the captain's quarters. He has a generous-sized room with varnished timber walls hung with nautical paintings. Apart from the double bed, there are bookshelves and an oak desk and chair. There's a sharp chemical smell in the room but she supposes that cargo ships would be host to many unpleasant smells. The crew are probably used to them.

Now the part she's been dreading. She tucks the torch back into her pocket and climbs slowly down the ladder into the hold of the ship. She can hear the scuffle of rats below, adding to the sense of foreboding. Her heart pounds, and not just from the strain of the climb. She has to fight off the feeling of being trapped down here.

When she reaches the bottom, she flashes the torch around the space. It's like being in the belly of a whale. She walks slowly around the perimeter of the hold, taking it all in.

It would normally be packed with wooden crates and sacks of goods but, apart from pallets, broken crates, cargo nets and rusting chains lying about, it's empty.

Finding nothing of interest, she undertakes the difficult task of climbing back up the ladder. By the time she reaches the top, she's exhausted. She sits down to take a breather. The air seems thick and stale.

After a few minutes she feels recovered and walks up the stairs to emerge on the deck and into the bracing night air. She takes a slow observational walk around the circumference, careful not to trip in the dark. She didn't really expect to find anything, when experienced police and customs officers have already been over it a dozen times, but wanted to get a better sense of where the robbery took place. The endeavour may have been an unnecessary risk but it hasn't been a complete waste of time. Everything on the wharves revolves around the movement of goods. Could the goods have been disguised in a way that allowed the thieves to move them around as the search progressed? Not as individual boxes, of course, but inside something else – like a Trojan Horse?

Up at the bow of the ship, she trains her torch down at the black water lapping against the wharf. The ship's anchor hangs limply on its chain between the water and the hull, a thick rope lashed to a bollard on the dock. The police divers have searched the area, so evidently nothing to be found here.

She hears a sound behind her. Before she has time to turn, she's grabbed by rough hands and heaved overboard. Tumbling through darkness, she hits the freezing water hard.

Shocked and disoriented, she flails about without any idea if she's sinking or rising. She can see a sprinkling of reflected lights above her and tries to reach the surface. Now she realises her coat is dragging her down. She struggles to undo the three buttons. Out of breath and fighting panic, she manages to undo the last button, but pulling her arms out is impossible. A calm clarity descends on her. She stops struggling, letting her arms hang by her sides, then kicks with all her strength towards the surface, allowing the coat to fall away behind her. Suddenly she's gasping a lungful of cold air.

Paddling with hands and feet to stay afloat, she pushes down the fears of sharks (the harbour is infested with them) and hypothermia. She dogpaddles desperately towards the dock and is soon exhausted. She pauses to rest for a moment at the bow of the ship, holding on to a rope tied off the anchor. Shivering violently now, she checks her bearings.

She can see a ladder attached to the dock. Heading for it, she leaves the safety of the rope and paddles frantically. It crosses her mind that if it wasn't for a calm sea this evening, she could be pushed under the wharf. It's not easy to count blessings in this situation but that's certainly one.

Finally, with numb hands, she manages to grasp the rough, barnacled rail of the step and pulls herself up in torturous steps to collapse gratefully on the solid timber of the wharf.

Now on solid ground, she feels an overwhelming desire to lie here and sleep. But she knows she has to fight off the fatigue and keep going. Shaking all over, her teeth chattering uncontrollably, she makes her way slowly towards the gates, sleepwalking on numb feet.

The nightwatchman sits in his hut, smoking and listening to the radio. The last thing she sees before her knees collapse is the shocked look on his face.

36

PIXIE HAS HER DOUBTS

Pixie wakes to the sound of Alice's sticks on the wooden floor downstairs in the showroom. She shuts her eyes tight, wishing herself back into sleep. The words 'you don't know what you don't know' keep coming back to her like a song she can't get out of her head. That's what the last few days have brought home to her. She hasn't thought this through properly, and she can see how reckless it was to rush into this. She doesn't know where to buy sewing machines or find machinists. She doesn't have enough money to pay wages for very long, and doesn't really know how piecework is managed. Her biggest mistake has been to try to do this without Gloria's know-how. And Gloria is not going to change her mind.

Pixie thought that working at Empire for two years would have taught her most of what she needed to know, but that was an established company, and she had flitted from one department to another. Now she's trying to do what her grandfather did twenty-five years ago and start something from scratch. The difference is that he was always cautious and thought things through carefully. He never leapt into anything, especially where money was involved.

'Cup of tea?' calls Alice up the stairs.

Pixie clears her throat, thick with tears. 'Yep! Be down in a sec!' she calls back, faking a cheerful voice, and rolls off the mattress.

Alice sits working at the old kitchen table that is now her desk. She gives Pixie a quizzical look as she walks in. 'All right, Pix? You look a bit peaky, as my mother would say.'

Pixie goes into the kitchenette, saved by the whistle of the kettle. She bites her lip hard to stop the tears. 'Yep, I'm fine.'

She makes the tea and brings two cups into the workroom. Giving one to Alice, she leans in the doorway and sips hers, comforted by the warmth. 'I can't believe that not one supplier will give us credit.'

'You know that's Dottie's doing, so don't blame yourself,' says Alice.

'I did some sums last night, and the money's going to be so tight. I didn't think putting the electricity on would be so expensive. And the hanging rails are way more than I thought.'

'We just need a few garments to get started, and then we'll get some cash in, and we'll be fine,' says Alice.

'Everything is more difficult than I thought it would be. I know what you're going to say – I've led a sheltered life—' Pixie stops at Alice's expression. 'Why are you smiling?'

Alice shrugs. 'Because you've already worked out the problem. You've had everything handed to you, and now it's a struggle. But that doesn't make it a mistake.'

'Morning, ladies!' calls a voice. 'Working on a Saturday?'

Pixie puts her head around the door to see Effie Finch striding through the showroom.

'I thought you'd have a room full of frocks by now,' says Effie, who Pixie has noticed never wears anything but trousers – men's, by the looks of them.

'There's a lot of work to do before that happens,' Pixie says defensively.

Effie puts a cake tin down on Alice's desk. 'Baked my special Jamaican ginger cake for you girls. Keep your strength up.'

'Ohhh, thank you, Mrs Finch,' says Alice, smiling.

'It's Miss,' says Effie. 'And call me Effie. We're neighbours now.'

Pixie levers open the tin and breathes in the sweetness of the warm cake, only now realising she's starving. She thanks Effie and, cramming a large piece of cake into her mouth, follows her out into the showroom.

'So, what are you planning to do in here, décor-wise?' asks Effie, waving her arm around the room. 'It's a bit sad looking.'

Pixie agrees. 'It needs painting. We might need to borrow your ladder again, if you don't mind. I don't suppose your dad had any left-over paint?'

Effie shakes her head. 'He's been dead five years, so it'd be stuffed by now anyway. Ladder you can have anytime.' After a moment, she looks Pixie up and down and adds, 'I can give you a hand with painting, if you want. There's a bit of a knack to it.'

Pixie's almost had enough of everyone thinking she doesn't know how to do anything practical, but she thanks Effie for the offer.

After Effie leaves, Pixie lingers at the front door, looking out at the bright winter's day, wishing . . . wishing what? That she was somewhere else with less responsibility? That's where she was until recently. She hears Alice behind her and turns, forcing a smile.

'Let's sit here in the sun for a minute,' says Alice.

Pixie offers her friend a steadying hand and they sit down together on the front step. Alice stares up at the sky in silence.

Pixie's certain she's about to quit. 'Just say it,' she says abruptly. 'Get it over with.'

Alice turns her gaze on Pixie. 'Stop panicking, Pix. You're wearing yourself out and wasting all your energy on it. Let me help you with the planning—'

'I'm supposed to be the business head. You're the creative genius.'

'I don't know anything about business, but I'm willing to learn,' says Alice.

'The biggest problem is not having Gloria on the production side of things. She could pull everything together, like that,' says Pixie, clicking her fingers. 'She knows everyone, and people trust her. She wouldn't accept not getting credit. She knows how to be pushy.'

'This is exactly what I mean. You're going over and over the same problems. We don't have Gloria, but we can ask her for advice, can't we? She didn't say we can't ever speak to her again. I'm sure she'd be happy to give us some direction.'

'That's true, I suppose,' Pixie agrees, a little annoyed she hadn't thought of that.

'I think you're taking the idea of "going it alone" too seriously. We're in this together. We should be working everything out together. You help with the designs, so why shouldn't I help with the business side of things?'

Pixie knows what Alice is saying makes sense, but there is some part of her that needs to prove something. Is it to prove to her parents that she's a competent adult, or to the world that she's a business whiz? It seems childish when she thinks of it like that, but that doesn't make it any easier to let go of.

'So, the "Summer of Love" range we talked about?' says Alice.

'Last night I did three designs that we can make quickly and cheaply. They're on my desk.'

Pixie gets up and brings the sketches back to their sunny spot. The designs are quite different from anything they've done before. Alice points out the features and adds, 'I was thinking, there's a man down at the markets who sells cabbage . . .' She pauses. 'You know what that is, don't you?'

'I know what a cabbage is, yes,' says Pixie, a little irritated.

Alice laughs. 'Not the vegetable. That's what they call the bits of spare fabric, offcuts or end of bolts that big manufacturers have left over. At Empire they don't have much waste, and that's mainly down to Maria's expert cutting. But it's a big rort in some of the larger places. And it sells cheaply at the markets.'

Pixie has never even heard the term. 'There's enough fabric to make a dress?'

Alice nods enthusiastically. 'I've designed these so we can have one fabric on the front and a contrasting one on the back.' She points to one of the drawings. 'This one could have different fabrics in the flounces in the skirt, and the sleeve. The Summer of Love range will have fringing and beading, uneven hemlines, fabric flowers . . . easy and cheap – and fun.' She stops. 'What's wrong? Don't you like them?'

'I do. They're gorgeous. I just can't stop thinking about the samples Dottie stole. They were so good. Now we're starting again.'

'Forget about them, Pixie. That's in the past. These designs are quick to make. Why don't we start with them and build up from there?'

Pixie turns to the empty showroom. 'It's so daunting to have to fill this whole space.'

Ignoring her, Alice continues. 'I think we should ask Maria if she can cut the patterns for us. Cash in hand. I'm sure she'll do it.'

'All right,' agrees Pixie, pushing herself to be enthusiastic. 'I'll call her.'

37

HAZEL BACK IN BUSINESS

Hazel gasps for breath. Her eyes snap open to find Betty's worried, tearful face hovering over her. Sunlight streams into the room. Hazel has vague, confused memories of dark water, the glaring lights of a hospital room, and kind voices in the background.

'Hazel! You're awake! Oh, thank goodness. Say something.'

'Hello, Betty dear,' says Hazel. Her voice comes out as a croak.

Sitting down on the bed, Betty takes her hand. 'How do you feel?'

'Not too bad. Happy to be alive.'

'You could have died of hypothermia. I can't imagine how you ended up in the water. I feel terrible,' Betty says tearfully. 'When I came home and you weren't there, I went to bed, so involved with my own problems. Silly little problems. I'm so selfish—'

Hazel holds up her hand to stop the flow of words, but Betty continues railing against her own insensitive behaviour. 'I'm so sorry, Hazel,' she says finally. 'I've brought you some clean clothes.'

'Forgiven, Betty dear. Now . . . I need you to help me with two things. I'd like to go home as soon as possible. And I need you to contact Detective Dibble. Could you ask him to come and see me at his earliest convenience?'

'They need to check your blood pressure,' says Betty. 'I'll go and find a nurse. Then we'll be off. Just wait there.'

Hazel sits up and looks around. She's in a ward with four beds, two of them occupied by sleeping patients and one empty. Almost as soon as Betty's gone, a man walks in, looks at each of the beds and then walks over to hers. 'Hello, Mrs Bates,' he says.

'Do we know each other?' she asks.

'Pickles, the nightwatchman at the docks. Just wanted to make sure you were all right. You were in a terrible state last night.'

At first Hazel doesn't remember this man at all. He's a weathered-looking fellow, with thinning grey hair, and if the pulpy nose and broken veins on his face are anything to go by, he enjoys a drink or two. Then she recalls his shocked expression in the yellow light of the nightwatchman's shed.

'Thank you, Mr Pickles. I probably owe you my life.'

He grins. 'I reckon you do. I thought you was drunk at first, then I see you're wet through. Put you straight in a taxi. Better than waiting for the ambulance.'

'I'm very grateful. And I'll make sure you're paid the fare.'

He brushes the offer away. 'No charge from the taxi. All's well that ends well, as they say. Funny time to take a dip in the harbour,' he says. 'Did you fall in or what?'

'No . . . no, I was thrown in the deep end, so to speak.'

'What were you doing out there at night?'

Hazel hesitates. 'I was just having a wander around. Silly, really. So you were at the gate all evening?' she asks.

'That's right. No one gets in or out without my say-so. Don't know how you got in.'

'Did anyone leave the docks before I turned up?'

He shakes his head. 'Normally there'd be crew on shore leave coming and going until the curfew at midnight. But right now there's not many ships in port, so it's quiet. No reason for people to be on the quay at night.'

Despite her jumbled thoughts, Hazel's ears are still doing their job. Pickles is lying, and she wonders why he's really here.

Mr Mulligan waits at the hospital entrance in his brewery van. Seeing Hazel, he gets out and helps her in. She slides along to the middle of the seat and Betty squashes in beside her.

'Quite a scare you gave us, ol' girl,' Mr Mulligan says, crunching into gear. 'What made you take a swim in the harbour at that time of night?'

'It wasn't voluntary, I assure you.' Hazel turns to Betty. 'I left my handbag in the office, so I'm wondering how they came to contact you.'

Betty smiles. 'You had a card from Boots 'n' All in your pinny pocket. Remember you took your shoes for new heel plates? They called and got our number. They'll be your lucky shoes from now on.'

'Bloody lucky yer still got feet,' chortles Mr Mulligan. 'Probably too cold for sharks this time of year. Not for tea ladies though, eh?'

'It's really not a joking matter,' says Betty coolly.

'I survived,' says Hazel. 'We might as well find some humour in it, I suppose.'

Betty says nothing but, when they're home, comments that Mr Mulligan's joke was in very poor taste. She insists Hazel sit on the sofa in the front room with her feet up and the gas fire on full blast, and she tucks a rug around Hazel before bringing her a pot of tea and two slices of date and walnut roll.

'Nice to be spoiled, dear,' says Hazel. 'But I'm really feeling fine now.'

'You can't be too careful,' cautions Betty. 'I'm going to get your wet clothes into the washing machine before they start to smell.'

'Before you do, can you check the pocket of my pinny for a folded hankie? Don't unfold it, whatever you do.'

Betty goes out for a moment, returning with the damp hankie. 'This is very mysterious, Hazel. Is it a clue?' She starts at a knock on the front door.

'You'll find out soon enough,' says Hazel.

While Betty's answering the door, Hazel flings off the rug and moves to her favourite armchair. A moment later, Dibble stands in the doorway, his face full of concern.

'Now, what have you been up to, Mrs Bates?'

'Something very silly, I'm afraid,' admits Hazel, directing him to the sofa.

'Let's hear it,' he says, sitting down.

'You remember I was curious about why Mr Cooper chose the spot he did,' she begins. 'Well, I may have found a clue, which I'll come to in a minute. I heard the *Cape Argus* had been released and would leave tomorrow – well, today now. And I wanted to take a look myself before it left.'

Betty comes back with tea and cake for Dibble and sits down to join them.

'You thought you'd explore on your own at night?' asks Dibble, shaking his head.

'That was very reckless,' adds Betty.

Dibble agrees. 'The ship has already been thoroughly searched. Why not come to me if you had any suspicions?'

'I didn't have any evidence. I knew it was my last opportunity to see the ship.'

'So this is to do with the Krugerrand robbery?' asks Dibble.

Hazel nods. 'But it could be more than that.'

'That would be enough,' says Dibble, settling back with his tea.

Hazel explains how she searched the ship, found nothing and was then thrown overboard. 'I didn't see who threw me over, but it was definitely two people – I was lifted up and bundled over so fast. This morning at the hospital, I spoke to the nightwatchman, Mr Pickles, and according to him, no one came or went. But I think he was lying.'

She picks up the hankie and carefully unfolds it to show Dibble the tiny stone. 'I found this a couple of days ago. I thought it could be a diamond.'

He takes it from her and peers at the stone. 'It's possible. I'm no expert, but I'll get it checked out. Where did you find this – on the docks?'

'Fallen into the timber decking where Mr Cooper used to wait for his birds. And you remember there was that note left by Mr Beauchamp.'

Dibble is silent for a full minute. 'So, if this turns out to be a diamond—'

Hazel nods. 'Our friend Mr Beauchamp may not be as squeaky clean as people seem to believe.'

38

IRENE GETS TO WORK

At 4 am on Sunday, Irene and the Neck sit in his car parked in Chapel Lane, silently smoking cigars and staring into the dark street outside.

'S'pose I'd better get on with it then,' says Irene, not keen to get out for a few reasons. Mainly the cold and the risk of getting stabbed to death by Malteses.

The Neck hands her a couple of tiny tubes of glue. 'You won't need any more. Just a drop in the locks. It'll take you less than a minute each.'

'How come I'm doing all the work?' grumbles Irene. 'You sit here all safe and warm while I risk me flamin' neck.'

'You'll be less noticeable. Also I'm driving the getaway car,' he says with a grin.

'Think yer funny, do yer?' says Irene, scowling at him.

'The whole job will take ten minutes. Got the list of house numbers?'

Irene tucks the tubes in her coat pocket and gets out the list. She peers at it in the dark. 'There's ten houses here. Reckon that's enough glue?'

'Yes, a little goes a long way. Don't get it on yourself – it's potent. Got your gloves?'

Irene holds up the white cotton gloves she used to wear to church. 'May as well get it over with,' she says, opening the door. 'Yers better bloody be here when I get back.'

'You can rely on me,' says the Neck.

'Yeah, right.' Irene gets out and quietly pushes the door closed. She tucks the list into the pocket of her coat and buttons it to the neck. She doesn't make a sound as she walks down to Woods Lane in her rubber-soled slippers. Not a whisper.

During business hours, Woods Lane is a lively spot. Tarts stand in the doorways, calling out cheeky comments to blokes wandering up and down, gawping and drooling. It's full of life and a darn sight safer than it is right now. Right now she could get shot down here and no one would know.

The front doors of the terrace cottages all open straight onto the street, so it'll be quick and easy to put a dot of glue on each lock. Irene feels around for the list and finds nothing but the hole in her pocket. Blasted thing. Lucky she put the glue in the other pocket. They were only planning to sabotage Joe Borg's houses, but she figures she might as well do every door in the lane.

Standing in the shadows, she fumbles around with the top of the first tube of glue. The gloves are slippery, and she takes off the right-hand one. Now she's got glue on her finger and wonders what 'potent' means. She puts the glove back on and squeezes a tiny bit of glue into the first lock. One down.

By the third house, the fingers of the left-hand glove are all stuck together. She tries to take it off and discovers one of her fingers is glued to the glove. She'll have to sort it out later. Keeping her mind on the job, she moves quickly from door to door, popping a blob of glue in every lock along the way.

When they're all done, she hurries back to where the Neck was parked and is relieved to see him still waiting there. She sneaks up the side of the car and taps on the driver's window – and is well rewarded for her efforts.

'Who's funny now?' she says, getting in the car.

Her backside barely touches the seat before he takes off.

'How did you go?' he asks.

Irene shrugs. 'No problem. Didn't see no one.'

'You didn't get any glue on yourself, did you?'

'Course not,' says Irene. In truth, the right-hand glove is stuck to her middle finger, and her left ring finger, middle finger and pinkie are all stuck to each other. 'Yer quite the gentleman, aren't yer?' she says, glancing at him. 'Yer married?'

He gives an amused snort. 'You're barking up the wrong tree, Mrs Turnbuckle.'

'Ah, yer bat for the other side then? Could'a guessed.'

His eyes dart to her and back to the road. 'How?'

'Yer nails are too clean for a bloke. And yer smell nice.'

'Is it really your business?'

'Mate, I'm a tea lady. Everything's me business. Makes sense is all I'm thinkin'. I mean, no risk of yers sampling the goods at Miss Palmer's.' Irene considers the possibilities. 'Yer interested in a bit a blackmail?'

He frowns. 'Am I interested in being blackmailed? No, but thank you for asking.'

'Nah, I mean there's potential, is what I'm saying. Yer know the punters at 555. Yer hang out with pretty boys in Darlo and know all the blokes in high places with dirty secrets. I've got a bit of experience in that area, as it happens.'

'I think we should just concentrate on this task. If you don't mind.'

'Don't mind at all,' says Irene, admiring his manners and minding her own.

At home in her attic room, she discovers the sleeve of her coat is glued to her wrist. No matter how hard she pulls, the thing won't come off. When she gets into bed, the coat comes with her, lying across the covers like a shadow attached to her hand. Still worth it. She can't help but grin, picturing the chaos when Woods Lane opens for business this afternoon – or doesn't open for business. Them Malteses will be hopping bloody mad.

After a nap, Irene heads around to Glade Street to find Hazel and Betty all cosied up in the front room by the gas fire, knitting and listening to a talk on the radio.

'What's goin' on?' Irene asks. 'Thought knitting was Merl's department.'

'We're making baby layettes for the auction,' explains Hazel, pointing out a pile of knitted bits and pieces all in pink, blue and yellow.

Irene had completely forgotten about the auction for the little no-hopers. 'I could auction off a couple of my old wigs,' she suggests.

Betty makes a face. 'I'm not sure people would go for those, Irene. I don't know why you even have them. I've never seen you wear one.'

'Probably yer didn't recognise me,' says Irene.

'What have you been up to, Irene dear?' asks Hazel, giving her a shrewd look.

'Nuthin',' says Irene. 'Not a thing.'

'Judging by your guilty expression, I very much doubt that,' says Betty. 'Are you aware Hazel nearly died of hypothermia?'

'Mild hypothermia,' corrects Hazel. 'I took a night-time dip in the harbour.'

'Someone push yers?' asks Irene. 'Who?'

'Not just pushed me, threw me.' Hazel pauses. 'I don't know, but I intend to find out. Are you staying, Irene? If so, why don't you take your coat off, dear? I was just about to make a cuppa, and Betty's made her special lemon drizzle cake.'

'In a minute, but I got a bit of a problem needs sorting out first.' Irene takes her glued hand out of her pocket and holds it up. It looks like a claw now.

Betty leans over for a better look. 'What on earth have you done?'

'Glue,' says Irene. 'Glued me bloody fingers together. And glued me coat to me arm.' She gets out the other hand with a glove dangling off it.

Hazel doesn't seem surprised. 'Betty, why don't you get your nail varnish remover, and I'll organise tea and cake. Then you can explain from the beginning, Irene.'

Irene agrees, more than happy with this plan.

Hazel comes back with the tea and Betty gets to work on the glued-up bits.

'Gawd that stinks,' complains Irene.

Hazel agrees. 'A nasty chemical smell.'

'Yer remember how I was worried about them Malteses?'

'*Not* the sweet ones,' confirms Betty.

Ignoring her, Irene explains how she and the Neck cooked up a plan (it was more him than her, but he's not here) and she'd gone out in the dark and glued all the locks shut.

'So, they'll have to have all the locks drilled out,' says Hazel.

'If Borg suspects Miss Palmer's behind it, won't that make things worse?' asks Betty.

'Nah, there's a second bit of the plan. The Neck has a mate at *The Mirror*. He's gonna feed him a story.'

'Oh, yes?' says Hazel, as if she doesn't have much faith in the Neck.

'Remember that fella? You know the one, he's the big banana up Kings Cross,' says Irene, racking her brains.

'Mr Borisyuk?' suggests Hazel.

'Yeah, that's him. The Tsar. The Neck's mate is puttin' out a story that the Tsar's the one tryna put Borg outta business. *The Mirror* love that stuff, can't get enough of it.'

'Turn the villains on each other,' murmurs Hazel. 'Interesting strategy.'

'He's not just a Neck, he's got brains as well,' jokes Betty, applying one last dab of nail varnish remover to Irene's finger.

'I reckon. That'll keep 'em busy for months.'

Irene wiggles her fingers, enjoying having them back in action. Betty offers to mend the hole in her coat pocket, so Irene settles in for a second cup of tea and another slice of cake.

39

BETTY'S SECRETS REVEALED

When Irene's gone home with her fingers all in working order, Betty suddenly bursts into tears. And much as Hazel would do anything for her friend, after her recent ordeal in the harbour, more water is not what she hoped for right now.

'I have a confession to make,' Betty sobs. 'It's so awful.'

'Betty dear, I think it's time you told me what's going on,' Hazel says gently.

Betty takes out her hankie, mops her face and blows her nose. 'I'm just so embarrassed . . . so ashamed. I don't know how this happened. I've made a complete and utter fool of myself . . .' Her words are lost in another flood of tears.

Hazel leans over and puts a comforting hand on her arm. 'You have no need to be ashamed or embarrassed with me, Betty. You are my dearest friend. Whatever it is, you already have my understanding.'

Betty nods and dabs at her eyes. 'It all started when Lucy joined the firm.'

'And very quickly became your friend,' confirms Hazel.

'You're right, Hazel. Too quickly. I was flattered and it went to my head,' says Betty. 'When I was young, lots of people wanted to be friends with me. People thought I was pretty and fun.' She stops as if the memory is painful. 'Then, without me even knowing it, I became invisible.'

'You're still pretty and fun, dear, and don't forget: invisibility is a special power—'

'Hazel, please don't try to make me feel better. You don't know what I've done, how silly and naïve I've been. I've humiliated myself, and probably brought tea ladies into disrepute.'

'I'm sure that's not true but tell me. Get it off your chest.'

'I took all my clothes off in front of people. Not just ladies, men too. There!'

Hazel is momentarily stumped by this extraordinary confession, especially from someone as modest as Betty, and she wonders if the recent drinking played a part. 'I can't quite imagine how this might have happened, dear.'

Words tumbling over each other, Betty explains how much she admired Lucy, so liberated and intelligent and open-minded, how flattered she was by the interest and attention. Not just from Lucy, but other people in the house too. They thought Betty had interesting things to say, and they particularly admired and envied her working-class background.

'If I can just stop you there for a moment,' Hazel says. 'What did they admire, exactly?'

Betty sighs. 'The struggle of working people, the proletariat. Salt of the earth.'

'I see. Go on,' says Hazel, bemused.

Betty continues the tale of her downfall – the parties, the drinking and the dancing – until she reaches the night in question. 'I didn't realise a life class involved . . . nudity.'

'Neither did I. So don't blame yourself there.'

'I thought they were going to paint my portrait, like the Queen. I wore my best blue frock – the one that brings out the colour of my eyes. Then I was sent behind a screen. Everyone waiting. I thought I was going to be sick – there was no getting out of it. I wore a robe at first . . . but then, well, I knew everyone thought I was being silly and childish. Lucy had all these artist friends there, and I was embarrassing her. So in the end I . . . I just did it.'

'I'm sure you looked splendid, dear,' says Hazel. 'I don't see any reason for shame. I think it was very brave of you.'

Betty shakes her head miserably. 'A lot of the pictures were nice, flattering, but this one fellow made me into a horrible caricature. He had everyone laughing. I was a joke.'

Hazel frowns. 'And what did Lucy say about this?'

'I don't know. I left straightaway and haven't seen her since,' says Betty.

'It sounds to me as if you were shoehorned into that situation, so I don't think you should be so hard on yourself.' After a moment of thought, Hazel asks, 'What do you think could make you feel better about it all?'

'To get another job and never have to see her again?'

'I'm not sure that's practical, especially when you think how long it took me to get another job. And there's no reason why you should have to make that sacrifice.'

'I suppose not,' says Betty.

Hazel picks up her knitting. After a moment, Betty does the same and they work in silence. The day outside has darkened and rain begins to fall, softly at first and then heavily. It bounces off the windowsills and gurgles down drainpipes, and Hazel's concerns turn to the broken roof tiles and the capacity of the buckets in the ceiling.

'What I want is that awful drawing destroyed,' Betty declares suddenly. 'And I'd like Lucy to apologise for humiliating me. And then I never want to see her again.'

'All right. That's a good start. Do you have her phone number?'

Betty turns pink. 'What, tell her now? Could you do it, Hazel? Please?'

Hazel slowly shakes her head. Betty's mouth pulls down at the corners.

After another bout of silent knitting, Betty gets up and walks out of the room. A few minutes later, Hazel hears her on the phone in the hall saying, 'This is Mrs Dewsnap.'

The conversation is short, and Hazel doesn't catch most of it. Betty comes back looking crestfallen and sits down on the sofa. 'She said I was being silly and taking it too seriously; it was a caricature. And that *awful* man is a very well-respected artist who's had exhibitions in galleries.'

'And what did you say to that?' asks Hazel.

Betty's head droops. 'Nothing. I just hung up.'

'Ah, well – at least she's got the message,' says Hazel. 'That's half the job done.'

Betty nods glumly, clearly feeling no better for having spoken to Lucy.

When Hazel arrives at Trades Hall on Monday morning, Yvonne looks up from her typing with a shocked expression. 'Mrs Bates. We didn't expect to see you today.'

'It would take more than a dip in the harbour to stop me,' says Hazel, curious that the news has travelled so fast.

'Did you fall in, or what? I heard you were in the hospital and nearly died.'

'Just a brush with hypothermia, but I'm back on deck now,' says Hazel breezily.

'Well, that's something. What about Rex? Have they charged him?'

There's something in Yvonne's tone that makes Hazel suspect she secretly likes the drama of having her boss arrested. Perhaps it's something to boast to her friends about. Hazel is noncommittal; it's not up to her to keep everyone up to date.

Passing through the office, she gets more attention than usual. Everyone seems to have heard the news. Teddy follows her down the hall to the kitchen for a private chat.

'I'm surprised that so many people know about the incident, and so quickly,' says Hazel, as she assembles the trolley.

'It's not every day a tea lady goes in the drink. Pickles has been spreading it about that he saved your life. What were you doing there at night?'

'It's a long story,' says Hazel evasively.

'I remember you said you couldn't swim,' he says. 'I'm amazed you survived. You could have suffered the same fate as Cooper.'

Hazel feels a chill at his words. She tries to remember who else was present when she and Rex had that conversation the day Cooper's body was found. Teddy obviously. Someone else, the bookie? Or one of the other fellows in the office?

'Perhaps you shouldn't go down to the port office again,' he says. 'You don't want to put yourself in harm's way if someone's got it in for you.'

'That's assuming someone pushed me,' says Hazel, glancing over at him.

'It's pretty obvious. You wouldn't go for a paddle voluntarily. You must have been poking your nose into something, and someone doesn't like it.'

Now she thinks about it, Teddy would have something to gain from Rex being out of the way. There could be a step up the ranks for him. The executive committee might have their own ideas but Teddy's known to be more moderate in his politics than Rex, so perhaps he's a desirable candidate to replace him.

'Rex thinks that having a tea lady down there one day a week is good for public relations,' says Hazel. 'That's what he asked me to do, and I intend to continue until I hear otherwise.'

Teddy shakes his head, obviously annoyed. 'Well, there's duty and there's being stubborn for the sake of it. If you want my advice, at the very least, stop poking your nose into things that don't concern you.'

Hazel forces a smile. 'I'll take that advice on board. Thank you.'

Teddy walks off, leaving Hazel to wonder why he's interested and what exactly he wants her to keep her nose out of. From now on she'll be keeping a close eye on him.

40

BETTY PUTS HER FOOT DOWN

When Betty arrives in the haberdashery section with morning tea, Lucy comes straight over to her. 'It's done,' she says. 'As you asked.'

'What exactly?' asks Betty in the coldest tone she can muster.

'He brought the drawing over and I burnt it myself. It's gone. Perhaps it didn't seem respectful to you, but he's made a sacrifice. His drawings sell for hundreds. I don't think you understand caricature.' She pauses. 'You will still come back and visit us, won't you? We all love you.'

'I think not,' Betty says, handing her a cup of tea.

The other staff in the section are looking over at them curiously, and Betty shudders at the thought that Lucy might start blabbing to them.

'I would appreciate you not mentioning this to anyone,' she whispers to Lucy.

'Could we at least discuss it?' asks Lucy. 'It's important to me.'

Betty shakes her head. She decides she'll collect the cups later and wheels her trolley into the hallway. Lucy follows her. Betty pushes the trolley briskly down the hall, but Lucy keeps pace beside her.

'I wanted this to be an awakening for you, Betty,' she says. 'The beginning of a love affair with your own body, so you can be truly liberated and free.'

Betty gives her a horrified glance and picks up speed. She breaks into a light jog, now worried about slipping on the polished lino floor.

Lucy matches her pace. 'There's nothing to be ashamed of. No one should ever be ashamed of their body!' she cries, loud enough for everyone to hear.

When Betty stops suddenly, the crockery keeps going, rolling and crashing all over the trolley. She only just manages to stop the urn tipping over. Turning to Lucy, she says in a quiet voice, 'For your information, that's not what I'm ashamed of. I'm ashamed I let you talk me into doing something I did not want to do. And you knew perfectly well I didn't want to do it. That just wasn't important to you.'

Lucy falls silent. Tears spring in her eyes. But Betty's too angry for tears. She quickly straightens the crockery and walks on without another word.

Over a delicious dinner of corned beef with mustard sauce, mashed potatoes and peas, Betty describes the scene. She adds a few dramatic touches for effect and enjoys Hazel's helpless laughter at the image of the two of them racing down the hall, neck and neck, the trolley rattling along at high speed.

'Very impressive,' says Hazel, mopping her eyes. 'You must be proud of yourself for telling her how you really felt.'

'I feel like such a dope for getting mixed up in it all in the first place, like a silly teenager. I don't know what I was thinking,' says Betty. 'I just lost myself for a while there. I'm glad it's over. I was out of my depth.'

Hazel gazes at her fondly. 'Well, I'm glad you're back, Betty dear, because I need your help to sort out this situation with Rex. I'm getting nowhere on my own.'

Hazel pours two glasses of mulberry wine and Betty fetches her notebook.

'You know I'm always careful not to leap to conclusions, thinking that things are necessarily connected,' says Hazel. 'We have a number of clues that I think *may* be connected, but there's no evidence as yet.'

Betty waits, poised, while Hazel gathers her thoughts and continues. 'I'd like to step through it, starting at the beginning, if you don't mind. Two things started it all. Detective Dibble told me about the missing gold coins – the Krugerrand. And Mrs Fletcher asked me to help find her son, Cliff. At that point the two things were not connected but were brought to my attention because of my new job.' Hazel takes a sip of wine and thinks about it. 'So that was coincidental because of the location. Mrs Fletcher heard Cliff could have found work on the docks. The people I asked all denied having seen him, but when I visited Rex in hospital, he implied that this lad was the person who assaulted him. Everything points to Cliff working for someone that no one wants to cross—'

'Which is why they denied any knowledge,' confirms Betty, making a note. 'Has Rex told the police about Cliff?'

'I don't know,' says Hazel. 'You would hope so, but whether they've found him or not is another question. Then we have Cooper, the pigeon man, murdered on the wharves, closely followed by the murder of the trader and owner of the stolen gold, Beauchamp. I think those two may have been connected by a smuggling racket.

So, if Beauchamp was not who he appeared to be, what else could he have been involved in? The robbery itself?'

Betty makes silent notes, not wanting to disturb Hazel's train of thought.

'Then I find the gun hidden in the kitchen cupboard, which happens to be the murder weapon in a bag belonging to Rex. I'm certain that bag was left peeking out so that I would spot it. It makes absolutely no sense for Rex to hide such an incriminating piece of evidence in the building, let alone so carelessly.'

'But why would they want you to find the gun?' asks Betty.

'To add credibility,' says Hazel. 'The union staff know I'm an old friend and great supporter of Rex's, so my finding the murder weapon adds extra weight.'

It crosses Betty's mind that Hazel does have a blind spot when it comes to Rex and she seems to be the only one convinced that he's innocent. Betty's eyes stray to this morning's paper sitting on the dresser and the headline, *'COMRADES IN CORRUPTION: Widescale rorts by union bosses revealed!'*

Hazel follows her gaze. 'It seems that the press is eager to convict Rex,' she says. 'They've even brought up his wife's death in a motor accident many years ago, now questioning his involvement. He was behind the wheel when they were hit by a drunk driver. He's always blamed himself for not being able to avoid the accident. It's appalling that the papers should dredge that up now. He presents a threat to a lot of powerful people – all the way to the Premier himself – and they're looking for an opportunity to break his grip on the union. So don't take too much notice.'

'I trust your judgement, Hazel,' says Betty, and she means it.

'We're dealing with a shrewd operator. Someone on the inside who knows that making Rex the scapegoat suits a lot of different people. And that redirecting police efforts will take attention away from the real culprit – or culprits.'

'What about these people throwing you in the harbour, Hazel?'

'I haven't forgotten that. Were they trying to kill me, in which case they would have knocked me out first, or did they just want to scare me off? It makes me wonder if there is still evidence on the *Cape Argus*,' muses Hazel, getting up to take their plates to the sink.

Betty reads out her list. 'Gold robbery . . . Mrs Fletcher missing Cliff . . . pigeon man Cooper murder . . . Beauchamp murder . . . Rex fingerprints, framed . . . Hazel scared off.' She stops and looks up at Hazel.

'I'm far from scared off,' says Hazel.

'And . . . where are the Krugerrand?' Betty adds that to her list.

'We're back to that. The key to everything,' says Hazel.

41

PIXIE STRUGGLES ON

Driving around town on errands, Pixie has a thousand worries on her mind. Top of the list is that Alice will leave and go back to Empire. Pixie can't shake the idea and keeps coming back to it over and over. The thought of it makes her chest hurt. Second on the list is that she will end up in debt that could take her years to repay and be humiliating.

She and Alice had so many ideas for decorating the showroom and fitting out the workroom upstairs. Pixie is supposed to make these things happen but so far all she's done is fly around like a bee in a bottle, not making any progress at all. She only has herself to blame, but it doesn't help to know that.

She arrives at the shop to hear Alice chatting to someone in the back room. She could not be more surprised to find Mrs Beauchamp, elegant as ever, sitting at the worktable having a cup of tea.

'Pixie! I'm so glad you're back. I was worried I'd miss you,' says Mrs Beauchamp. 'I heard about your boutique and wanted to see for myself.'

'Oh, that's nice,' says Pixie, tongue-tied.

'I was just looking over Alice's drawings and marvelling at the originality of them.'

Pixie nods. 'I know. She's brilliant.'

Mrs Beauchamp gestures to a chair and Pixie obediently sits in it. She starts to relax as they look through some of Alice's designs and Mrs Beauchamp exclaims over them. Then the older woman puts her cup down very slowly, and Pixie knows from their previous meeting that it's time for business.

'Look, I understand you're having a bit of a struggle getting the show on the road,' says Mrs Beauchamp. 'Quite understandable. You've taken on an ambitious project.'

Pixie gives Alice a betrayed look and gets an embarrassed shrug in return. It's not like Alice to be blabbing. Mrs Beauchamp must have charmed it out of her.

Mrs Beauchamp picks up one of Alice's most colourful designs and holds it up. 'I adore this outfit. What are you calling it?'

'It's a jumpsuit,' says Alice. 'An all-in-one, like overalls.'

'According to Dottie it's a children's playsuit,' says Pixie.

Mrs Beauchamp laughs. 'I don't agree with that. Women wore this type of suit in the war because it's comfortable and practical. Does anyone else have designs like this?'

'In London, yes. It's based on a Biba design,' says Alice. 'But I haven't seen any here.'

'I think it's an absolute winner – young women will go mad for it.' Mrs Beauchamp lights a cigarette and leans back in her chair, as if she has all the time in the world.

Pixie picks up the drawing and examines the design again. It's a long-sleeved jumpsuit in a psychedelic pattern of purple, pink and blue with a pointy collar, a zip down the front and flared bell-bottom pants. She'd loved it when Alice first showed her but, with Dottie's comments and the business worries, she'd lost confidence in it and put it aside for something safer.

'As I'm sure you know, I've been going through a very difficult time with the death of my husband and all the attention in the press and interest in his business – not to mention the gold robbery.' For a moment Mrs Beauchamp looks sad and tired. Then she forces a bright smile. 'I want to get back to the things I do the best and make a fresh start. I'd like to help you girls get this business started, and help it grow.'

Alice and Pixie exchange looks.

'What would that involve?' asks Alice cautiously.

'Business advice, if you're open to that. And . . . I might be interested in investing. I'd need to discuss that with your accountant and get a better picture, but that's a possibility.' Mrs Beauchamp gets a tiny gold case out of her handbag, stubs her cigarette into it and puts it back in her bag. 'I wouldn't involve myself in the actual designs. That would be left completely to you. I can see you know what you're doing.'

'So . . . my parents would have nothing to do with it?' asks Pixie, wondering if this offer is too good to be true. 'It would be just you?'

'Just me,' Mrs Beauchamp reassures her. 'You don't have to make a decision now, of course.'

Pixie looks at Alice and gets a nod in return. Pixie can't believe it. This is the break they need – someone who's on their side, older and more experienced. There is no one in this city more influential with women than Mrs Beauchamp.

'We're definitely interested.' Pixie hesitates, not knowing how much to reveal but at the same time wanting to put her trust in the woman. 'We've been a bit lost, to be honest. We don't even have a name for the shop.'

Alice gets out a stack of papers. 'We have thrown some ideas around and I've done some logo designs,' she says, spreading the papers across her worktable.

Mrs Beauchamp picks up each design, considers it carefully and puts it down before picking up the next one. Finally, she holds one out. 'They're all good, but my vote goes to this one. Simple, tells you where it is, and I think it's memorable.'

'Vine Street Boutique,' says Pixie, to hear how it sounds. It's perfect.

42

HAZEL GETS A NASTY SURPRISE

'Your friend Mrs Fletcher – she is back,' says Mrs Babinski, pushing a bucketful of carrots in Hazel's direction with her foot. 'Not here. I see her downstairs.'

'She's staying in the hotel section this time?' asks Hazel, taking off her coat.

Mrs Babinski purses her lips and nods slowly, as if to imply something sinister when all it really means is that Mrs Fletcher has money to spend on accommodation this time. Hazel wonders what's brought her back to town.

Mrs Babinski gives Hazel a shrewd glance. 'You don't believe this lady.'

'It's not that she's a liar exactly, she just left some important details out of her story.'

Mrs Babinski gives a grunt of laughter. 'Lies, these are the weeds hiding in the flowers. The liar is good, we cannot see the difference.'

'I'm sure you're right,' says Hazel. 'Perhaps she wasn't deliberately dishonest.'

'Mrs Bates, I work here many years. I meet many different people. They make dishonest thoughts. No one tells me: "This is my fault. I make mistake or I make bad decision." No, no, it is always some other person is needing blame of the trouble.'

Hazel puts on an apron and picks up a handful of carrots. 'I know what you're saying, but many of the women here have escaped from violent husbands. That's not their fault.'

'Make mistake to marry this idiot man. Bad decision.' Mrs Babinski shrugs. 'Chop the carrots small for stew,' she adds. 'I have mutton neck. Very nice.'

Hazel gets to work. Ten minutes later, Mrs Fletcher herself appears in the doorway. 'Mrs Bates?'

'You not to come in here, madam.' Mrs Babinski waves a bloodstained cleaver at her. 'Is dangerous. For staff only.'

Hazel wipes her hands and goes out to talk to Mrs Fletcher in private.

'I came to tell you to stop looking for Cliff,' says Mrs Fletcher, sounding agitated.

'Oh, has he been found?' asks Hazel. 'That's wonderful news.'

Mrs Fletcher nods. 'Yes, he got in touch with me. I'm seeing him this evening.'

'And where has he been all this time?' asks Hazel.

'He was fine. He has a good job. He was just too busy to get in touch.'

Hazel's ears are tingling but it's impossible to tell which of these three statements are weeds and which are flowers.

'Well, it's quite normal for a mother to worry,' Hazel says sympathetically. 'It's a shame he couldn't have let you know earlier. When he knew you were looking for him.'

Mrs Fletcher sighs impatiently. 'There was that letter. I feel embarrassed about asking you to look for him. He's very annoyed about it.'

'Is he now? How does he know I was looking for him?' asks Hazel.

'Just stop asking about him, all right? And can I get the photograph back from you?'

'Of course,' says Hazel. 'It's in my bag, I'll get it.'

Impatient now, Mrs Fletcher says, 'You can leave it at reception on your way out.'

'Will do,' says Hazel. 'I'm glad you found him.'

The woman gives her a cursory nod and walks off.

In the kitchen, Mrs Babinski looks up with interest. 'She has weeds or flowers for you, Mrs Bates?'

'Weeds, I'm afraid,' says Hazel.

Mrs Babinski gives a knowing smile. 'After carrot is celery. Don't take out strings. Is all food by grace of God.'

Hazel goes back to the carrots, wondering what that conversation with Mrs Fletcher was really about. She'd been instructed to get Hazel out of the picture — but why?

When the carrots are done, Hazel gets stuck into the bunches of celery, chopping at high speed. When she's finished, she tells Mrs Babinski she has to leave early this evening. The cook heaves a great sigh, as if disappointment is all she's ever known in this world. But as Hazel puts her coat on, she comments, 'Take care, Mrs Bates. May God watch over you.'

Hazel thanks her and hurries downstairs. At the main desk, she asks for an envelope and puts the photo of Cliff inside. 'Is Mrs Fletcher in?' she asks. 'Perhaps I could give this to her personally.'

Glancing at the register, the clerk turns to study the board behind him, which is covered in room keys on hooks. 'Yes, she is.

There's a phone in the hallway but not in the room, so it might take a while.'

'Never mind.' Hazel passes the envelope over and thanks him. Buttoning up her coat, she goes outside to wait across the street.

Fifteen minutes later, stamping her feet and clapping her gloved hands together to keep warm, Hazel has begun to wonder if this is a waste of time. However, she's very curious to know what's really going on with Mrs Fletcher so decides to wait another ten minutes.

The time is almost up when she sees Mrs Fletcher in the foyer handing over her key and collecting the envelope. She sets off along the street and Hazel follows, staying on the other side and hanging back a little. They leave the central city area, heading towards Millers Point, in the direction of the port. The streets are empty and darker now. Hazel stays close to the tight rows of workers cottages and terrace houses, all packed together and following the line of undulating streets.

Finally, Mrs Fletcher pauses in front of one of the cottages. There are houses on one side of the street, and on the other is a cast-iron fence atop a cliff, with the port down below. She gets a note out of her pocket, perhaps to check the address, but continues to stand in the street for a couple of minutes as if she's nervous about entering. Then she knocks on the door. It opens quickly and she steps inside.

Hazel hovers in the shadows. If Mrs Fletcher is being reunited with Cliff, she could be in there for hours. Hazel walks past the house and makes a note of the number. She passed a phone box down the street and decides to call Dibble to report Cliff's whereabouts.

As she walks back to it, she hears voices behind her and turns to see the front door of the house open, Mrs Fletcher roughly thrust out into the street, and the door slammed behind her. Mrs Fletcher stands there for a moment, as if she can't believe what just happened.

Hazel quickly glances around for cover. Beside her is a row of terraced flats with external stairs leading to an upper balcony that runs the width of the building. She ducks in and up the stairs. From the balcony, she watches Mrs Fletcher walk on past, her head lowered, sobbing quietly. There's no point in tailing her now; the meeting is over and clearly didn't go well. But was it Cliff, or someone else who threw her out of the house?

Hazel glances at her watch. It's a little after six-thirty. Normally she would be home by now. Betty will be worried. She goes down the stairs and along the street to the phone box she passed earlier. By some miracle it hasn't been vandalised and the light even works. Hazel finds a coin in her bag and calls home.

'Oh, Hazel,' Betty answers breathlessly. 'I was starting to worry.'

Hazel explains what's happened and asks her to make a note of the address Mrs Fletcher visited. 'I'll ring Detective Dibble now and wait here for him.'

'I'm worried, Hazel. Couldn't you call him from home?'

'Don't worry, if he doesn't answer, I'll come straight home.'

Hanging up, she hears the tap of footsteps approaching. A second later, a face appears, staring at her through the glass, and Hazel realises she's stumbled into terrible trouble.

43
HAZEL CAUGHT IN A TRAP

The face disappears into the darkness. The footsteps break into a run. Taking out her lipstick, Hazel quickly scrawls a name on the window. She opens the door and dashes back towards the city as fast as her legs will carry her.

She's barely got a hundred yards before she hears the roar of an engine.

A white van pulls up beside her and two people leap out. One throws a blanket over her head and the other grabs her from behind, roughly tying her wrists together. She's shoved into the back of the van and her ankles are tied together.

They take off at speed. Hazel, lying on her side, bumps along on the hard metal floor, trying to stop herself sliding around. She can hear her kidnappers talking in the front. The man she assumes to be Cliff Fletcher, but the woman's voice is all too familiar.

'She's the nosy old lady who's been asking about you!' shouts Yvonne. 'Why is she here? How did she find you? What have you done?'

'You told me to make my mother stop asking questions,' says Cliff. 'I couldn't speak to her at the hotel, so I got her to come—'

'You're a bloody idiot. Now we've got to get rid of this one! How stupid can you get? She must have followed your mother.'

'All right, all right. Stop shouting. It's not my fault. Who is she anyway?'

'She's the tea lady,' says Yvonne bitterly. 'Now she knows everything.'

'I don't really get it,' says Cliff in a bewildered voice.

'The one who's trying to get Commie Rex out of trouble. Just shut up and let me think,' says Yvonne. 'We can't afford another body turning up right now. But we have to get rid of her.'

'Can't we just keep her at the house?' asks Cliff. 'We're leaving tomorrow night.'

'Too many stickybeaks around here,' argues Yvonne. 'It was a big risk grabbing her. Anyone could have seen. She was making a phone call. Bugger. This is your fault.'

On the brink of making an argument for herself, Hazel decides to remain silent. Anything she says is only going to enrage Yvonne, and she runs the risk of being gagged. She will save her energy for whatever comes next.

'We could take her out to sea – throw her overboard,' suggests Cliff.

'Too complicated,' says Yvonne. 'Too risky.'

'What about—'

'Just shut up, will you? I need to call the boss. Pull over near that pub . . . Not under the streetlight, you dunce. Up the street where there's no cars. I don't know why I've got to tell you everything.'

While Cliff's parking the van, Hazel peers out the back window, trying to work out where they are exactly.

'You may as well come in,' says Yvonne. 'And lock the van.'

'All right,' says Cliff testily. 'You don't have to tell me everything. Do we gag her?'

'You got a scarf? Hankie?'

'Not on me,' admits Cliff.

'Forget it. No one will hear her from here. She's not going anywhere.'

When they've gone, Hazel rolls around painfully on the floor until she manages to get on her knees and then prop herself into an uncomfortable seated position. With her wrists and ankles tied, there's not much more she can do. The only things in the back of the van are a toolbox and a couple of old blankets. She wriggles around and tries opening and then kicking at the back door, but it doesn't budge. The street is empty. Not one passerby to call for help.

In the dim light, she spots her handbag flung in the corner, and shuffles on her bottom over to it. Positioned with her back to it, she fumbles at the clasp until she gets it open, then she feels around inside for her lipstick. Once the tube is in her grasp, she pushes the bag as far under a blanket as she can.

Hazel is in no doubt now that Cliff was Rex's assailant, but Yvonne's involvement is a complete shock. It's clear from their conversation and the deferential way he spoke to her that she wields the power. It seems she's his boss, but not the big boss.

The two of them arrive back, bringing the smell of beer and cigarettes with them. Cliff glances over at Hazel, sitting with her back against the side of the van. 'Should we blindfold her?' he asks.

'Got a blindfold?' asks Yvonne furiously. 'Stop making stupid suggestions. She's already seen us, you idiot. Anyway, she won't be telling anyone. You've made your last cup of tea, Mrs Bates.'

Cliff starts the engine. 'I feel bad about getting rid of a sweet old lady.'

'She's not sweet. She's bloody annoying.' Yvonne lights a cigarette. 'We'll be doing her a favour putting her out of her misery. It's terrible being old, you know. Life's not going to get any better from here on.'

'Life's going to get a lot better for me,' says Cliff with a bark of laugher.

'Yeah, all right. Just get on with it,' snaps Yvonne.

They drive in silence for twenty minutes or so, arriving in a suburb Hazel doesn't recognise. Yvonne instructs Cliff to stay where he is and disappears inside. Five minutes later she comes back and tells him to get moving.

'Got it?' he asks.

'Yes, of course. Now get cracking,' she says.

They drive on and, when they eventually slow down and stop, Hazel can see out the back window that they're down near the port, pulled up at the gates.

Yvonne gets out and greets the nightwatchman. 'We've got some pamphlets to drop at the office,' she tells him.

'Is that right?' says a voice Hazel recognises as belonging to Mr Pickles. 'Funny time of night to be doing it.'

In the silence that follows, Hazel can only assume money is changing hands.

'That'll do nicely,' says Pickles. 'I'll get this gate open for you.'

Once on the dock, they head in the opposite direction to the office, stopping at one of the wharves, where Yvonne gets out.

Hazel can't see much through the back window. Twisting around, she gets on her knees and, through the windscreen, can see Yvonne unlocking the huge sliding doors of Shed 5.

Finding the door is too heavy to move, Yvonne gestures urgently to Cliff to come and help, and he gets out. Hazel's fingers curl around the tube of lipstick, slide off the top and give the case a couple of turns. With some difficulty, and working backwards, she does her best to write the number 5 on the white metal floor. She only has a moment to wriggle around and check it's legible and to push the lipstick under the blankets.

Cliff drives the van into the shed, then the two of them slide the door shut from the inside. Now Hazel is completely trapped. She takes a deep breath to keep a calm head.

The back doors of the van open. Yvonne holds a torch and Cliff tries to work out what to do. 'I can't carry her like that, bent backwards.'

'Just put her over your shoulder,' snaps Yvonne.

Ignoring her, Cliff unties Hazel's wrists, reties them at the front and lifts her out.

'Go on then, where to?' he asks aggressively.

Yvonne leads the way with the torch and Cliff follows, carrying Hazel in his arms like a child. They weave their way through crates and boxes stacked high, collapsed piles of loose papers and folders, army blankets tied with rope, and broken crates overflowing with books.

'No one ever comes in here. It could be months before they find her body. Or years,' Yvonne comments.

Hazel tries to take in as much as possible. She knows that these enormous goods sheds are filled and emptied constantly by the tides of imports and exports flowing through them, every item scrutinised by customs officers. But, if the thick smell of rats and the layers of filth are anything to go by, the goods in this warehouse have been here for a very long time. Yvonne is probably right. No one comes in here.

When Cliff stumbles against a broken crate, Hazel takes the opportunity to push one shoe off in the wild hope that someone might come looking for her.

'Here we go. Stick her in here.' Yvonne opens the door of a wooden wardrobe.

'She's not going to fit in there,' argues Cliff.

'Just put her in and stop arguing.'

Cliff obediently lowers Hazel gently onto the floor of the wardrobe. It's clear to Hazel that he doesn't want to do this. He is her one hope right now but she stays silent, waiting for her opportunity to speak and make her words count for something. Waiting for a moment alone with him – but how could that happen?

'Seems a bit cruel,' he says. 'Do we have to kill her?'

'Do you think it's better to starve to death?' asks Yvonne. 'Where's the gun?'

'Um . . . in the glovebox,' he says.

'Oh, for God's sake! You're so frigging disorganised.'

'You were rushing me! I can get it, okay?'

Leaving the wardrobe door open, they walk off arguing, their voices receding into the distance. A faint hope rises in Hazel's heart that they'll change their minds and just leave. She'd have a chance to get out and possibly find a way to break the ropes binding her.

But a few moments later, the torchlight appears again, bobbing along. Cliff's dark shape comes into view and then he's standing over her with a pistol.

Hazel looks up at him and speaks for the first time in the last hour. 'We haven't been introduced, Cliff. But my name is Hazel Bates.'

'I don't care, lady,' he says, levelling the gun at her head.

Hazel speaks calmly and quietly. 'You should know the name of a person you murder. I will be on your conscience every day for the rest of your life.'

He hesitates. 'Shut up, will you?'

In the distance, Yvonne shouts for him to hurry up.

'Your mother asked me to look out for you. She was worried about you,' Hazel explains. 'I was concerned—'

Cliff leans in, pressing the barrel of the pistol to her head. 'Shut up. I don't care. It's your own fault for sticking your nose in other people's business. There's nothing I can do.'

'Of course there is—'

'Shut up,' he says again. But still he hesitates, his face contorted.

'I'm a mother, and a grandmother. That's why I wanted to help Flo find you.'

'Hurry up. What are you doing?' screams Yvonne, her voice closer. 'Get on with it!'

Cliff's hesitancy and agitation tell Hazel that he might have given Rex a beating, but he's never pulled the trigger on someone. She has to give him a way out.

'Cliff, even if I could escape from here, it would take me days. You'd be well clear by then,' she says quietly. 'My blood will be on your hands, not Yvonne's. She won't even know you didn't pull the trigger on me.'

Yvonne shouts at him again. He reacts by violently kicking the wardrobe door shut, leaving Hazel in complete darkness. She hears the key turning in the lock, then two shots are fired into the door at close range. The explosion is deafening and she can't hear anything for a good minute. She's aware of a sharp pain in her shoulder but, in the blackness, can't see anything.

A few minutes later, she hears the thudding of the shed door sliding open. The van drives out and the door slides closed again.

44
BETTY CALLS FOR HELP

After Hazel's call, Betty can't settle to anything. She sits down to work on her knitting and the next minute finds herself standing at the front window, watching the street. Did Hazel manage to reach Dibble? If she had, she would have given him the address, not waited around all night. Either way, she should be home by now. It's after ten.

Betty finds Detective Dibble's number in the teledex on the hall table and calls. No answer. That tells her nothing. Coming up with another plan, she puts on her coat, goes next door and knocks at the Mulligans' door.

Maude answers it. 'Something wrong, Mrs Dewsnap?'

'I think Hazel's in trouble,' says Betty.

Maude beckons her inside and Betty explains the situation, recounting her last conversation with Hazel. 'She gave me the address of the house this Mrs Fletcher visited.'

'I reckon we go down there ourselves. We can take Dad's van.'

Maude pulls on her coat and swaps her slippers for shoes. She calls out that she's giving Mrs Dewsnap a lift, and Mrs Mulligan shouts back to drive carefully.

The little Morris van with 'Tooheys Brewery' painted on the side is parked on the street. They get in and Maude flicks on the interior light. She pulls a map book out of the glove box, hands it to Betty and they set off.

With trembling hands, Betty flicks through the book. The thought of something happening to Hazel makes her feel panicked and teary but she pulls herself together. She needs to be strong and concentrate on guiding Maude through the city to Millers Point.

They drive slowly until Betty spots the phone box Hazel must have called from. Maude pulls over and stops the car.

Getting out, Betty can see they're on the top of a cliff, looking down over the wharves and harbour, all in darkness with a sprinkling of lights. She goes into the phone box, finds a coin in her bag and calls home to see if Hazel's arrived. She listens to the sound of the phone ringing in the empty house. As she waits in hope, she casts her eye over the dozens of names scratched into the paintwork and on the windows, wondering who all these people are and why they feel the need to make such a mess.

'Any clues?' asks Maude when Betty gets back into the van.

Betty shakes her head, a lump rising in her throat. 'This is all my fault. I've been so selfish, gallivanting around thinking I'm twenty again and not paying attention and letting Hazel down . . . We always did everything together, and now something terrible's happened.'

Maude pats her on the shoulder. 'We don't know anything bad has happened, Mrs D.'

Just then a white van speeds past, does a U-turn and parks across the road in front of a row of houses. A young couple get out, walk inside and close the door.

Betty sighs. 'She's not here. I've brought you on a wild goose chase.'

'What was the street number she gave you?' asks Maude.

Betty gets out the note she made. 'Two forty-two.'

'I'll go and check which one it is.'

Maude pulls a torch out from under the seat and gets out of the van. She crosses the road and works her way along.

A few minutes later she's back. 'It's the house those two people went into.'

'Do you think she could be in there?' asks Betty. 'She wouldn't go willingly. This fellow Cliff Fletcher is dangerous by all accounts.'

Maude thinks about it. 'They just came back from somewhere, so if they have her, it doesn't make sense that they would leave her and go out. I suppose there could be someone else in the house. I think we should check out the van first.'

Maude gets out, crosses the road and looks around the van.

'It's locked,' she says, getting back in the car. 'I could probably break in, but then I might lose my job . . .'

Betty wonders when Maude became so grown up that she started overcomplicating things. They need to find Hazel, that's all that's important. But there's no point in arguing, and Betty does not want Maude to lose her job. 'We need Irene,' she says.

'Good thinking,' says Maude, starting the car again.

Betty hurries into the Thatched Pig, which is crowded with suspicious-looking men. More than one of them look at her as if she's the first hot dinner they've seen in weeks. She glances around for Irene's wizened little face, long black coat and her usual hat. She notices the fellow they call Big G sitting in the corner with another man who looks like his bodyguard. They're the sort of men Betty usually goes to great lengths to avoid, but not tonight.

Ignoring all the gawkers and grubby invitations, she goes over. 'Excuse me, Mister . . .' Betty falters. Mr Big doesn't sound right, and she has no idea of his name. 'Mister G. I'm wondering if you've seen Mrs Turnbuckle in here this evening?'

Both men stare at her blankly, then Big G asks, 'You are?'

'Mrs Dewsnap.' Betty offers her hand, only to be ignored. 'A tea lady friend.'

Big G pulls a face. 'Bloody tea ladies. They're everywhere.'

'Like cockroaches,' suggests his offsider.

'Or spring flowers,' says Betty, with a tight smile.

'She just left,' he says, nodding at the back door.

Betty thanks him and goes outside to the small parking area. No Irene.

She loops around to where Maude is waiting. They drive around the nearby streets and eventually find Irene sitting at a bus stop with a large square object wrapped in a towel on her lap.

'Irene!' calls Betty, opening the door and half stepping out. 'We need you!'

'What for? Goin' home to watch me telly,' Irene says, staying put.

Betty goes over. 'Hazel's missing. We need your help.'

Irene peers past her into the brewery van. 'Is that Mr Mulligan driving yers around?'

'No, it's Maude.'

'If yer got the girl copper on the job, why d'yer need me?'

'Please, Irene. It's important. I'll explain on the way. We can drop you home with your telly after. Save you getting it on the bus.'

Irene thinks about it and gets up reluctantly. 'I s'pose.'

Betty opens the back doors of the van and they tuck the television safely inside a beer crate. Betty then slides into the middle seat, and Irene takes the outside one.

'What was that you put in the back?' asks Maude.

'Won the chook raffle,' says Irene, not missing a beat.

'Big chook,' says Maude, with a snort.

'Reckon,' agrees Irene. 'What's goin' on?'

As they drive back to Millers Point, Betty explains the situation to Irene. 'Have you got something to pick a lock with?'

'Yers want me to break in with a cop as a witness? Is this a joke, or what?'

When Irene lived with Hazel, she'd become friendly with Maude. She often boasted about 'taking the girl under me wing', which meant teaching her dodgy things like lock-picking. But when Maude joined the police force, Irene's opinion of her went downhill and stayed there.

'Mrs Turnbuckle, I'm off duty and this is unofficial—' begins Maude.

'All right.' Irene digs around in the pocket of her pinny, brings out a couple of thin metal picks and squints at them. 'Usually keep something handy for emergencies.'

They arrive at Millers Point and Maude parks down the street from the van. 'I'll keep watch,' she says, handing Betty the torch.

Irene gets out her flask and takes a swig, shaking the last drop into her wide-open mouth. 'Not exactly how I planned to spend me evening,' she grumbles.

'Your chook will still be here when you get back,' says Maude.

'Me what? Oh yeah. Let's go.'

Betty holds the torch and keeps an eye out while Irene opens the door of the van. Flashing the torch around the interior, Betty can see tools and some old blankets.

Irene gives her a sharp poke in the rib and hisses, 'Hurry up, will yer?'

Betty notices an S written on the white metal floor. She shines the torch on it and touches it with her finger; it's greasy and pink. Prodding the blankets aside with the torch, she gives a gasp at the sight of Hazel's handbag. She lifts up the blankets and shines the torch underneath. There's a tube of lipstick. The colour is Sweet Cerise. Hazel's lipstick.

45

NO WAY OUT FOR HAZEL

It takes all of Hazel's mental stamina to breathe slowly and keep herself calm so she can think clearly. Her wrists are tied tightly, but at least they're in front of her, not behind as before. Even working in the dark, untying her ankles is not that difficult. Freeing her wrists will be harder.

Her neck is excruciating from being hunched in an unnatural position. Her shoulder throbs but she's fairly sure the bullet only grazed her. It would be much more painful if she'd been shot.

Her hands are not as flexible as they once were; arthritis has crept in over the years. She focuses all her efforts on using the fingers of one hand to tug at the knot binding her wrists. When that hand tires, she swaps to the other and back again, on and on. Persistence wins the day, she tells herself, and it calms her to be working on her release.

After a while, she feels a loop has formed and continues to pull at it, digging in with the tips of her fingers to open it out. A few more tugs and the rope falls away and her wrists are free. She rubs her arms and shoulders to get the circulation going.

Reaching inside her coat to touch her throbbing shoulder, she finds the fabric of her dress is stiff with blood. She could weep with fatigue but can't afford the time or spare the energy. The fear of dying in this box is stronger than the exhaustion.

She pushes at the door, but it's definitely locked. She tries to remember if the wardrobe was up against a wall. If she positioned her back against one side and her feet on the other, could she rock back and forth and tip it over on its side? The worst thing that could happen would be it falling forward – then she would be in a coffin. She tries kicking at the side of the wardrobe, but she's so cramped it's hard to get any momentum or force.

She had almost no time to examine her prison before being plunged into darkness, but generally wardrobes have a solid timber door with some decorative work or a mirror on the front. The unseen parts, the sides and the back, are usually made of a cheaper, more flimsy material that might possibly break on impact. Pulling her knees up, she rocks backwards and forwards, throwing her weight against the side wall, dreading the moment it might tip over. But it's a very stable piece of furniture. It doesn't even budge.

Exhausted from her ordeal, she leans back to rest for a moment. She's thirsty and the wardrobe is dark and airless. To keep her spirits up, she tries to imagine Betty finding the name she scrawled in the phone box and calling Detective Dibble for help. But it's a stretch to believe they could put all the pieces together and find her. All she can do is hope.

She remembers something she once heard about survival times: three minutes without air – she has a little air – three days without water, three weeks without food. The last one she won't have to worry about.

She closes her eyes, gathering her strength. Disappointingly, her life doesn't flash before her – perhaps that only occurs in sudden near-death experiences. For Hazel, it's quite the opposite. She realises she forgot to put the bin out, and wonders if Betty will remember it. When her thoughts return to the present, it's to reflect on possible reasons why this shed is packed to the rafters with useful things that have somehow been forgotten. She suspects the existence of these goods has been forgotten between government departments, and the rent is being paid with taxpayers' money.

Finally, back to her current predicament. While she would have preferred to pass away somewhere more pleasant and among friends, she doesn't fear death as she might have expected. Her thoughts are with the people left behind. The mystery of her disappearance will haunt them for the rest of their lives. Even when her body is eventually found, the question of how she got here will remain unanswered, the culprits long gone.

Norma has her own family to comfort her, but Hazel *is* Betty's family, and Irene's too for that matter. Her disappearance will break their hearts. The important places in their lives will never bring the same pleasure. Their regular table at the Hollywood Hotel will always have an empty chair. With a pang of nostalgia, Hazel remembers the many companionable evenings they have shared together in her front room. Ordinary times, unremarkable and taken for granted. While she would never consider herself an important person in the world, she's an important person in their world – a responsibility that hardens her resolve to escape this dark prison.

46

IRENE FINDS A TREASURE

Irene's squashed in the front seat of the grog van between Betty and Maude, all sitting in a row like the Three Stooges. One of them is blubbering over a lipstick and it's not Irene.

'Now that we have the evidence of Hazel's possessions, we should try Detective Dibble again,' says Maude, sounding worried.

'Yeah,' Irene agrees. 'Let's get proper coppers onto it.' She wonders how long it will take to set up her telly and what's on at this time of night.

'They could have thrown her in the harbour!' wails Betty.

Irene's had enough. 'Jesus wept. Yer were the ace detective. Now yer a big cry-baby.'

'It's just I've never had to do this without Hazel!'

Irene gives her a little pat on the knee. 'There's three of us, yer dope, not just you.'

Betty stops crying and blows her nose. 'All right,' she says, getting out her notebook. 'Read out the number plate of the van, and I'll make a note and call Detective Dibble. I'm sure he'll help.'

Maude reads out the plate and asks, 'Do you have his home number?'

Betty nods. 'It's in my address book.' She pats her handbag. 'Come with me, Irene.'

'The bloody phone box is right there,' argues Irene. 'We can watch yers from here.' She suddenly notices the door of 242 opening. 'Get down!'

They slide down in their seats out of sight. Irene takes a quick peek and sees a woman walking along to the phone box.

'She's makin' a call,' Irene informs the others.

'Now what?' asks Betty, squashed on the floor.

'She's still making a bloody call. I'll tell yers if anything changes.'

'Thank you, Irene,' says Betty.

'We could just drive off,' suggests Maude, half under the steering wheel.

'Too suspicious,' says Irene. 'All right. She hung up. She's just standing looking at something in the phone box.'

'What's she looking at?' asks Betty.

'Dunno. Now she's having a bit of a clean-up,' reports Irene. 'Wiping the glass with her sleeve. All right, she's finished. She's going back in the house.' Irene gives Betty a nudge. 'G'on, now's yer chance.'

Betty gives a frightened squeak, but she gets out of the car and jogs over to the phone box. Irene and Maude watch her make the call and hang up.

'Now *she's* staring at something on the window,' says Maude, puzzled.

'Quite the detective, aren't yer?' says Irene.

Betty gets back in the car, out of breath. 'That woman was trying to rub off a name written on the window in lipstick!'

'You've lost me,' says Maude.

'Sweet Cerise! Hazel's lipstick! She wrote the name "Yvonne". I saw it earlier! It's all smeared, but you could still see it and spelt incorrectly with one 'n' – you know Hazel's spelling is not the best.'

'Who the hell is Yvonne?' asks Irene.

'I don't know.' Betty stares at her own finger. 'And the letter S was written in pink lipstick on the floor of the van.'

Irene's losing patience. 'What does it all mean?'

Betty sighs. 'I have no idea.'

'No answer from Detective Dibble?' asks Maude.

Betty shakes her head. She gets out her notebook and scribbles away while she talks. 'Clue number one, Hazel's handbag. Number two, the name "Yvonne" and number three, the S, both in Hazel's lipstick. We've got a registration number and an address.'

'And we can establish that Hazel was in that van,' says Maude. 'But since Detective Dibble's not around, I think you two should go down to Central Station and report it.'

Irene's tired and desperate for a smoke. 'Who's gunna believe us?'

'Oops, get down!' snaps Maude, sliding back under the steering wheel.

Irene and Betty bang heads as they scramble onto the floor. Car doors slam and headlights sweep past as the white van drives off. Maude scrambles back into position and starts the engine.

'Hold on, ladies!' She swings into a U-turn and takes off after the van.

'Yer don't think they might notice being followed by a grog van?' asks Irene.

'Maybe they will, but it's worth a try,' says Maude.

'Don't s'pose there's any booze in the back, is there?' asks Irene, peering over her shoulder.

'Irene, may I remind you that we have a job to do?' says Betty, annoyed.

'Little sharpener wouldn't hurt.' Irene twists around. Half-kneeling, she feels around behind the seat. Her hand finds a wooden crate and in it a cardboard box.

'Irene! Just sit down, will you? We're on the Harbour Bridge!' cries Betty. 'You'll end up through the windscreen.'

Ignoring her, Irene leans back over and opens the cardboard box. Inside the box are tiny little bottles. She lifts a handful out and drops back into her seat.

Maude glances over. 'One of Dad's sidelines for private hotels.'

Irene can't believe her luck. In her lap are half-a-dozen tiny bottles of Scotch. She offers one to Betty, who shakes her head angrily. But Irene knocks back three of them and pops the others in her coat pocket for later. This adventure is getting better by the minute. Not as good as watching her telly, but not as bad as five minutes ago.

Now they're driving through narrow streets on the north side of the harbour.

'They're heading into Waverton, by the looks of it,' says Maude.

Maude's not bad at this tailing business, ducking behind other cars but keeping the white van in sight. When the van turns down a small street towards the water, Maude drives on and parks further down the street. 'Now we go on foot,' she says.

'On second thought, I'll have that drink now, thank you, Irene,' says Betty.

Irene hands one of the bottles to her. Betty gulps it in one and gets out of the car, spluttering and coughing.

They follow Maude back to where the van turned off. The

street is short and steep, ending at the water, and the white van has disappeared.

'Stay close to the fence line,' whispers Maude as they walk quietly along the street.

There are only three houses here. The last one, closest to the water, has a high brick wall with tall wrought-iron gates. Behind them is a very fancy-looking house, the sort of place where old people with old money live. The white van is parked on the driveway.

Maude beckons and they follow her down to a small sandy beach. They can see from here that the house has a private dock. And tied up to the dock is a good-sized yacht. Irene's no expert on boats but this one looks top notch, all polished wood and tall masts. Probably sleeps a few, in comfort too. You could sail pretty much anywhere in the world in a boat that size.

'Now what?' Irene asks.

'We need to get help,' says Maude in a worried voice. 'Urgently.'

47
HAZEL FIGHTS FOR HER LIFE

This wardrobe was once hung with clothes but now the only smell is of wood and glue, and the faintest whiff of mothballs. Hazel wonders how long it will be before she runs out of oxygen. There might be a tiny amount leaking through the joints in the timber and a slight gap under the door, but not much. More activity means more oxygen expended. She has to use it wisely. She gathers her strength, then pushes her feet against the side of the cupboard again, feeling hopeful at the slight flex of it. She regrets dropping that shoe; she could use it now.

She tries again, pushing her feet with all her strength against the side. It flexes but comes nowhere near breaking. There's not enough force behind it. She takes off her remaining shoe, which has a low heel with a brand-new heel plate. She tries using it like a hammer to weaken the timber and then drags it like a scraper. Her shoulder throbs with pain.

After some time, she feels the roughness of broken fibres under her fingertips. All she needs right now is a small hole to let some air in.

On and on she works, stopping now and then to gently touch the surface, taking care not to pick up a splinter. Eventually she has shredded an area the size of a football.

She puts the shoe back on and, with great difficulty and pain, twists herself around into a different position, imagining herself like a baby turning in the womb. Once she's on her hands and knees, she feels around for the roughened patch and gives it a tentative kick with her shoed foot. It lands awkwardly. She needs to hit it harder with her heel.

She gathers herself and kicks hard with every bit of strength she can muster. On the fourth or fifth attempt, she hears a slight cracking sound. Energised, she kicks at the timber again and again. When her right foot is too painful to go on, she swaps the shoe to her left foot and continues. Now every kick rewards her with a cracking sound until, finally, her foot goes right through the side of the cupboard.

All that effort has yielded the reward of a hole a little larger than her foot. At this rate, to make one the size of her body will take days. But with some fresh air and a sense of hope, she twists back to the seated position and uses her shoe to hammer at the splintered plywood, pulling shreds away with her hands.

Her hands are soon bleeding and her whole body in pain from the cramped position and wounded shoulder. She needs to rest and gather her strength for the next stage. She makes herself as comfortable as possible and, as she closes her eyes, her thoughts turn to Betty. She focuses her mind and endeavours to send a telepathic message, but the problem with telepathic messages is not knowing whether they're received. What she does know for certain is that Betty will be looking for her. This will be the biggest test of her friend's detective skills yet.

48

BETTY ON THE CASE

When Betty tries Detective Dibble again he answers, sounding cross and half asleep (not surprisingly at one in the morning).

'Hazel's missing,' Betty tells him. 'Something bad, really bad, has happened.'

Twenty minutes later, Maude, Betty and Irene sit across from him at police headquarters, recounting everything they know so far about Hazel's disappearance. Dibble peppers them with questions about times and locations and asks Maude to write up the report.

'She could be anywhere, but given the episode with her being thrown into the harbour, it's possible that Mrs Bates has been taken to the docks area,' he says. 'We'll get someone down to talk to the nightwatchman. We can certainly impound the van. You left the handbag in there?'

'Where I found it,' Betty confirms.

'And the messages were in the lipstick belonging to Mrs Bates?'

Betty puts the tube of lipstick on the table. 'Sweet Cerise. Her favourite colour.'

'All right,' he says. 'We can bring in Cliff Fletcher for questioning now we have his whereabouts. And hopefully this Yvonne person.'

'Do you think the mansion in Waverton is part of it?' asks Maude.

'Hard to know, but since the van was there, that might be grounds to search the property. You'll have to be patient, ladies,' says Dibble. 'With Mrs Bates' disappearance this has become more complicated. We need to be careful we don't get into a hostage situation, and we can't afford to rush in and scare them into hiding. I need to consult my superiors. I suggest you go home. Get some sleep and we'll be in touch.'

'Oh, Hazel, where are you?' Betty asks herself aloud. She lies in bed, tears dripping onto the pillow as she tries to order everything in her mind. Hazel's last words. The bag with the gun. The name scrawled in the phone box. The white van. Everything's all jumbled up and makes no sense. She knows that Hazel is depending on her, but where does it all lead?

She falls into a disturbed sleep and wakes to a gloomy day, rain threatening. With renewed determination, she calls in sick, has a fortifying bowl of porridge and sets off to the wharves.

She's never had reason to visit the waterfront before and had no idea of the scale of the place. There are any number of offices and huge two-storey warehouses lining the docks and the many jetties. There are enormous cargo ships in port and the whole place teems with men and trucks unloading goods.

Keeping out of the way of the workers, Betty asks a man for directions to the Dockside Union office.

'See that sign? Shed 2,' he says, pointing through a maze of buildings. 'Go past that and then you'll see the office straight ahead.'

Betty follows his instructions and quickly finds the union office. Entry to the offices is barred by a long counter, but there's no one in attendance. She gathers her courage, ducks under the counter and continues into the office. There's only one fellow at his desk and he glances at her briefly and without interest.

'Hazel's away today,' explains Betty, trying to keep the nervous wobble out of her voice. 'I'm taking her place.'

'Kitchen's down there, last door,' he says, nodding towards a hallway.

The kitchen door is locked, and she goes back to the office to ask the fellow for a key.

He shrugs. 'No idea. Yvonne will be here shortly. She'll have one.'

Shock runs through Betty's body like an electric current pinning her to the floor. The man doesn't seem to notice her reaction.

'Take a seat if you want,' he says, turning back to his work.

Betty stands there for a good minute, not knowing what to do. Should she call Dibble from the office? Not if this Yvonne is about to arrive. She'll leave and find a phone.

She goes back out through the front office. As she lifts up the counter to make her exit, a woman walks in through the door. Betty only saw her briefly in the phone box from a distance, but there is no doubt in her mind that this is Yvonne.

'Can I help you?' Yvonne asks.

Not a single response comes to mind, and after an awkward silence, Betty says, 'No, thank you very much.' She forces herself to smile. 'Looks like rain, doesn't it?'

'I s'pose,' says Yvonne as she passes.

Stepping outside, Betty can hardly breathe. Large drops of rain splatter on the concrete. What to do? Get off the docks. Then call Dibble.

Following that thought, she half runs out through the gates. She spots a phone box further up the street and hurries towards it. She calls Dibble at headquarters but he's out. Betty explains to the operator that it's urgent. Very urgent. The woman takes the number of the public phone and says she'll try to contact him.

Rain is belting down now. Betty feels marooned, waiting in the smelly phone box for a call that may not come. She stares out through the filthy window. There's a high barred fence between the street and the waterfront, and her view is blocked by one of the long goods sheds running along the perimeter of the wharf.

She feels dismay at the thought that Hazel could be down here somewhere. It's like a city within the city, with hundreds of men moving goods to who knows where. Ships coming and going. Hazel could be anywhere. She could be taken away on one of those ships.

Fighting tears of frustration and despair, Betty watches the raindrops slide down the windows and waits. The rain finally stops. She steps out for some fresh air. Propping the door open so she doesn't miss the call, she wanders up and down outside.

Her gaze turns again to the long sheds on jetties that stretch out into the harbour; each has a number painted six foot high on the end of the building. Her jangled thoughts come to a sudden halt. Every shed has a number. Somehow that seems important. What does it mean? All the confused thoughts tumbling around in her head suddenly crystallise into one.

The phone rings. She rushes in to answer it.

'Mrs Dewsnap?' asks Dibble.

'Five! Not S! It's five!' Betty shouts. 'Shed 5! Hazel must have known where they were taking her and left that clue for us!'

Before he can respond, she slams down the receiver and hurries back through the main gates, passing all the sheds until she reaches number five. The giant sliding timber doors on all the sheds she passed were open, with workers going in and out, but Shed 5's doors are locked and bolted. She thumps pointlessly on the door with her fist, hoping for a response, but there's nothing. She walks around the entire shed and finds other entrances, but they're all locked too.

By the time she's completed the loop, Detective Dibble has arrived in an unmarked car, accompanied by another officer. Betty explains about the shed numbers, and he sends the officer over to the Maritime office for the keys.

While they wait, Betty tells him that Yvonne works at the union office.

Taking it all on board, Dibble radios for reinforcements while Betty waits anxiously. Finally a fellow from the Maritime office appears and unlocks the door.

'Doubt you'll find anyone in here,' he says. 'It's been shut up for that long.'

The shed is the size of an aircraft hangar and crowded with crates and cartons, hundreds, if not thousands, of them, piled high. Betty looks around, realising the enormity of the task of finding Hazel in here – if she's here at all.

'What is all this stuff?' Dibble asks the Maritime man.

'It's all earmarked for bush communities out in the middle of nowhere. The Education Department hasn't got around to sending it.

Been sitting here for a couple of years at least. Waste of taxpayers' money,' he grumbles, flicking on the overhead lights.

Betty and Dibble and the Maritime man spread out, trying to be systematic in their search. The sounds of sirens in the distance are getting closer by the minute, and Betty wonders if Hazel can hear them.

There are crates big enough to hold an entire family. Sacks filled with blankets that look horribly like bodies. Betty calls out Hazel's name over and over. When there's no reply she begins to fear the absolute worst. It takes all her strength to hold back tears as she looks around in despair. This search will take hours, if not days. They need more people on the job, many more people.

She cups her hands around her mouth and trumpets, 'Cooooeeeee! Cooooooeeee!'

Even if there was a response, it would be impossible to hear it with the commotion of sirens and people shouting outside. Betty calls again and again. Dibble must have had the same thought because she hears the thud of the doors sliding closed. The noise outside is abruptly silenced. Betty immediately hears a faint tapping sound from deep in the shed. Like a bird pecking on wood. She calls out to Dibble. Together they make their way between the crates and boxes, stopping now and then to listen.

Betty calls again. 'Coooeeee!'

Now the tapping is louder, a banging and the muffled sound of someone calling back.

'It's coming from this direction,' says Dibble, striding ahead.

Betty follows him to an old timber wardrobe against the back wall of the shed. The door is locked but, from inside, she can hear Hazel calling her name, then a hand reaches out from a hole in the side.

Overcome with emotion, Betty kneels down and clasps it in both of hers. 'Hazel. Oh, Hazel.'

'I knew you'd find me sooner or later, Betty dear,' says a familiar voice.

49

HAZEL SEES THE LIGHT OF DAY

From the loneliest place in the world, Hazel emerges into the blinding light of day and complete chaos. Police cars, lights flashing, are parked across the main gates. Uniformed officers hold back a crowd of onlookers who watch as Hazel and Betty are ushered into the back of an unmarked car. Dibble gets in the front.

'We'll go straight to the hospital to have that wound looked at,' says Dibble.

'How is Rex Shepperton?' asks Hazel.

'He's been discharged from hospital and is in custody. He was due to be questioned today,' says Dibble. 'Once you've been checked out by the doctor, we'll get you up to headquarters to make a statement.'

'Before we do that, where is the *Cape Argus* now?' Hazel asks.

Dibble turns to look at her. 'Why?'

'I had a lot of time to think in there, and I have an idea,' says Hazel.

'I understand it's gone into dry dock over at Cockatoo Island for repairs,' he says.

'Ah, of course. We need to go there immediately,' says Hazel.

'Can you tell me why?' asks Dibble.

'It will be quicker and easier if I show you,' explains Hazel. 'I could still be wrong.'

'You need to go to the hospital to have that wound dressed and then home for a nice bath and food,' says Betty, firmly.

'There'll be time for that, Betty dear. If I'm right, this will take an hour at most.'

Fifteen minutes later, Betty and Hazel are speeding across the harbour in a police launch with Dibble and three uniformed officers on board.

The day is fresh and bright, with a salty breeze blowing off the harbour that washes over Hazel, reviving her in body and spirit. She's concerned she could be wrong and wasting police time but is nevertheless enjoying being back in the world and very much alive.

Hauled up the slips, the *Cape Argus* is exposed as a knocked-about old vessel, its white-painted steel weeping tears of rust.

They all follow Dibble up the gangplank to the deck, which is littered with cranes and winches, just as Hazel remembers from her night visit. Then, at Hazel's instruction, they troop down the stairway to the lower deck and along the passageway to the captain's quarters.

As soon as she steps into the room, Hazel's certain that her theory is correct. The timber walls had previously appeared to be a permanent fixture. But looking carefully, it's clear to Hazel that they are made up of wide individual panels dovetailed into one another.

'Can we remove one of these panels?' she asks.

Dibble gives the uniformed police a nod. One of them levers off a panel and the other places it aside. Behind the panel is the painted metal wall. But Hazel's pleased to note that the panel was not fixed directly to the steel wall but to slim battens bolted in, creating a space of half an inch between the two surfaces.

She goes over to examine the wall and Dibble, looking mystified, joins her.

'Look here. Every six inches or so, there's a spot of black where something was glued to the wall and pulled off.' She scrapes at one of them with her nail and shows him the black velvet fibres. 'There are hundreds of them.'

'At regular intervals,' adds Dibble.

'There could have been a couple of hundred boxes glued to the wall behind this one panel. Imagine how many you could conceal in this room.'

A smile dawns on Dibble's face. 'Thousands,' he says. 'Close to seven thousand even.'

'I think this wall was constructed specifically for this purpose. Or perhaps it replaced an existing one. It looks quite new to me. When I was here last, I noticed the sharp smell of glue in this room, but didn't think much about it at the time. It's a precise job to remove and replace these panels so neatly, but Cliff Fletcher is a carpenter. He could have done it during the trip between Darwin and Sydney.' She points at some of the panels that have been jammed back in place. 'But he wasn't available for the removal of the coins, and the panels have been hastily taken off and replaced by someone much less skilled.'

Dibble nods. 'We have him in custody, along with Yvonne Cassone. The question is, where are the coins now?'

'I'll leave that to you, Detective,' says Hazel.

He turns away to instruct the other officers to find out who has visited the *Cape Argus* since it arrived at Cockatoo Island.

The captain needs to be brought in for questioning, the fingerprint team brought over, and the vessel put under police guard.

Back up on the deck, Betty asks Hazel how she's feeling. It's only now that Hazel realises her shoulder throbs painfully and every bone in her body aches. A crushing fatigue washes over her, making her feel almost faint.

'Grateful,' she says, with a sigh. 'And a bit tired. Let's go home.'

50
IRENE REAPING THE REWARDS

Irene's enjoying a Cuban cigar and a can of baked beans for breakfast when Miss Palmer walks into the kitchen at 555, holding a newspaper. She's frowning slightly, at the sight of Irene smoking client cigars or maybe because she doesn't believe in eating out of cans.

Irene gives her a friendly nod. 'Yer back then?'

'Maurice tells me you are something of a heroine,' says Miss Palmer.

Irene frowns. 'Who the heck's Maurice?'

'He's my driver. Did you never introduce yourselves?'

Irene shrugs. 'Nah, we got a . . . yer know, a professional relationship.'

'He tells me you saved my Chapel Lane house from being firebombed and likely saved Bunny's life. I wanted to thank you for your courage and quick thinking.'

Irene has a puff of her cigar. 'Don't say I didn't warn yers. I said them Malteses were gonna come after yers. Everyone knows about 'em.'

'I may have underestimated the situation. You did mention it, and I didn't take it seriously enough,' she says. 'I'm sorry.'

It occurs to Irene that there might be a bonus coming her way. She's busy calculating the possibilities when Miss Palmer adds, 'In future, feel free to help yourself to client cigars, Mrs Turnbuckle. But please stop substituting them with cheap ones.'

That's a better offer than anything Irene could have hoped for. 'Deal,' she says.

'I thought you might like to see this morning's paper.' Miss Palmer drops the newspaper onto the table.

MAFIA MADNESS!
Darlinghurst residents were too terrified to leave their homes last night as violence erupted between rival criminal gangs with members of the Maltese/Sicilian mafia, known as the 'stiddari' having declared war on Sydney's notorious crime boss, Alexander Borisyuk, a White Russian also known as the Tsar.

Two men were fatally injured in a shootout outside the Tradesman's Arms Hotel. An illegal brothel in Woods Lane, belonging to mafia boss Joe Borg, was firebombed in the early hours of this morning with no fatalities. A resident action group has called on the police to curb this growing threat that is endangering ordinary citizens going about their daily business.

Irene chuckles. All it takes to start a gang war is a tea lady and a tiny tube of glue.

51

IRENE DOES THE HONOURS

Saturday afternoon, Irene puts on her best hat and the button-up leather shoes she inherited from her mother. She takes off her pinny and puts on the dress she usually saves for funerals. She only has one coat, so that has to do.

She arrives at the registry office early and sits in the foyer watching all the suckers going in to get hitched. Blokes in borrowed suits. The girls in their best dresses, clutching bunches of flowers. Half of them likely up the duff and some already showing.

Sometimes mums and dads trail behind, no one speaking. They leave the registry office looking desperate for a drink. While Irene wouldn't mind a wrestle in the sack with a decent-looking bloke now and then, sitting here watching this lot makes her happy to be a free woman.

Bunny and Dimples arrive in the foyer holding hands, looking for all the world like movie stars stepping onto the red carpet. Lieutenant Watts wears a sharply ironed uniform, and Bunny has poured herself into a sparkly blue dress, the bleached hair up in stiff petals on top of her head. Both beam with happiness.

'Thank you so much for being our witness, Mrs Turnbuckle,' says Bunny.

Leaning down, she gives Irene a kiss, smelling like a flower shop. Irene puckers up for a decent smacker from Dimples, but he laughs and brushes a kiss on her cheek.

The three of them head into the registry office. After a bit of muttering from the registrar bloke, Bunny and Dimples repeat his words and they're hitched. The newlyweds, Irene and a staff member sign the papers and it's all over.

Irene half expected them to take her to the pub and shout her a drink or five, but Bunny explains they are off on a two-day honeymoon to the Central Coast before Dimples gets shipped back to Vietnam.

'Well, good luck to youse,' says Irene, hiding her disappointment.

Dimples hands her an envelope. 'Just to show our appreciation, Mrs Turnbuckle.'

'We wouldn't be here today if it wasn't for you,' says Bunny, with a smile.

Before Irene can bask in more compliments, the two of them run off hand in hand, pausing only for Bunny to turn and blow a kiss Irene's way.

Irene looks in the envelope to find a wad of twenties. She quickly slips it into her coat pocket and heads down the Thatched Pig to celebrate.

'Yer welded to that stool?' Irene asks, finding Arthur Smith in his usual seat at the bar, staring at his drink.

'I hope this is the full extent of our conversation,' says Arthur. 'I'm not in the mood for your witticisms today.'

'Mate, that was a proper question,' says Irene. She signals to the barmaid and orders a whiskey. 'Same for me friend here.'

Arthur stares at her, bleary-eyed. 'I'm struggling to imagine what would inspire generosity of such magnitude from you, Mrs Turnbuckle. Apart from the fact that you still owe me some forty-five dollars.' He glances down at her feet. 'And wearing actual shoes? Wonders will never cease.'

Irene takes a sip of her drink. 'Well, I started a bloody gang war, saved a brothel and just sent a soldier and his sweetheart off on their honeymoon. After that, he goes back to the war to be shot at. She'll probably end up preggers or run off with some other bloke. But I've done my bit.'

'Ah,' sighs Arthur. 'The wandering heart of things that are, the fiery cross of love and war—'

'No idea what yer on about. Everyone thinks they're a bloody poet these days.'

'GK Chesterton.' Arthur tips his glass to hers. 'To love and war.'

'To love and war,' repeats Irene, clinking glasses.

52

BAD NEWS FOR PIXIE

Pixie's battling to fit the jumpsuit onto the mannequin when Effie Finch strides into the showroom, as she often does on her way home from work.

'That's definitely a two-man job,' she says.

'And I'm not much help,' says Alice, watching on.

'Two would make it easier, thank you,' says Pixie. 'I'm worried about ripping it.'

Effie puts down her shopping bag and takes hold of the mannequin, allowing Pixie to slip the suit up the legs and onto the torso and feed the sleeves onto the arms.

'I wore one of these overalls in the fire service in the war. Didn't look as pretty as this one.' Effie looks around. 'I keep expecting to see this place populated with nice frocks.'

'Sore point,' says Alice.

Effie laughs. 'All right, I'll keep my dreams to myself.'

'It won't be long now,' Pixie assures her. 'The patterns are cut. We've got two sewing machines arriving this week, and we've hired a couple of machinists.'

Effie raises her eyebrows. 'Watch this space, eh? A couple of go-getters.'

Pixie smiles. Everything has changed in the few days that Mrs Beauchamp has been involved. She's given them business advice and negotiated credit with suppliers. More importantly, she's given Pixie the confidence to move forward with everything. It seems she's serious about investing her own money in the business, and Mr Levy is helping to work out the arrangements. But Pixie doesn't mention any of this to Effie. They're sworn to confidentiality. That's how Mrs Beauchamp does things.

'So what's happening to this little lady?' asks Effie, putting her arm around the mannequin's shoulders.

'We're going for dramatic effect in the window,' says Pixie.

Effie helps carry the mannequin over and, between them, they get it set up in the display window. Then they step outside to view it from the street.

'Hmm,' says Effie. 'She's a bit lost. Wait here, I'll be back in a minute.'

True to her word, Effie returns a few minutes later carrying a battered lamp on a stand. 'My dad's old work-light,' she explains. She carries it inside, plugs it in and switches it on, pointing the beam towards the mannequin.

Joining Pixie outside again, Effie says, 'I've got another idea.' She heads back home.

Pixie goes inside. 'She's got another idea,' she tells Alice.

'Well, that was a pretty good one,' says Alice. 'What do you think, Pix?'

Pixie smiles. 'I think it's good. It looks really good.'

Effie arrives back carrying her ladder and a bag of tools and brings them into the showroom. 'Let's get this little lady flying,' she says.

An hour later, with the base of the mannequin removed, the figure is suspended from the ceiling by fishing line and hangs in the shop window as if leaping through the air. The lamp lights up the jumpsuit and casts the leaping shadow of the figure on the white wall.

Alice joins Pixie and Effie outside to admire the effect. 'It looks wonderful!' she says.

'All part of the service,' says Effie. Within minutes she has packed up and gone.

'Let's walk down the street a bit, and then come back and surprise ourselves with the window display,' suggests Alice.

Pixie laughs. As they walk up to the corner of Vine Street, she notices the trees in the scruffy little park on the corner have a dusting of pink blossom. Spring is not far away.

As they reach the corner, a van pulls up and a stack of evening papers, tied up with string, lands on the pavement beside them.

Pixie glances at the front page and one name jumps out at her. 'Oh, no . . . no,' she whispers, kneeling down to read it.

BEAUCHAMP BUSTED! MULTIPLE ARRESTS!

The Beauchamp murder and gold robbery that has held the entire country in thrall has taken a surprise turn with the arrest of Mrs Angela Beauchamp, who, along with her alleged lover, Mr Tony Rizzo, has been charged with the murder of her husband, gold and diamond trader Mr Charles Beauchamp. Both have also been charged with fraud and with the murder of a second man, Mr Albert Cooper. The gold Krugerrand coins have been recovered from the Beauchamps' property in Waverton. Several others, including the captain and a crew member of the cargo vessel *Cape Argus* and Mr Rizzo's niece, Yvonne Cassone, as well as two members of the Painters and Dockers Union, have been charged with crimes related to the robbery.

53

TEA AND REVELATIONS

Keen to make up for lost time and take better care of Hazel, Betty bustles around the kitchen preparing afternoon tea. There's a knock on the door and she hurries to answer it, ushering Detective Dibble and Maude (in uniform as Officer Mulligan) into the front room. While they get settled, she brings the tea and two sorts of cake (Irene not lifting a finger to help as usual).

'So you've all heard the news, I imagine,' Dibble says, glancing around.

'That was quite a shock,' says Hazel. 'I haven't met Mrs Beauchamp myself, but I know she's very highly regarded.'

Dibble nods. 'It's been a shock for many people. I wanted to fill in some of the blanks for you today, given your contribution. We don't have all the information yet. Three of the suspects have confessed, but Mr Rizzo and his niece, Yvonne Cassone, are not cooperating.'

He picks up his cup of tea and settles in. 'I'll start right at the beginning. It seems the Beauchamps were in serious financial trouble. The company owned a diamond mine in what was the

Belgian Congo, now the Republic of Congo, and the government seized it during the political upheaval there last year. Beauchamp had invested a big pile of money in it and was suddenly in debt and faced losing everything. So, in desperation, he looked for other ways to stay afloat.'

Betty wonders if Dibble intended that as a pun but no one laughs so she doesn't either. It's probably not the time or place.

'That's when he got involved with Cooper?' suggests Hazel.

'It seems so. Beauchamp had plenty of contacts in the business, and Cooper was using his pigeons to smuggle in diamonds and precious stones in tiny pouches,' continues Dibble.

'Just to avoid import duty?' asks Hazel.

Dibble shrugs. 'Possibly. Depending on the category of goods, there could be up to a thirty per cent tariff. But more likely Beauchamp was a "fence" – receiving stolen goods from incoming ships. Then he decided to step it up with a plan to import the Krugerrand, steal it and claim the insurance.'

Irene gives a grunt of approval.

'How did he get the funds to buy the Krugerrand if he was broke?' asks Betty.

'That's where Mr Rizzo comes into the picture,' says Maude.

'Correct,' Dibble confirms. 'Long-time crook and fixer for criminals and unions alike, Rizzo raised the funds from his cohort in return for a split. But then it all got very messy. It seems Cooper caught Rizzo and Angela Beauchamp in a compromising situation and decided to blackmail Rizzo.'

Hazel gives a shudder. 'That wasn't his best idea.'

'No. After an ugly dispute with Rizzo, Cooper went to Charles Beauchamp and told him everything in return for protection. Next thing Cooper's dead. Rizzo is now being charged with his murder.'

'And how did Mr Beauchamp's murder come about?' asks Hazel.

'Angela Beauchamp has admitted to killing him but is claiming self-defence,' says Dibble. 'She maintains that he had confronted her about her relationship with Rizzo, threatening her with the gun, and it went off accidentally.'

'That's what they all say,' scoffs Irene.

Dibble agrees. 'She knew all about the diamond smuggling and was involved in the Krugerrand plan. It's possible that she and Rizzo planned to double-cross Beauchamp and reap the profits for themselves. As a by the by, the entire six thousand, seven hundred coins were not recovered. They had a portable smelter on the property and some of them had already been melted down and gone into circulation, probably as gold bars.'

'Mrs Beauchamp was already profiting from the situation,' muses Hazel. 'But perhaps she wanted to get out of that marriage – and saw her opportunity.'

Dibble agrees. 'She's a smart one. Rizzo, being the shrewd fellow he is, came up with the plan to frame Rex Shepperton – who was a thorn in his side in any case – for Beauchamp's murder and, by association, the robbery. A clever tactic to turn attention away from Angela Beauchamp.'

It occurs to Betty that if there were fewer dead people involved, it would be quite a romantic story. Now it will be years before the lovers even see each other again.

'I'm interested to know how they came up with the plan to hide the gold on board,' says Hazel. 'They must have been on the ship before, or was it the captain's idea?'

'The Beauchamps went to Durban to arrange the purchase and shipment of the Krugerrand, and they inspected the ship.

The captain was a contact of Rizzo's, so he was in on it all along. The timber panels were installed in Durban for this express purpose – so quite a sophisticated plan. The initial focus of our investigations was on a deck hand who left the *Cape Argus* in Darwin. When he was finally tracked down, he claimed he was fired for no reason.'

'And then Cliff Fletcher took his place?' asks Hazel.

'That's correct. Fletcher was flown up to Darwin for the job of concealing the gold. Also, as an aside, during questioning, one of the crew had mentioned there was a "relationship" between the captain and Fletcher. On night watch, he'd seen the young man entering and leaving the captain's quarters. At the time, it didn't seem relevant, but now we know why he spent time in there. Between the ports of Darwin and Sydney, Fletcher removed the timber panelling, glued the presentation boxes to the wall and put it all back together. No one would suspect anything was hidden inside the walls because they looked like a permanent fixture.'

'But why all this business declaring the goods as souvenirs?' asks Hazel.

'The *Cape Argus* is what's known as a lighthouse tender, a tough little cargo ship that can take on any sort of seas and loads. But it's the last vessel anyone would use to import something as valuable as the Krugerrand. Beauchamp argued the subterfuge was to prevent a robbery – but in fact it was to *stage* the robbery, then claim the insurance and double his money. The coins were listed as souvenirs to put the captain in the clear. Supposedly he wasn't aware of the value of the cargo he was carrying.'

'That part of the plan almost worked. The captain could have got away if his ship had been released sooner,' adds Hazel.

'Yes,' agrees Dibble. 'Once they left Australian waters he could have disappeared.'

'That waterfront property in Waverton belongs to the Beauchamps,' says Maude. 'So as soon as the *Cape Argus* went into dry dock, Rizzo, and the other couple of fellows we've also arrested, took the Beauchamps' yacht across to Cockatoo Island, removed the coins and brought them back without anyone noticing. They were no doubt expecting that Cliff would remove and replace the panels – but he was in custody.'

Betty looks over at Hazel and her heart swells with pride at her friend's clever deductions. But she also gives herself a quiet pat on the back for the role she played in finding Hazel and saving her life.

'It's been a complex case, and no doubt more details will emerge in time,' says Dibble. 'There were a lot of players and plenty of red herrings but we got there in the end, thanks to all of you.' He looks around, giving each of them a nod of acknowledgement. His gaze comes to rest on Betty. 'And very special thanks to Mrs Dewsnap for excellent detective work in locating Mrs Bates.'

Betty thanks him, glowing in the spotlight. If nothing else, this whole dreadful business has reminded her that this is where her strengths lie. She's a natural born detective. All this silly mourning for her lost youth. She could never have done this as a young woman. She wasn't strong or brave or clever. She lived in a dream where other people were in charge. Now her time has come, and she's not going to waste another minute of it.

'More tea, anyone?' she asks.

54

HAZEL HAS AN UNEXPECTED VISITOR

Hazel answers the door on Saturday morning to find Rex Shepperton on her doorstep, holding a bouquet of flowers. 'Come in, Rex dear,' says Hazel. 'It's so good to see you.'

Without a word, he steps inside and takes her in a warm embrace. When he releases her, Hazel takes the flowers and hurries to the kitchen, staving off tears.

'Betty has baked and the tins are full,' she says, getting out a vase.

Rex takes off his coat and sits down at the table. 'Words can't express how grateful I am to you, Hazel. When I heard what you went through . . .' He stops, choked up. 'I wish I'd never brought you onto the docks. They say it's no place for a lady—'

'Don't talk nonsense, Rex,' Hazel says. 'No such place exists. We belong everywhere that men do. What you need is *more* women working down there, not less.'

Rex smiles wearily. 'You could be right there, Hazel.'

Hazel cuts two slices of cake, pours the tea and sits down. 'That said, I hope you don't mind but I've decided to resign. With one thing and another, I'd be happy never to set foot on the wharves again.'

'I understand completely. It'd be more surprising if you wanted to return.'

'Even a tea lady has her limits,' says Hazel with a smile. 'Rex, something that puzzles me is that when I first asked you about that young man, Cliff Fletcher, you denied having seen him . . .'

'Still can't get away with anything, can I?' Rex pauses to select a piece of cake. 'You're right, of course, but I was trying to protect you. Fletcher was just a lackey, but I knew he was working for Rizzo, who was *the* most dangerous bloke on the waterfront.'

'Had you guessed it was Rizzo who framed you?' asks Hazel.

'It did cross my mind, but I would never have guessed that Yvonne was the one who put the plan into action. I had no idea they were related. I don't think anyone did – they kept it very quiet, for obvious reasons. I only realised later that she started with us around the time that I began campaigning to have the Painters and Dockers Union deregistered because of their criminal activities. Not coincidental, I suspect.'

'It would have been helpful for Rizzo to have inside information,' agrees Hazel. 'I must admit, for a while I suspected Teddy was involved.'

'Teddy! Never. He's a loyal foot soldier of the union movement.' Rex pauses. 'There's been so much fallout. I understand Mr Pickles, the nightwatchman, has lost his job for accepting bribes. He worked down there for thirty-odd years.'

'Oh dear. I suppose he was facing retirement and needed a few extra dollars in the kitty. You can't blame him, I suppose.'

Rex shrugs philosophically. 'He's probably been on the take for thirty years. Just got caught this time.' He gives a sigh. 'What will you do now, Hazel?'

'I have a lot to be going on with. For a start, the Tea Ladies Guild have an auction next week to raise funds for the new orphanage, so I need to get more involved – there's a lot of work still to be done.'

'Anything you want from me, Hazel – trip to the moon – just ask. It's yours.'

Hazel laughs. 'Thank you. What about you? You'll continue with your crusade?'

Rex considers this for a moment. 'If anything, I'm more committed than ever. When working people have decent conditions and pay, there's less incentive to turn to crime and the Pickles of this world won't face a life of poverty when they retire.'

'It's your calling, isn't it?' says Hazel.

Rex smiles. 'It is. But right now, there are piles of paperwork calling me.' He stands and puts his coat on. 'Thank you for the tea, and please pass on my compliments to Mrs Dewsnap for the excellent cake.'

At the door, Hazel gives him a hug. 'Don't be a stranger, Rex.'

'I promise,' he says, giving her a fond smile.

55

LET THE BIDDING BEGIN

Hazel couldn't be more surprised and delighted at the turnout for the auction; there must be a hundred or more people here this evening. The church hall is overflowing, every seat filled and people standing at the sides and back of the room.

Sister Ruth has been greeting arrivals at the door. Betty dashes about handing out lists of auction items. Effie Finch directs the crowds. Irene sits in the front row smoking a cigar. The only empty seats are on either side of her, and Hazel takes one of them.

The entire Mulligan family and other neighbours from Glade Street are here but, sadly, no Merl. Hazel feels her absence keenly. While Merl can be difficult, she's part of the Tea Ladies Guild and it will be a shame if she's too proud to forgive and forget.

There's a buzz of excitement in the room when Rex Shepperton appears at the lectern. He taps his finger on the microphone and gets a satisfying sound in return. 'Good evening, ladies, gentlemen and everyone in between! It's wonderful to see so many local residents and familiar faces attending this evening. As you know, this auction has been organised by the indefatigable Tea Ladies Guild—'

'Stick to plain English, mate!' shouts some wag, getting a laugh.

'I'll do my best,' says Rex, laughing. 'We're here tonight raising funds for beds and blankets at the new orphanage wing at the Sisters of Hope Convent. There are plenty of us in this community who spent time in orphanages and know firsthand how tough it can be. It's projects like this that the community needs to rally—'

'We know all that, now get on with it,' heckles Irene from the front row.

'All right. I will heed Mrs Turnbuckle's excellent advice and get on with it,' he says.

Behind the lectern, two long trestle tables are piled high with donated items. Rex walks up and down the tables, highlighting some of the items on offer.

There's everything imaginable on those tables, from lacy white communion dresses and patent leather shoes to encyclopaedias, a set of crescent spanners from the local hardware shop, packets of tea from the grocers, four gift sets of talc and soap from the chemist. There are six bottles of Hazel's homemade wine, a three-tiered Black Forest chocolate cake baked by one of the Defence tea ladies, a tin of Violet's rock cakes and packets of sweet biscuits made by the Italian ladies. Mr Kovac has made a generous donation of a large tin of Nescafé, and Hazel has her eye on some beautiful lace doilies made by Mrs Babinski.

'We have a very special item donated by someone who wishes to remain anonymous,' Rex says. Lifting the cloth covering the largest item, he reveals a small portable television, which ignites a murmur of excitement in the room.

'Goodness,' says Hazel, surprised. 'That's very generous!'

'Bloody generous,' says Irene. 'Must be a saint, I reckon.'

'Not sure it would qualify for a sainthood,' says Hazel with a chuckle. 'But definitely a special thank you – if we knew the person's identity, of course.'

'We also have another very exciting surprise for you,' Rex continues. 'But I'll leave you in suspenders about that for the moment.'

When the chatter dies down, the auction begins. Rex takes the bids and members of the Guild collect cash and cheques, handing out items to each bidder on the spot.

Finally Rex gets back to the television set. A hush falls over the room and the mood of the auction takes on a new seriousness. The bidding starts at fifty dollars and goes up ten at a time, then five dollars until just two men are battling it out, raising their bids a dollar each a time until it sells to Mrs Babinski for a hundred and fifty dollars, raising almost half the fundraising goal.

'Yer'd have to be happy with that,' says Irene, shooting Hazel a sidelong glance.

'I'm delighted,' says Hazel. 'Thank you, Irene.'

'Don't thank me. Don't give a stuff about the little beggars.'

Hazel knows that's not true. She knows from a reliable source that Irene's early years were spent in an orphanage – one that is notorious for its poor treatment of children. Then, when she turned sixteen, her dreadful grandmother put her to work in the brothel. But that's Irene's business, and Hazel's not about to argue the point.

'Now we come to our final surprise of the evening!' says Rex.

Up the front of the room, Alice sits near the record player. Obviously nervous, she carefully lowers the stylus and the Beatles song 'Penny Lane' begins to play. At a sign from Rex, she turns up the volume. He directs the crowd's attention to the main doors. Heads crane towards the back of the room.

Pixie opens the doors and a model wearing a bright patterned jumpsuit struts down the aisle to the stage, followed by three more models wearing jumpsuits in different colours and patterns. The room explodes with excited chatter that almost drowns out the music.

Quietening everyone down, Rex explains that a jumpsuit will be made to order for the lucky bidder by a local firm. He beckons Pixie up on to the stage and introduces her.

'I believe this outfit is also available in a new shop . . . or should I say *boutique*,' he adds. 'The Vine Street Boutique – which I probably don't need to tell you is just around the corner in Vine Street. So even if you are not the lucky bidder this evening, you still have the chance to purchase these from the shop. Just pop by and see Miss Karp to place your order.'

The bidding is slow at first, with women perhaps wondering if they would dare wear this outfit, but soon their confidence grows and so does the bidding. Finally the jumpsuit goes to the highest bidder at forty dollars, which Hazel knows is much more than Pixie plans to sell it for.

It had been Hazel's idea to launch the brand at the auction after she heard that Pixie had been counting on Mrs Beauchamp investing in the business (probably planning to launder some of her ill-gotten gains). As a result of this evening, at least a hundred people are aware of the new enterprise, and they will no doubt tell two hundred more.

Sister Ruth comes up to the lectern and warmly thanks everyone for coming. She talks about the strength of the Surry Hills community, one that has seen more than its fair share of hard times over the last century. 'Thanks to your generosity, the children we care for and educate will not only have comfortable beds to sleep in but will grow up with the knowledge that they are part of a close-knit community where people care for each other. These children will become a new generation who may well choose to settle here and spend their lives among you good people.'

Irene gives a wet sniff and wipes her nose on her sleeve. Hazel would like to give the dear old battle-axe a comforting pat, but that's the last thing Irene would want.

The audience clap heartily and begin to make their way out of the hall. Once they're gone, the Guild ladies swoop in to tidy up, stacking chairs and putting the hall back to rights. Before they leave, they gather to watch Hazel count the cash while Betty tallies up the cheques. To everyone's jubilation, they have raised $495.50 – almost a hundred over the goal. Sister Ruth thanks them all again and leaves with the funds tucked safely in the pocket of her habit.

Hazel looks around at the familiar faces – Betty, Irene, Mrs Li, Effie, Violet, the Italian ladies, the Defence ladies, and half-a-dozen others she doesn't know quite as well – and she realises that the Guild has finally become a community. They may be of different nationalities and different backgrounds, but the common thread is the role of tea lady: someone who nurtures workers with a hot beverage, a sweet biscuit and a kind word. And now these women have opened their generous hearts to the wider community, for the benefit of kiddies with no place to call home. The project may have got off to a bumpy start, but there's no doubt it's been very successful, and Hazel hopes it's the first of many.

56

SPRING COMES TO GLADE STREET

It's been a long, bitter winter. Spring has crept in quietly, sprinkling the odd blossom and bud along the streets of Surry Hills. This evening at 5 Glade Street, the front room window is open for the first time since last summer, and Hazel can smell the night-blooming jasmine that grows wild over the front fence. Sitting at her card table with a glass of mulberry wine, she looks over the Great Wall of China jigsaw, now close to completion.

Betty sits in the armchair near the lamp, knitting a jumper for the orphans – her new mission. 'You know, I think I'm almost as fast as Merl now,' she says.

'You might win her over with a knitting race,' says Hazel.

Betty sighs. 'She doesn't even come to the laneway for lunch any more.'

'I'm very surprised she hasn't been able to put this little setback behind her.'

'Her ego is bruised,' says Betty.

A knock on the front door gives them both a start.

'Oh, fudge! Oops, sorry, Hazel, I just dropped a stitch.'

This particular curse has been the extent of Betty's swearing; it's a sweet one as curses go, but she seems to relish it all the same. Hazel tells Betty she's forgiven and goes to answer the door.

On the front step stands a young woman dressed in a long cheesecloth skirt and a T-shirt displaying a Ban the Bomb symbol. Thick tawny-coloured hair frames a fine-boned face without a skerrick of make-up. She holds a large flat package, wrapped in brown paper and tied up with string.

'Hello,' says Hazel, already guessing her identity. 'Can I help you?'

The woman holds up the package for Hazel. 'This is for Betty . . . Mrs Dewsnap. I hope she likes it.'

'She's here,' says Hazel. 'Would you like to give it to her yourself?'

The woman ducks her head as if considering the idea. 'No, that's all right,' she says softly. 'Just tell her . . . I'm so very sorry. If she doesn't like it, she can burn it.'

Suddenly feeling sorry for her, Hazel gives her a quick smile. 'I'll pass that on. You're quite sure you don't want to come in?'

Shaking her head, she raises her hand in a farewell gesture and walks away.

Hazel takes the parcel, heavy and large enough to be awkward to get inside.

'Who was that?' asks Betty, glancing up from her knitting. 'And what's that?'

'I think that was your friend Lucy,' says Hazel.

Betty's face turns scarlet. Her hands fly to her face in horror, letting her knitting drop to the floor. 'Oh no, don't look at it, Hazel! I'm taking it straight out to the incinerator.'

'Don't be too hasty, Betty dear,' says Hazel. 'I'll wait in the hall while you look at it in privacy. Then, if you really want to burn it, wrap it up and we'll get rid of it together. But you should definitely give it a chance.'

Betty stares at the package with trepidation. But when Hazel returns a few minutes later, she is sitting on the sofa holding the painting in front of her. She turns it around for Hazel to see. 'What do you think?'

'Oh, Betty! It's . . . beautiful,' says Hazel, surprised and almost tearful. Whatever else she may be, Lucy is a real talent. She has captured not just Betty's likeness but her character, her sweet smile and generous, loving nature within. 'I'm sure any art gallery would be glad to hang it on their walls.'

'Is that really what I look like?' Betty asks anxiously.

'She has captured you to perfection. And you're right, that blue frock really does bring out the colour of your eyes. It was a good choice. And look, she's even detailed the lacework on the buttons.' Hazel takes both Betty's hands in hers. 'Now, I think we should hang it somewhere everyone can see it.'

Looking around, she notices a bright patch on the wall where an old photograph used to hang. Together they lift up the portrait to hang it in its place.

Betty can't stop looking at it. 'Are you sure it's a good likeness?' she asks again.

Before Hazel can reassure her, there's a thump and crash in the hallway and a moment later, Irene sticks her head around the door. She comes into the room to see what they're looking at. 'Who's that then?' she asks, looking at the painting.

'You really don't know?' asks Betty.

Irene grins. 'Just kidding, yers look like a bloody film star.'

'Oh, Irene, I think that's going a bit far,' says Betty, stifling a giggle.

Irene peers at it up close. 'It's bloody good. How do yer do that, d'yer reckon?'

'Betty's friend Lucy did it. She's a very talented artist,' says Hazel.

'I might give it a go meself,' says Irene, reaching out to touch it.

'Irene! Keep your mitts off it,' snaps Betty.

'Keep yer hair on. Anyway, I got yers a present too,' says Irene. She pulls a flat packet out of her coat. 'For yer record player.'

'Now, Irene dear, I don't want you to think us ungrateful,' says Hazel. 'But I would like to be assured the record was lawfully obtained.'

'Guaranteed. Yer can ask old Gibson. I'm back watching the telly out the front of the shop. So I thought I'd buy something to . . . you know . . .'

'Soften the blow?' suggests Betty.

Hazel takes the record from her. She puts it on the new record player and lowers the stylus. Petula Clark's warm, melodic voice fills the room. The experience is marred by Irene's extremely unmelodic accompaniment. It's so awful, Betty gets up and closes the window to spare the neighbours, and it's quite a relief when the song comes to a shrieking end.

'Lovely,' says Hazel, not wanting to encourage Irene to do an encore. 'Why don't I get us a glass of the good stuff to celebrate?'

'Now yer talkin,' says Irene, sitting down.

When everyone has a drink, Hazel settles back in front of the jigsaw, Betty picks up her knitting, and Irene makes herself comfortable with her feet up on the sofa.

'Here's to us,' says Irene, lifting her glass in a toast.

Hazel and Betty raise their glasses. 'To us.'

'And to women everywhere. In all our struggles, may we find strength in our friendships,' says Hazel, taking a sip of whiskey.

'Ohhh . . . that was so lovely, Hazel,' says Betty in a wobbly voice.

Irene pulls out a huge cigar and gives it a sniff. 'Yeah, well, no need to start blubbing and wreck the mood.'

'They're called emotions, Irene,' says Betty crossly.

As they sit in companionable silence, Hazel experiences a moment of the breathless panic she felt trapped in the blackness of that wardrobe. It's the memory of loneliness, more than the fear, that comes back to her vividly in the night, and occasionally in the day. She takes a deep breath and calms herself.

Glancing up from her jigsaw, she looks across the room at Irene stretched out on the sofa, puffing away on her cigar, and Betty, busy knitting for the orphans. She takes a moment to appreciate the ordinary loveliness of this time together and feels a sense of contentment settle on her. She is home in the truest sense of the word.

She picks up the last piece of the puzzle. With a happy sigh, she snaps it into place.

ACKNOWLEDGEMENTS

The Tea Ladies series owes much of its success to the expertise and enthusiasm of the team at Penguin Random House. Many thanks to my publisher, Ali Watts, for her incredible support over many years; editor extraordinaire Amanda Martin; designer Debra Billson, whose gorgeous covers define the series; and proofreader Sonja Heijn, whose imprimatur is always a vital link in the chain. Also vital are the creative contributions and hard work of publicist Laura Nimmo and marketing manager Rebekah Chereshsky.

Many thanks to Julie Burland, Holly Toohey and Dorothy Tonkin for their support. To Veronica Eze and the audio team, Sarah McDuling and her Rights team, and Janine Brown and her sales team. Special thanks to Zoe Carides, who brings the tea ladies to life in the audiobook.

Thank you to the early readers of *The Deadly* Billie Trinder, Joe Harrison and Diana Qian for their valuable and insightful feedback, and members of the Wondering Women book club: Anna Loder, Gayle Banfield, Liz Hogan, Michele Giblett and Fay Levi.

Special thanks to Laurence Burgess, former NSW detective, for helping with my criminal plots, Neale Towart of Unions NSW for the informative history tour of Sydney Trades Hall, Elliot Lindsay, historian and archaeologist, for the tour of East Sydney and my nephew, Adam Hampson, for checking the accuracy of all things dockside.

To the booksellers who hand-sold and personally recommended *The Tea Ladies* series to their customers – thank you! A special thanks to our online supporters, the fabulous bookstagrammers: an army of reviewers who share our work far and wide.

And thanks to you, my readers, for taking the time to enjoy my books and recommending to your friends and family.

I am forever grateful for the support of my wonderful children and their partners: Tula Wynyard, Joyce Cheng, Milan Wynyard, Hayley Farrell, Darren and Tonia Gittins, my grandchildren Claudia, Ollie and Chelsie, and my sister, Kim Hampson.

This book was written on unceded Wurundjeri Country. The author acknowledges First Nations people as the custodians of this land, and pays respects to Elders past, present and emerging.

BOOK CLUB QUESTIONS

1. Do you think the main characters have evolved over the series, and in what ways?
2. What elements of the story captured the mood of the sixties for you? Do you think these were better times?
3. 'Even a tea lady has her limits,' says Hazel. Do you think that's true?
4. Betty's only ambitions were to get married and have children; now she feels life has passed her by. Do you think this was a common regret for women of that generation?
5. It seems to Betty that young people understand the world much better than her generation ever did. In what ways does she see this, and is it still true today?
6. The friendships of the tea ladies suffer an upheaval in this story. Do you think Merl could return to the fold?
7. Betty makes the comment that it's 'a man's world' – a common phrase of the time. Do you think it's still true today?

8. Do you think the characters are representative of older, highly capable women of their time? How do they compare with older women today?
9. 'It's the clue right under your nose that's the hardest to see.' How does this play in out in *The Deadly Dispute* and other books you have read in *The Tea Ladies* series?
10. Have you read other books by Amanda Hampson, and which is your favourite?

THE OTHER BOOKS IN
THE TEA LADIES SERIES

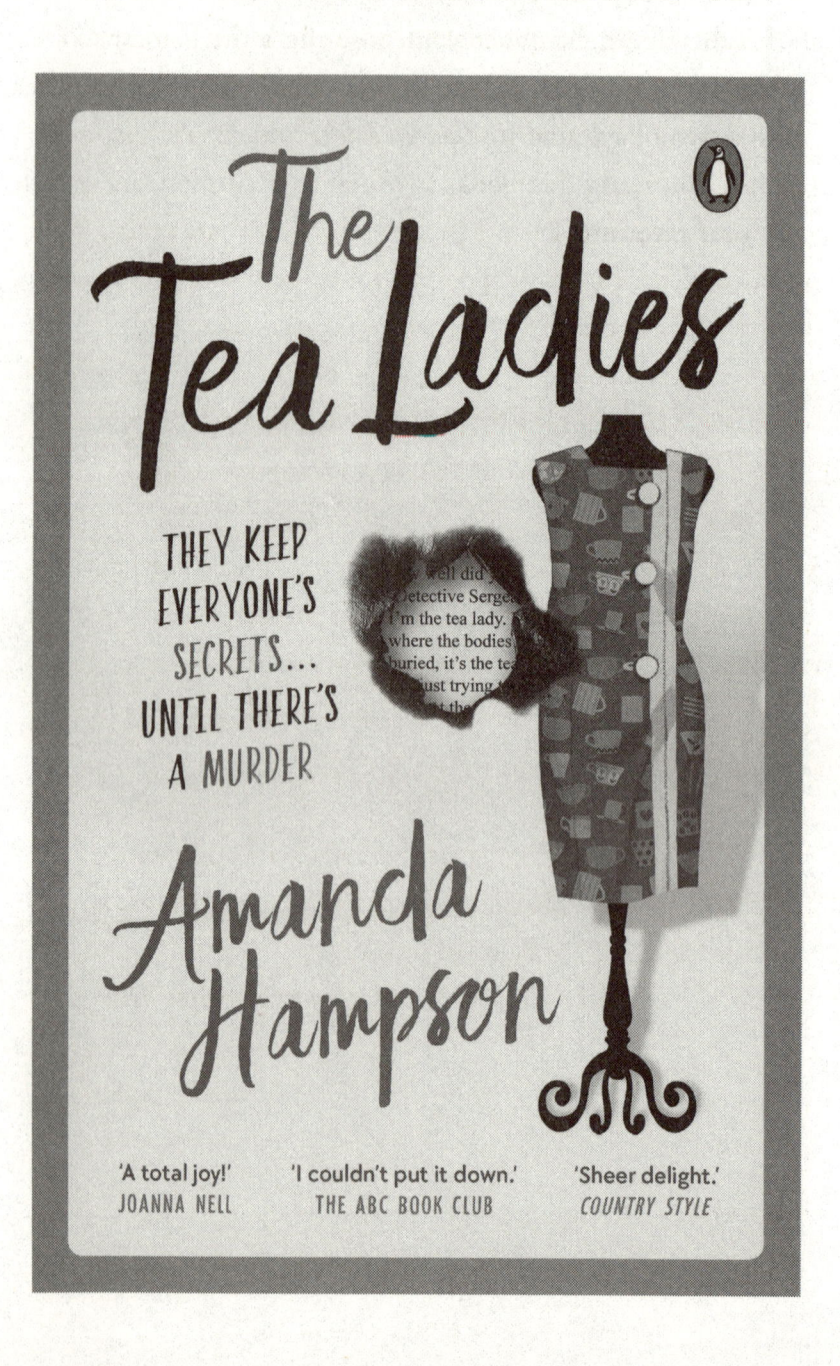

The Tea Ladies

THEY KEEP EVERYONE'S SECRETS... UNTIL THERE'S A MURDER

Amanda Hampson

'A total joy!'
JOANNA NELL

'I couldn't put it down.'
THE ABC BOOK CLUB

'Sheer delight.'
COUNTRY STYLE

They keep everyone's secrets, until there's a murder . . .

Sydney, 1965: After a chance encounter with a stranger, tea ladies Hazel, Betty and Irene become accidental sleuths, stumbling into a world of ruthless crooks and racketeers in search of a young woman believed to be in danger.

In the meantime, Hazel's job at Empire Fashionwear is in jeopardy. The firm has turned out the same frocks and blouses for the past twenty years and when the mini-skirt bursts onto the scene, it rocks the rag trade to its foundations. War breaks out between departments and it falls to Hazel, the quiet diplomat, to broker peace and save the firm.

When there is a murder in the building, the tea ladies draw on their wider network and put themselves in danger as they piece together clues that connect the murder to a nearby arson and a kidnapping. But if there's one thing tea ladies can handle, it's hot water.

WINNER 2024 Danger Awards – Best Fiction
SHORTLISTED 2024 Sisters In Crime Davitt Awards – Best Adult Crime
SHORTLISTED 2024 Ned Kelly Awards – Best Fiction

The Cryptic Clue

A TEA LADIES Mystery

LOOK WHO'S BACK IN HOT WATER!

Amanda Hampson

'The Thursday Murder Club wish they had Hazel.' GOODREADS

In ZigZag Lane, in the heart of Sydney's rag-trade district, tea ladies Hazel, Betty and Irene find themselves in hot water. Having already solved a murder, kidnapping and arson case, and outwitting an arch criminal, they have proved themselves a useful resource and earned the respect of a local police officer. Now he needs their help to solve a plot that threatens security.

As if that's not enough, Irene gets a coded message directing her to the spoils of a bank robbery, which sends the tea ladies on a treasure hunt with an unexpected outcome.

There's also trouble brewing within the walls of Empire Fashionwear, where an interloper threatens not just Hazel's job but the very role of tea lady. It's up to Hazel to convince her friends to abandon their trolleys and take action to save their livelihoods – before it's too late.

Powered by Penguin

Looking for more great reads, exclusive content and book giveaways?
Subscribe to our weekly newsletter.

Scan the QR code or visit penguin.com.au/signup